AF442391

CODE NAME: LIBRA

USA TODAY BESTSELLING AUTHOR

JANIE CROUCH

CODE NAME: LIBRA • SPECIAL EDITION

To all Libras out there…
Thanks for keeping the scales balanced and trying to make the world
a better place.

CHAPTER ONE

TAKING a bullet to the chest sucked.

Taking a bullet to the chest from someone who was your friend *really* sucked.

But worse than either of those were the side-eyed glances he got from everyone around him as he recovered.

The *whoa, is he going to topple over?* side glances and winces after people slapped him on the shoulder, worried they'd hurt him with the friendly gesture.

Landon Black had become way too familiar with those over the past six months.

Worse than the bullet hole itself—and that had been pretty damned painful—was the fear that no one was ever going to treat him normally again. That he was never going to remember he was once a deadly Navy SEAL, then had become an agent for one of the top security firms in the world.

Because that person felt pretty long gone.

But smiling through it all? *That* was the absolute worst.

Smiling was what he did. It was what he was known for. He was the charmer, the peacemaker. The one who made everyone laugh and was tactful and charismatic.

The *Libra*.

It was his code name there at Zodiac for that very reason. He was all of those things.

And now he was expected to be all of those things with a bullet scar on his chest only a few centimeters from his heart.

Honestly, the scar he didn't mind so much. It could've been worse. He knew that every single day.

But he'd been relegated to desk duty for the past six months since "the incident." *That* was driving him nearly insane.

Zodiac Tactical was a world-renowned private security contractor started by his best friend and former SEAL teammate, Ian DeRose. The company provided expertise in tactical work of all types: risk consulting, intelligence gathering, private and corporate guarding, international hostage negotiation and rescue.

If the law couldn't—or wouldn't—handle it, Zodiac Tactical could.

And *did*, on a regular basis.

But they'd taken some hits of their own over the past year: kidnapped employees and loved ones, criminal masterminds attempting to take them down, bullet holes to the chest.

They were only now finally finding their footing again, putting Zodiac back on track and stronger than ever. The threat was over, eliminated by them. Everyone was free to return to their regularly scheduled programming.

Except him.

Every time he looked at the active mission calendar, his name wasn't on it. For the past four months, he'd been traveling around to the different Zodiac offices, helping rebuild morale and take the emotional temperature of each group of people.

Flashing 'em the famous *Landon Black smile*, complete with dimples he knew how to use to his advantage.

Hopefully, no one noticed if it was a bit frayed around the edges.

Today, he'd been called into the Los Angeles office by Ian. Until "the incident," he'd mainly worked in the Denver office. But since that was where he'd gotten shot in the chest by the woman his best friend loved, it had made the place a little haunted for both of them. Neither of them had spent much time there since.

It was Saturday, which meant none of the regular staff was around the office. But when Ian had asked Landon to come in and meet with Callum Webb, he'd agreed. Callum was a federal law enforcement agent with the Omega Sector task force, or he had been until he'd been fired for helping Zodiac rescue one of their own a few months ago.

"Anybody here?" The empty reception area didn't answer him. "Yo, Ian?"

"Conference room," he called.

Even though he was the owner of the company, Ian didn't keep a real office here. He'd been spending most of his time in New York, wanting to be near Wavy and her newly prosperous art career.

The conference room at the end of the hall held a big, shiny mahogany table and expensive leather chairs.

"Morning." Landon walked into the conference room and smiled at the coffee and pastries on the table. "Nice."

"Help yourself." Ian motioned for the food. "Callum stepped out to take a phone call."

"What's going on?" He stuffed an icing-coated cinnamon something in his mouth and moaned in pleasure. He tried to eat healthy as much as possible, but damn he had a sweet tooth.

"He wanted to wait for you to explain it all." Ian cracked a grin as he watched him eat. "You need some time alone with that?"

Landon laughed and washed the pastry down with the coffee—black, hot, perfect. "No, but you knew bringing anything cinnamon in here would tempt me."

He nodded. "I did, indeed."

Before he could press him more about that, the door at the back of the conference room opened, and Callum walked in. He looked the very picture of a federal agent: hair cropped short, tie wrung to the side where he'd pulled at it, exhaustion bracketing his mouth.

He and Ian both stood, and Landon held out his hand to greet their friend.

"How's it going, Webb? You here to ask for a job?"

They'd both give him one in a heartbeat. Callum may not have been a SEAL like he and Ian, but he was someone Landon would trust at his back during a fight.

"No, I've thankfully been reemployed by Uncle Sam, at least for the time being. The fact that we put Mosaic away for good helped get me out of the doghouse."

Mosaic—a pretty name for an ugly group of scumbags— had been the bane of their existence for nearly a year. They were the reason he'd been shot and the reason why Ian now had a little gray in his dark hair.

Landon reached for his coffee cup and held it up as a toast. "To doing what we can to stop the bad guys."

"I'm hoping maybe you'll be interested in stopping some more bad guys." Callum fixed his serious gaze on him as they sat down around the conference table. "You specifically, Landon. Some undercover work on a tropical island."

Landon glanced at Ian out of the corner of his eye. He didn't look surprised as he took another sip from his mug. Which meant he knew from the beginning Callum had been there to see him.

He ran a hand through his hair and let out a sigh. "No need for a pity fuck, you guys."

Callum laughed as Ian spewed his coffee. "I'm pretty sure

Wavy wouldn't approve of me fucking you in any way, pity included."

He leaned back in his chair and kept his eyes pinned on Ian. "Did you offer me to the Feds because you know I'm going crazy on desk duty?"

Callum held out a hand in a gesture of peace. "Hang on. Ian didn't contact me. I gave him the mission parameters and asked him who he thought was the best fit."

Landon raised one eyebrow so high he was afraid it might get stuck there. "And surprise, surprise, Ian thought of his friend Landon for a gig on a tropical island. Sounds like a way to get me to take a paid vacation."

He'd had enough vacation sitting in that hospital a few months ago. He was tired of feeling useless.

Ian crossed his arms over his chest. "Why don't you hear Webb out, then you can decide if you're interested in this particular fuck. Which, I can promise you, is not pity."

Ian and Landon stared each other down. They'd known each other for nearly twenty years. Had saved each other's lives more times than either of them kept track of.

But the last few months had been hard for both of them.

"You don't owe me anything, Aries," he muttered, calling Ian by his Zodiac code name. "Wavy doesn't either. What happened, happened."

He gave him a short nod. "I'm not sure she sees it that way, but I'm not trying to babysit you. Callum came to me, and you're the best fit for the mission. If you don't want to take it, that's no problem."

He stared at Ian a couple more seconds before turning to Callum and flashing him a full-dimple smile. "Woo me."

Callum chuckled. "Imagine the beautiful sandy beaches of a private Channel Island…"

Off the coast of California. Known for their beauty and privacy—particularly catering to the rich and famous. "Sounds good so far."

"Now imagine a high-level member of the Frey Cartel being there, ripe for giving up information to us."

Landon sat up straighter in his seat. Callum was talking about one of the biggest organized crime syndicates in California, probably in the entire United States. "Seriously?"

"Yeah. The Frey Cartel was in bed with Mosaic. We didn't have enough intel to make arrests, but they've been on federal law enforcement's watch list for a while."

"And they're going to be hanging out in the Channel Islands?" he asked.

"Vincent Frey, third-highest member of the cartel, is going to a wedding there. Oliver Thornton, father of the bride, was connected to him in the past."

"Is Thornton a criminal also?"

"Not as far as we know. He's a financial investment guru. In the past, he's offered financial advice to the Frey Cartel for their freshly laundered money. Ethically questionable, maybe, but not illegal."

Callum opened a folder on the table in front of him and slid several pictures toward them. "Thornton's daughter Christiana is getting married. They're doing an over-the-top, weeklong celebration on the island, and our intel tells us Vincent Frey is on the guest list."

"Do you have enough to arrest him?"

"We could arrest him at any time, but not for anything significant, and it wouldn't bring down the cartel. So what we need you for is an info-gathering mission. The main objective is to put a nano transmitter on either Frey's phone or computer."

Ian and Landon exchanged a glance. Nano transmitters were virtually untraceable once placed and would allow Callum and his team to gather important intel—track locations, record calls, access any apps or websites that were opened on the electronic device to which it was attached.

But Frey wasn't just going to offer up his phone to a

stranger. Computer would be even more difficult. "Good idea. But that's not going to be an easy task."

Callum rubbed the back of his neck. "Very true. If it were easy, we'd have already done it. We're hoping the wedding will put everyone a little more at ease. Thornton has rented out the entire island for the event, which is, of course, invitation-only. And security will be top-notch. Nobody is getting on that island if they're not part of the wedding."

Ian slid the tablet to him, and he flipped through the pictures. The first few were various angles of Vincent Frey. The last one was of a family. He focused on it.

The caption said the man in the center was the financial adviser and host of the wedding, Oliver Thornton. To his right were two women who looked like they'd stepped out of a trophy wife catalog—identical younger and older versions of each other. Perfectly coiffed blond hair, pencil-thin figures, heels that had to be nearly impossible to walk in. Their clothes were tailored to fit them, and the perfection in their faces screamed expensive spas and high-end cosmetics.

To Oliver's left was another woman, not quite as impeccable as the other two. Her hair wasn't truly blond, but it wasn't brown. It was pulled back and over one shoulder in messy curls. She wore a tailored dress as well, but where the other two women's were deep blue, hers was a cheery, pale yellow. She also had several more pounds on her than the other two—not fat by any means, but...*softer*.

While the whole appearance worked well for her, she looked out of place in a photo obviously meant to show off the family's level of wealth and prestige.

"Meet the Thornton family," Callum said. "The one with curly hair is Elizabeth. She goes by Bethany and is who you'll be focusing on. The other daughter is Christiana, the bride, and next to her is Thornton's wife, Angelique."

"Why are we focusing on Bethany?" And why did she look like the odd man out in her own family photo?

Callum shrugged. "Intel suggests Bethany is not close to her family. She owns a bakery about an hour north of here."

Landon slid the tablet back to Callum. "Why aren't you handling this in-house?"

He leaned back in his chair and ran a hand down his face. "We have a mole—someone in the department is leaking intel. I know it's not me and am certain about my direct supervisor, but that's it. He gave me permission to outsource this and is securing funding our department won't be able to trace."

Callum glanced quickly at Ian then back to him. That probably meant Ian wasn't charging Callum anywhere near what Zodiac would normally charge for a mission like this. Ian was a billionaire and could afford to take the loss. He also knew Landon would work for free if it meant helping take down the Frey Cartel.

They were all sorts of bad news—weapons and information sales, drugs, backing terrorists. It would be his pleasure to do this small part in helping to shut them down.

"How are we going to get invited to this high-society wedding?"

Callum tapped the picture on the screen again. "Bethany."

He raised an eyebrow. "I'm not interested in some sort of Romeo seduction mission."

Ian smiled. "Speaking of pity fuck…"

Callum shook his head. "No, romance is not our in, but Bethany's business is. She's a baker. While investigating the family, I found that one of her employees has a record. And, conveniently enough, a bench warrant for unpaid child support."

He hissed. "Asshole."

Callum waved it off. "Best I can tell, he paid it. But the idiot didn't do it through the courts, so the ex is claiming he never did. I've already talked to him and got him on board. The bench warrant goes away and his record will be cleared if he helps us get someone inside Bethany's baking business."

"That doesn't get us to the island."

"It does if she's doubling as both the bride's sister and as the primary dessert-provider for all the week's events. Christiana hired Bethany's Slice of Heaven to cater."

Landon frowned. "Why would someone with so much family money open a bakery?"

Callum shrugged. "The family has millions, so I don't know why the elder Thornton sister opened her tiny bakery at all. All I know is we're going to use it if we can."

"How? I may love to eat sweets, but I'm never going to pass for a professional baker."

"You don't need to be. The employee of Bethany's we're putting pressure on, Harley Winterfield, is an older guy who assembles her intricate cake stands and towers—something that will definitely be needed for the wedding. It involves carpentry and basic mechanics."

Landon looked over at Ian. "This is why you suggested me."

Ian had known him long enough to know that carpentry was a side passion of his. He loved tinkering—putting things together, figuring out how they best fit, making them beautiful. It was something he'd done since back in the Navy. It was a great hobby for when his insomnia kicked in and he wasn't getting much sleep.

"See?" Ian raised an eyebrow. "Not a pity fuck, asshole. Your skills are needed."

Callum smiled. "So, you'll do it?"

No mention of his injury. No questions about whether he was up to it. He wasn't sure if Ian had coached him on what to say or if Callum had faith he could handle it.

To be honest, Landon didn't want to know the answer.

It was a real mission, it was important, and it involved his expertise. He would take it.

"Hell yeah, I'm in."

"Bethany was due to fly out with Harley in two days." Callum pulled some papers out of his folder. "Here's the address of the bakery and a few small details about Harley that will help prove you know him. As soon as I give the go-ahead, Harley is going to call Bethany with some excuse about why he can't go to the island, but explain you're willing to step in."

Landon nodded and looked over the info. It said he and Harley had met at a home improvement store in the Valley and had traded a few jobs over the years, more acquaintances than anything.

Callum pulled a small jewelry box out of his suit pocket.

Landon already knew what it was, but he allowed his eyes to get wide anyway. "Callum, oh my God, don't you make me remember this cinnamon roll forever by proposing to me."

Ian laughed and coughed over words that sounded suspiciously like *pity fuck*.

Callum took it in stride and dropped down on one knee next to him. "Libra, would you do me the honor of"—he popped open the jewelry box to reveal the nano transmitters —"helping us catch some real dickheads and making sure they go to prison for a long time?"

He put his hand up to his mouth and batted his eyes at him. "I'd thought you'd never ask. This is the happiest day of my life."

Callum snickered and handed the box to Landon before dropping back into his chair. It contained three clear pieces of what looked like tiny strips of tape with a wire in them that was just as translucent.

"Phone is best, followed by a computer," Callum said.

He studied the transmitters more closely. "Getting close to Frey isn't going to be easy. These cartel guys are well guarded, wedding or not."

Callum waggled his eyebrows. "That's why we came to

you. My fiancé is good with people. If anyone can get close to Frey, it'll be you."

Before being shot, Landon would've said that was true. Now it felt like his people skills were as rusty as his smile. "Yeah, that's me. People person extraordinaire."

"You're going to have to be," Ian put in. "Because if you get caught, Frey won't hesitate to take you out—and I don't mean on a date—and you're not going to have any backup that can get to you quickly."

Callum flinched. Ian knew what it was to work under-cover—for the very law enforcement team Callum was a part of—and for them not be able to get to him in time to stop him from going through hell.

He didn't want Ian's past to spiral into him needing a babysitter. "I can handle it."

For just a second, it looked like Ian was going to argue, but he nodded instead.

"Once you get on the island, before you get anywhere near Frey, you'll need to hack into the resort's security feed," Callum said. "Frey's people will be watching it, and we don't want to make them suspicious. I'll talk you through it once you're on the island."

Didn't sound too hard. "Okay."

"But first, you need to get Bethany Thornton to agree to take you with her. Her employee was sure she knows nothing about any cartels when we explained Oliver Thornton's connections. Says she's one hundred percent on the up-and-up."

"You concur?" Ian asked.

Callum shrugged. "It's hard to say with these kinds of people. Don't assume anything." He slid the whole file over to Landon and stood. "Everything I know that could help you is in there. Memorize it. Don't take it with you."

Landon made a face as he stood also. "Not a rookie, asshole."

Callum shot him a grin. "That's fiancé asshole to you, lover."

"Bigger problem is that you're pairing sweet tooth here with a baker," Ian said. "He may weigh three hundred pounds by the time this is over."

Callum shot Landon a smile. "Fine with me as long as we take down the bad guys."

CHAPTER
TWO

"BETHANY, YOU THERE?" Harley's voice came over the answering machine and filled the kitchen. "Pick up if you are."

Bethany Thornton hurried toward the landline on the wall, mixing spoon in one hand, spatula in the other, and hit the speaker button with her elbow. "I'm here."

"Sorry to call you like this. I didn't know if you'd answer."

Harley knew she usually came in for prep and to freeze cakes for the week on Sunday mornings before they opened. "Only for you. What's up?"

Sunday was the only day they kept reduced store hours, and she never answered the phone if the shop was closed. She'd learned that lesson quickly—keep regular hours and stick to them. Everyone deserved downtime, even store owners.

Maybe especially store owners.

"Bethie…"

She knew right away she was in trouble. Harley and her other employee, Michele, only called her Bethie if they were about to break bad news.

"I'm really sorry to do this so last minute," he continued, "but I'm not going to be able to go with you to the wedding. I've got a family emergency I just can't get out of."

Bethany nearly dropped the spoon as she stared at the phone.

No. *No, no, no.*

Any time one of them wasn't able to work unexpectedly, it threw a kink into their well-oiled machine. Slice of Heaven required Michele, Harley, and her to do their individual parts at the required times. One of them not being able to do it put undue pressure on the other two—made life hard.

But this was much worse. *This* was a disaster.

Bethany brought her hand up to her forehead to rub at the stress pooling there already, then snatched it back down when she realized she still had the spatula in it. She tossed both utensils into the sink.

"Harley, no. Please. I can't pull this off alone."

Especially not this. Arguably the most important event of her career.

"Bethie, I know. I'm so sorry. I…I can't get out of this. Believe me, if I could, I would. I wouldn't do this to you if it wasn't a noose around my neck."

He sounded so contrite she couldn't get angry with him, but she couldn't stop the dismay washing over her. What Harley did with the cake stands was beyond her expertise. She was a baker, not a carpenter. The complicated cake stands he put together took more than just understanding of how to use a drill.

She turned on the sink to wash the flour off her hands. Harley had worked for Bethany for the past year, and every time he went on a job and did his magic with the cake stands, she wondered what she'd done without him for the year before when he hadn't been around.

Actually, she knew exactly how she'd done it. Her cakes, while still delicious, hadn't been showcased well, and they had sold accordingly. Her business had increased considerably over the last twelve months, and Harley's contributions were no small part of that.

She let out a sigh. "There's nothing you can do?"

"Family emergency. Believe me, I wish I could do something about it."

The word *family* almost seemed like a curse. *That* she understood, even though she'd never even heard Harley mention having one. He'd taken a few days off for fishing trips over the past year, but never for family.

He was a good employee overall. But this was leaving her hanging in the worst possible way. Her own family emergency.

Bethany dried her hands and rubbed her forehead again. "I don't know what I'll do."

"It's not total bad news. I've got a carpenter friend." He paused for a second, then continued. "He's available and needs the work. He'll be coming by later to introduce himself."

"One of your fishing buddies?" That was the last thing she needed.

"No, definitely not. His name is Landon Black. I'm sure he'll do just as well as I do."

"I doubt that. But I don't have much of a choice, do I?"

"I'm so sorry, kiddo. I was looking forward to heading to the island too. I'll see you when you get back."

"Yeah, Harley. Talk to you later."

She hit the button on the phone to disconnect the call and pressed her forehead into the cool kitchen wall, fighting the urge to bang it instead.

Harley knew this job would put Slice of Heaven in the black, finally.

Yes, it was her sister's wedding. And yes, her relationship with her family left something to be desired. But the connections she would make by providing the most delicious of desserts all week would hopefully catapult the bakery to the next level.

Harley knew that. But he didn't know the bad part. That Christiana was marrying Bethany's ex-boyfriend.

It wasn't as seedy as it sounded. She and Simon had dated years ago and discovered pretty quickly they weren't meant for each other romantically. She hadn't cared when the two of them started dating. Their getting married wouldn't have been her first preference, but overall, it didn't bug her too much.

But oh, how the gossipmongers loved to make it into a *thing*. She was already the black sheep of the family because she'd done something as squalid as actually *working* for a living. Then her younger, thinner, more attractive, more exotically named sister *stole her one true love*.

Eye roll. It wasn't like that at all; Simon was very definitely not someone Bethany was pining over. But nobody cared because…never let the truth get in the way of a good story.

But it was critical nothing go wrong with the desserts she was providing. Harley not being there meant they were off to a banging start.

She and Christiana may not be close, but they were still sisters. She'd done Bethany a huge service by hiring her to create the multiple cakes for her wedding reception, as well as the baked desserts for a number of events throughout the wedding week.

There would be so many wealthy, influential people in attendance, most of them from right there in California. If she did this right, word of mouth from this particular group of people would propel Slice of Heaven to an entirely new level.

So, Bethany had accepted the job when Christiana had asked behind their mother's back. She wasn't sure she'd wanted to, but she couldn't turn down the exposure. She needed Slice of Heaven to grow.

There was no way she would ever go back and ask her

family for money, no matter how much of it they had. No matter how many eighteen-hour days Bethany had to work in a row to make Slice of Heaven successful.

For two years, she'd been chipping away at her personal savings, not taking any sort of salary, to get the bakery off the ground. And now, this was her chance.

Bethany knew the exact point her mother had found out about Christiana's choice of her as baker. Three weeks ago, a friend of hers from culinary school had called to tell Bethany her mother tried to hire her to provide the cakes for the wedding.

She'd expected it to happen sooner, if she was honest. Christiana must have done a spectacular job keeping her a secret. And three weeks out from the wedding, Mother hadn't been able to find someone of caliber who could fill in.

She'd thrown a fit that Christiana had hired her. Bethany hadn't lost any sleep over it. Just like she hadn't lost any sleep over her parents partially disinheriting her when she'd gone this route.

The commoner's route. Her mother had had the actual gall to use those words, as if they were the Bridgertons or something.

As if Bethany pursuing her passion for baking—*owning her own damned business*—rather than marrying and playing tennis at the club brought embarrassment onto their family.

For shame. For shame.

With a sigh, she turned back to her cakes and got busy. She couldn't truly be mad at Harley. He'd been far too good to her. He'd worked insane hours helping her, and he hadn't stopped with carpentry. He'd done dishes, watched the front of the shop, and once had even helped her bake, though he hadn't liked it.

And when their business was at its leanest, he'd let Bethany pay him late. She'd vowed then that she'd never forget that, and she never planned to.

She couldn't pretend to be happy now, though. Harley's announcement was just the, pardon the pun, icing on the cake. Things had been steadily going downhill for the past three weeks since Mother found out she was providing the wedding desserts.

First that, then her boyfriend had dumped her. He'd decided he was tired of always coming in second place to her business. He didn't like the hours Bethany had to put in there.

There was no point in reminding him that she'd said no to going out with him six months ago because she'd known it would be unfair to any relationship to have to play second fiddle to her business. But Brad had insisted it wouldn't always be that way and that she was worth the wait.

Evidently, she was only worth six months of a wait.

Bethany hadn't even cried. She'd honestly been more upset that she'd lost her date for the wedding than that their relationship was over. She'd envisioned herself standing proudly on Brad's arm while everyone oohed and aahed over her delicious creations.

Everyone, including her mother and father, bride and ex-boyfriend groom, would make their way over to her to show their amazement. They'd gush about how she was not only a fantastic baker, but a savvy businesswoman and someone who obviously had her personal life together.

She'd graciously accept their praise and smile up at Brad, who would stand supportively beside her, stating he'd never doubted this was how it would all turn out.

And...*scene.*

Yeah, maybe Brad had been more of a prop than an actual boyfriend.

But now, Bethany was going to show up at the wedding not only as the hired help, but without her *plus-one.*

Mother would revel in it.

She'd already tried a power play. When Christiana

wouldn't let her fire Bethany, she'd decided to change the entire concept of the wedding cake design.

Every single bit of it. From size to tiers to structure to flavors. Then she'd announced she and Christiana would be coming to the bakery three days later to taste and see the conceptual design.

Brad should be glad he had broken up with her, because she didn't leave the bakery for a full seventy-two hours, working her ass off to get everything ready for their visit. By the time they'd walked through the door, she'd had a completely new design and several prototypes.

Mother hadn't said one nice thing about it, but she knew she loved it because she'd also not said one negative thing.

Not about the cake, anyway. Her shop, her hair, and her hips were another story.

Story of her life. Always closer to a size twelve than a size two.

But hey, never trust a skinny baker.

Bethany sighed and got back to work making cakes for that week. Her other part-time employee, Michele, would be keeping the shop open while she was gone. No way could they afford to close for a solid week, even with the new business the wedding would hopefully bring in.

If this carpenter friend of Harley's worked out and the entire event didn't fall apart.

Her mother would have a field day if it did.

She heard the back door unlocking. "Morning," Michele called as she walked through. "How was your weekend?"

Bethany worked weekends whenever possible to give Michele that time off. She winced. Maybe if she'd saved a couple of weekends for Brad, he wouldn't have broken up with her.

"Well, there's good news and bad news." She grimaced at her friend and employee.

"Oh shit. How bad is the bad news?" She hung her purse

on the hook by the door with hers. "On a scale of dang-it to jump-off-the-nearest-bridge?"

"Closer to bridge than dang-it."

She shook her head and grabbed a clean apron with *Slice of Heaven* embroidered on the breast. "That doesn't sound promising. Start with the good news."

"I got a lot baked and frozen for this week."

"You didn't have to do that." She bumped Bethany with her hip. "I'm capable of baking everything on our menu. It's the fancy cakes I'm no good at."

"I know," she said. "But you're going to be working more hours than normal this week, so I wanted to do what I could."

"You do too much. Okay, bad news?"

Bethany returned to the mixer and added a few spices, following the recipe exactly. "Harley called."

Michele was busily wiping down the glass fronts of their display cases. She glanced at the clock on the wall and realized it was time to open. Good grief. She finished the mix and got the cake in the oven, setting one of the many timers.

"Is he okay? I thought he would be here so you guys could finish your prep for tomorrow."

"No. He's got some sort of family emergency and can't come with me to the wedding."

She froze and looked up at her with her jaw hanging open. "You're joking."

Bethany shook her head slowly. "Nope. He said he's going to send someone to talk to me who can do the job for him, but I don't know. A stranger?" She rubbed her eyes again, headache creeping back. "And I can't afford to close the shop and take you with me, even if you could do the stands."

Michele rounded the counter and put the cleaning supplies away as Bethany stared at the front window, running possibilities through her head.

A car pulled into the parking lot. Usually she was happy to see the first customers right as they opened, but today, she could use a little more time to figure out exactly how she was going to handle this situation.

"First customer," Bethany muttered, then plopped down onto the stool behind the counter. "Maybe I should cancel entirely."

Michele snorted. "You know you're not going to do that. One, your cakes are fucking awesome, and it's time for you to show both your family and all their bougie friends that. Two, there is no way you're going to give your mother a reason to say I told you so."

Bethany straightened her spine. Michele was right. Well, sort of. If she canceled now, Mother would never say a thing. But her smug silence would be so much louder than her screaming *I knew it!* over a loudspeaker.

But she was really in a lot of trouble. The stands Harley was responsible for were elaborate and a huge part of the floating design Christiana and Mother had approved. Bethany could probably do it herself, but it would take her five times as long. She was going to need that time for dessert preparation and decor.

The elaborate floating design with multiple arms and moving parts... she wouldn't even know where to begin.

The pain in her head was back with a vengeance. "I could go with a different design and just deal with my mother's fury afterward."

Michele wasn't listening to her; she was studying the man who'd gotten out of the car and was walking toward the door. "Damn. He's freaking hot. Ten bucks says he wants a red velvet cupcake to put an engagement ring in."

It happened at least once a month. A guy wanted to be original, and nothing said love more than decadent chocolate cake with cream cheese icing. They usually helped by providing a heart-shaped box.

She glanced in hot guy's direction, but she couldn't even force herself to focus on him or his engagement needs. What was she going to do? What if Harley's carpenter friend wasn't as talented as Harley was? Or what if he didn't show up at all?

Bethany hunkered down on the stool behind the back of their display, hidden from the door. She didn't care about a hot guy. She was about to show up at her sister's wedding as both a personal and professional disaster.

The bell on the door rang as it opened, and she could hear the smile in Michele's voice as she called out her greeting. "Welcome to Slice of Heaven. Have you been in here before?"

"No. This is my first time." A smooth, deep voice washed over her like a blanket of soft silk, almost making her forget her misery for a second.

Almost.

"Let me guess, you're looking for a red velvet cupcake."

"That sounds delicious. But actually, I'm looking for Bethany."

Bethany froze and hunkered down farther. What did he want with her? Why did he know her name?

"Harley sent me."

Holy shit. The gorgeous man with the equally sexy voice was Harley's replacement?

CHAPTER
THREE

SLIDING OFF HER STOOL, Bethany peeked through the crack in the cardboard display to get a truly good look at him, knowing he couldn't see her. He definitely was not one of Harley's fishing buddies as she'd been expecting.

Brownish hair with some gold highlights. Eyes streaked with gold and green. One of those fascinating granite jaws, covered with just a little bit of stubble, that made you want to scratch your nails gently down it. A mouth spread into a wide, handsome smile. Complete with dimples.

If those weren't overkill, she didn't know what was.

And that wasn't even taking into consideration his broad shoulders and long legs. His long-sleeved shirt was rolled up to expose the muscles in his forearms, wrists, and long, trim hands.

"Uh, Bethany was just here," Michele said. "Let me see if I can track her down."

He shot her another smile and turned to look around the shop. So, Bethany did what any reasonable woman would do when faced with handsome charm personified.

She dropped to the floor and crawled into the back room so he wouldn't see her.

Once the door shut behind her, she straightened up and tried to look normal.

Michele busted through the door. "Did you become a magician? How the heck did you get back here without us seeing you? I turned around, and you were gone."

"I cannot deal with a man like that," she declared. "Tell him to go away. I'll figure something else out."

How could someone who looked like him be willing to take a short-term carpentry gig that didn't even pay that much?

Michele looked at her like she'd lost the last bit of sense she had to begin with. "A man like what? Drop-dead gorgeous? That's his crime? You're telling me if he had a dad bod and adult-onset acne, you wouldn't have a problem with him working for you?"

Bethany crossed her arms defensively. She did not need Michele pointing out how unreasonable she was being. "Might as well be. Bad things always happen in threes. First Brad, then Harley. Now this dude? No thanks. One look at him and I know he's bad news."

"You are being utterly ridiculous." Michele put her hands on her hips and stared at her. "Stop it right now."

She sucked in a deep breath. "I swear, Michele, this is too much."

All of it was too much. It was bad enough Bethany had to deal with her family all week, maintaining the highest level of professionalism. But add Mr. September to the mix and she could smell the fiasco coming a mile away.

She could not show up to the wedding dateless, with a gorgeous assistant in tow who may or may not know how to do his job.

Michele grabbed her upper arms. Bethany had her in height by about four inches, but she wasn't about to let go. "Get out of your own head. I know you think of yourself as the ugly duckling, but enough is enough. He's hot, yes. But he's just a guy, and if Harley sent him, you need to give him a chance."

She glared at her until she squirmed. Who was the boss here anyway?

But damn it, she was right. She'd judged him in the way she didn't want people to judge her: on looks alone. Appearances could be very deceiving. Bethany knew that better than anyone. Looking at her, nobody would've ever guessed she came from a wealthy and prominent Los Angeles family.

She let out a sigh. "I guess insanely hot is better than nothing."

"That's the spirit!" She gave her a thumbs-up and an eager grin before pushing her toward the door. "Now get out there before he thinks you're insane."

"I am," Bethany grumbled as she pushed the door outward to go into the front.

The man was staring at their different desserts like he'd like to take his sweet time savoring each one.

What would that sort of intensity mean if it was focused on a woman?

She resisted the urge to fan herself. *Business. Focus on business.* Jeez.

Bethany stayed on her side of the counter. There was no way she was walking around to his side. She needed to keep an expanse of glass and metal between them. "Hello," she said. "I'm Bethany."

He held out his hand across the counter. "Nice to meet you. Harley told me you needed some help this week with carpentry."

She shook his hand, trying not to be distracted by his broad shoulders, deep hazel eyes, or those damned dimples. Tried and failed.

She cleared her throat. *Business.* "Yes, I do need some help. Do you have carpentry experience?"

He ducked his head. "I'm not a professional, but yes, I

believe I have the experience you need. Since I left the Navy, I've been trying to figure out where I want to land in the civilian world. This job would help me out a lot, let me get a feel for carpentry work again."

Bethany winced. "I'd hoped for a professional carpenter."

"I've always been very good with my hands." Was that a double entendre? Did she want it to be? She schooled her features and didn't acknowledge his choice of wording.

He'd been a service member. Now she had to deal with her imagination trying to conjure up an image of him in his uniform.

His *well-fitting* uniform.

Her brain easily succeeded in imagining it. Then it changed, conjuring up a Navy uniform from days past, white with blue accents. A blush crept up her neck, but she ignored how hot he was in her imaginary uniform. This was going to be a lot of trouble.

Business. Business. Business.

And it wasn't as if she could say no. What kind of heartless bitch would she have been if she didn't give him a chance? A man who had defended their country. He was a veteran. A hero. He deserved at least the opportunity to prove his abilities.

"Would you mind giving me a demonstration of your carpentry skills?" She asked in the politest voice she could muster. Her mother would've been proud of her cool tone. "It's important that I don't head off to the event without being certain you can do the job."

"I'd be happy to," he exclaimed. "What do you have in mind?"

Bethany turned to discover Michele behind her with an enormous shit-eating grin on her face. "Shut up," she hissed as she walked through the door and held it open for the mystery sailor carpenter. Turning her attention to him, Bethany tried to smile, even though she knew it had to be coming across like a drunken grimace. "I didn't get your name."

To get between her and Michele at the door, he ended up sliding very close to Bethany. She could've sworn she felt heat coming off his body.

As she tried to convince herself it was all her imagination, he stopped and looked down at her. His dark hazel eyes twinkled, and his gaze lingered on her mouth. "You've got a bit of flour there on your lip," he murmured. "And my name is Landon."

Bethany's breath caught in her throat as he moved farther into the kitchen. She released it and swiped at her lip, pushing the door closed in Michele's face so she wouldn't have to keep looking at her goofy smile.

"Through here," she said, motioning to the left to the large supply closet. All of Harley's tools and equipment were in there.

He seemed at ease as he followed her, looking around in interest. "I've never done any work at a bakery," he said. "If I worked here all the time, I'd have to spend every other moment in the gym."

"Oh?" she asked. She didn't look at him as she pulled out one of their simpler stands, and she forced her mind *not* to imagine him at the gym.

Too late.

"Yeah, I have a major sweet tooth. Especially for cinnamon."

Bethany grabbed the small toolbox that Harley had put together and set it on the table in the middle of the room. "We have a delicious cinnamon roll cake you'll have to avoid, then."

He let out a groan that sounded actually pained.

Straightening, she spun around with her arm out. "The instructions are there on the table." The timer she'd set in the kitchen went off. "I've got to get some stuff out of the oven. If you could put this stand together, that would be great."

He saluted and turned toward the stand.

She wasn't sure she was meant to see that part, so she hightailed it out the door and focused on her cakes. She needed to get a couple more in the oven before calling it a day, as well as frost a few she'd baked yesterday.

Bethany didn't even get all her ingredients out before Landon walked into the kitchen. "All done."

He couldn't have been. That had been faster than Harley even, and Harley had a year's worth of experience with these stands. She followed him back into the storeroom and looked at the stand in shock. It was perfect.

"Did you use the instructions?" They didn't look like they'd been moved at all.

He shook his head. "No. This was fairly simple."

She tried to contain her amazement. "Wow. Okay. Yeah, that was one of our simpler stands, but you still did it really quickly. Interested in trying a more complex one?"

She wanted him to show her what he could do, but she didn't want to seem like a jerk.

"Sure." Dimples beamed. "Point it out. You don't have to get the materials. I know you have things to do."

Bethany pointed to the shelf with their most complex stand, one she'd be taking to her sister's wedding. "And, I hate to ask, but if you could dismantle this one?"

"No problem." Landon turned to get to work, so she stammered a quiet thanks and made her exit.

As she measured ingredients, she fully expected him to come to ask for a helping hand. There were intricate parts that Harley said needed two people.

But after a few minutes, she lost herself in her baking. That was what almost always happened. It was what had drawn her into the business in the first place. Mixing and measuring, focused only on what was in front of her, was like her therapy. Nothing existed but her ideas for treats, the ingredients, and making it all come together.

Everything else—pardon the pun—melted away.

Bethany was well into frosting the mini-cakes the shop would be highlighting tomorrow when Landon stuck his head in.

"Bethany? I'm ready."

She set down her spatula. "You're finished? You didn't need help with the second level?"

He shook his head. "No. I developed a work-around."

A work-around. She was staring at him. "How long has it been?"

He gave her a half smile. "About an hour."

An hour. It would've taken Harley at least twice that, even with her help. Not that she'd ever complained about Harley's work. But Landon was faster by far.

Which was good. He'd need to set up nearly a dozen of these stands, and a couple much larger ones, while at the wedding.

"Let's have a look at it." She had a sneaking suspicion she didn't even need to check. She'd walk into the room and find it perfect. She wasn't sure if that reassured her or made her more nervous.

Michele walked through the door from the front. "Landon, we've got a couple cupcakes that we have to throw out today. Would you like one?"

His eyes lit up. Then he glanced at her and shook his head. "Not right now, but I appreciate it."

Bethany laughed and took pity on him. He'd said he had a sweet tooth. "Go eat a cupcake. I'll come out when I'm done." She glanced at Michele. "That mix should be ready. Can you throw it in the oven?"

"Of course." She still had that giddy look on her face—like she knew if Bethany hadn't thrown Landon out by now, she wasn't going to do it.

Bethany hated that Michele was right.

Landon had erected the complex stand perfectly. She had no reason to deny him the position. He'd done an exemplary job, was utterly polite, and he'd look amazing in a suit setting up at the parties.

She wanted to bang her head against the wall.

"You have to hire him," Michele hissed as she walked back in. "He's perfect."

"Simmer down over there. Perfect is pretty extreme." Bethany rolled her eyes at her. "But yeah, he did a great job."

"I know how important this wedding is to you. Impressing your family. Getting our name out there." Michele bent over and studied the underside of the stand. "This thing is exactly right, isn't it?"

"Yes." Of course it was exactly right. Was there anything about Landon Black not exactly right? "And yeah, this wedding is important."

"So, you're going to hire him?" Michele stood up and clasped her hands together. "C'mon, hire the hottie."

"You've got to stop." But a little laugh escaped despite herself. "You're going to get me sued for sexual harassment."

Michele giggled and grabbed her hand. "Come on, live a little, Bethie. Give yourself some eye candy while you're having to deal with your stressful family."

"This is my chance to prove to my family that I made the right choice in opening my bakery," Bethany said. "I'll hire him because he did a good job. Not because he's gorgeous."

"But you do think he's hot?" she asked.

Bethany rolled her eyes. "Of course, I think Mr. September is hot." She made a sizzling sound as she pressed her finger against her hip, and Michele laughed.

A throat cleared in the doorway.

Aw hell.

"Sorry, I finished my cupcake and wanted to make sure you didn't need me for anything else."

There was no way he hadn't heard what she'd just said. Bethany wanted to melt into the floor. Instead, she squared her shoulders and turned to face him as if she hadn't just made a completely inappropriate statement.

And lawd, he really was attractive. She gave him a brisk nod as she got her hormones on a tighter leash. "If you want the job, you're hired. We leave for the Channel Islands tomorrow."

He nodded back, all sexy hazel eyes and dimples. "I want the job."

"Michele will get you the info you need for this week." With that, she turned and walked with whatever scraps of dignity she had left back into the prep kitchen.

Crisis averted. Bethany had a skilled carpenter who was going to help her make sure her desserts were nothing less than showstoppers at the wedding events that week.

What could possibly go wrong?

Everything.

And then some.

CHAPTER
FOUR

BETHANY THORNTON WAS NOT what Landon had expected.

She'd looked a little out of place in the picture Callum had shown him—a little less glamorous and a little more sunny than the rest of her family. But she was coming from a lot of money, at least some of it gained illegally, so he'd been expecting someone at least partially closed off or defensive.

Bethany hadn't been either of those things. She'd been stressed by his presence and a little flustered, but she definitely hadn't come across as criminal in anything she'd done or said.

Of course, that didn't necessarily mean she was innocent. The last time he'd hung around a woman who'd seemed lively and creative and innocent, she'd shot him in the chest.

Things weren't always what they seemed.

But they weren't always what they didn't seem to be either. He could wax poetic about that for a while.

After she'd hired him yesterday, Landon had taken the stands down and loaded a van with them and several more, along with a host of supplies. Evidently, Bethany didn't trust the island would have the specific ingredients and materials she needed to make her desserts. It seemed like she was taking most of her shop with her.

After they'd loaded everything nonperishable, she'd thanked him—still not quite making eye contact—and paid him cash. It had been his instinct to refuse since he was making a lot more money to infiltrate her company, but that would've been a dead giveaway. In the end, Landon thanked her graciously and promised to meet her there at the airport bright and early that morning.

She touched his arm as he turned to leave. "Don't be late. This wedding is…important."

Her voice was soft, a little hesitant, very un-criminal. She seemed quite young and unsure, and all he wanted to do was what came naturally to him: pull her in for a hug and let her know she could trust him.

Which she could. Sort of. At the very least, she could trust he was going to show up.

"I'll be there."

She nodded and attempted to tuck a strand of that riotous mess of curls into a braid behind one ear. She turned away, then glanced back at him over her shoulder. "Thank you. For showing up tomorrow. For your service to our country. For diving in and helping me out of a tight spot."

And didn't he feel like an ass?

Landon spent all last night studying the files Callum had given him. He knew more than he ever wanted to about Vincent Frey and the Frey Cartel. He read up on the Thornton family and Santa Catalina Island.

The information about Bethany herself hadn't been very thorough. She hadn't visited her parents in a couple of years, so obviously, they weren't close. There didn't seem to be much of a financial connection between them either.

Slice of Heaven was barely making it. Her parents could've helped out and at least eased the burden of the start-up loans Bethany was paying, but they either hadn't offered or she'd turned them down.

He saw her as his cab pulled up to the private jet section of the Long Beach airport. This airport was nowhere near as big as LAX, but it was definitely bigger than most regional airports in the country. Regular flights took off from here daily, but this section was reserved for private flights. No long-term parking that required a shuttle. No TSA security lines.

He'd gotten used to using Zodiac's private jet for a lot of his travel, although it was set up for meetings and strategy while getting from one place to the next. So, private jets weren't new to him. But they would be new to Landon the carpenter—he'd have to act the part.

Bethany stood beside a white van, checking things off a list on a clipboard while two men in yellow vests unloaded the van and loaded the items onto the plane. She shaded her eyes and turned to watch him step out of the cab, giving him a little wave. Relief was clear in her features. She'd been worried about whether he would show.

Landon grabbed his duffel and garment bag and looked around before pretending to notice her and returning her wave. The bay bustled with activity, boxes being loaded onto the plane, flight attendants and people in uniforms walking on and off the private jet.

Bethany walked toward him. He widened his eyes and nodded toward the plane. "We're flying on a private jet?"

She grimaced. "I may not have mentioned that the wedding we're catering is my sister's. And my family is..." She trailed off and turned to look at the jet with a lost expression on her face.

"Wealthy?" He supplied.

"Yeah. *Wealthy.* I'm not, but they are, and since I'm doing all the desserts for the whole week and technically a part of the family, we get the jet."

He whistled through his teeth. "You won't see me complaining."

One of the workers called over to Bethany.

"Go find a seat," she said. "We'll be taking off in a few minutes, but I want to personally make sure everything we need from the bakery is on board."

Landon boarded the plane and sat in the back, where he'd be able to observe everyone coming and going. The jet wasn't that big and had been built for luxury more than function. There were only a handful of seats in the passenger area. He wondered how large the cargo area was.

His answer came when the men in vests began loading boxes into the passenger area. Bethany came in and directed them while he sat back quietly watching.

With every second she worked, he could see why Harley had been convinced she was innocent. Why would someone put this much effort into a front? She obviously loved her bakery and took it seriously. Thankfully nothing about this mission should affect her business. He would be in and out without her ever being any wiser.

If it all went as planned.

He rubbed his chest over the bullet scar. It was a reminder that sometimes things went the complete fucking opposite of *as planned*.

It wasn't long before Bethany collapsed into the chair across from him. He grinned to cover his surprise that she sat with him instead of across the cabin.

"It's not even ten, and I'm already exhausted," she complained.

"You should've let me help."

As she rubbed her eyes, she smiled behind her hands. "This was more supervisory. I needed to make sure we have everything. But don't worry, there won't be as large of a staff at the island airport to help unload. I'll need your assistance there."

Which was unfortunately where Landon would need to get to his real work as quickly as possible, but he wasn't going to leave her in the lurch. "I'll be ready."

It wasn't long before the plane began to move, and he pretended to be excited to build his cover. "I'm used to flights on big Navy planes, strapped in and crammed next to my buddies."

Bethany peered out the window closest to her, then shut the shade. "This was the only way I traveled until I was eighteen and moved away from home to go to school."

"Are you excited to be catering the wedding?" he asked.

She sighed. "That's a loaded question. We're not catering the whole thing. Just the desserts, but…yes, I'm eager to show what I can do."

"Your family must be so proud and excited to have you serve your delicious treats—if they're anything like the cupcakes I tried yesterday."

She crinkled her cute little nose. "My family wasn't exactly supportive of my choice in career. My sister hired me without telling them."

"Your sister obviously has more sense than the rest of them." He gave her an encouraging smile. "This will be your chance to show them what you can do. And probably bring in more business from word of mouth."

Her eyes lit up. "Exactly. My parents have booked the whole island for Christiana's wedding. There will be so many potential clients there, I knew I had to get in on it."

"Are you in the wedding also?"

"No, Christiana isn't doing a traditional wedding party. But I'll be part of the multiple events. There's going to be a luau as a welcome reception, a masquerade ball in place of the rehearsal dinner, and various other events."

Landon already knew about those from the file.

"Are you and your sister close?"

Bethany turned toward the window. "Not really. She and I

are very different. I…" She trailed off with a sad shrug. "We're just very different. You'll understand when you meet her."

"I'm looking forward to it."

If anything, her eyes got a little sadder. "Christiana never disappoints. I'm sure you'll be charmed by her."

So, definitely tension between the siblings. That could possibly be used to his advantage later. But, looking into Bethany's green eyes, those thoughts made him feel less strategic and more like an ass.

So he shot her a smile. "If she's anything like her sister, I'm sure I will be."

The words were more real than his smile. Everything about Bethany seemed authentic and likable. Landon wished he were sitting there under different circumstances. He'd seen Christiana in the photos. She was beautiful, thin, with perfect…everything.

Under different circumstances, he'd assure Bethany that he would take her *real* over Christiana's *perfect* any day of the week.

Not the mission, asshole. Focus.

Bethany pulled out a pad of paper and read over it. A small wrinkle appeared between her eyes. "I hope I didn't forget anything."

"You didn't."

Her brows furrowed deeper as she continued to study the list. Her fingers were gripping it tighter as each moment passed.

"Hey," he said. "It's going to be perfect."

She bit her lip, drawing his attention there.

Her lips are definitely not the fucking mission, Black.

"It has to be perfect. It has to be. It has to be."

She was working herself into a panic. The least he could do was help head it off.

"Hey, you've got it all ready. You're prepared."

She looked up from her list. "What if I forgot something? What if it all falls apart? What if—"

Landon poked her gently on the knee to stop the escalation. "Can I give you some sailor advice?" Actually, it was Navy SEAL advice, but that wasn't part of his cover.

"Sure."

"You prepare as much as you can for the mission at hand, but then roll with the changes when that mission inevitably alters. You've already prepped to the fullest. Now, you'll work the problems as they come."

She set her pad next to her in the seat. "I guess you're right."

He winked at her. A wink he'd used hundreds of times with both men and women to make them feel comfortable, let them know he liked them, help them feel at ease.

This was the first time he'd ever felt like shit using it.

"Tell me more about your family. That'll take your mind off the catering."

She laughed. "Sort of like how a beautiful woman takes your mind off your headache by lighting your bed on fire?"

Surprised, he laughed out loud. This woman was so genuinely real. "Wow. Is your family that bad?"

"My family basically disowned me because I started a *commoner's* business." She rolled her eyes. "And not only is my sister—gasp, the younger daughter—getting married first, she's also marrying my ex-boyfriend."

Oh shit. That hadn't been in the report. "Wow," he repeated, genuinely at a loss for what else to say. "Is that a problem for you?"

"Nah. Simon and I weren't a thing for long, and we were never serious. But still, you know, I've kissed my sister's fiancé." She made a gagging sound.

He chuckled again. "Speaking of lighting the bed on fire."

But at least she was relaxing into her seat. Family stress wasn't as overwhelming as family stress *plus* business stress.

"Then, a couple weeks ago, I lost my plus-one. My boyfriend and I…"

Landon's phone buzzed in the middle of her sentence, and he glanced down to find a text from Callum.

Package One confirmed on island.

Good. Vincent Frey had arrived. If he'd changed his mind at the last minute, this would've been for nothing.

He looked back up at Bethany. She'd been saying something about her boyfriend, but she'd stopped when he'd turned his attention away.

"What were you saying?"

"Nothing." She shook her head. "Nothing important."

He could press. He wanted to press. He wanted to know more about her. This friendly, hardworking woman who'd turned her back on extravagant wealth to follow her dreams.

She was soft and sexy and alluring. And seemed to be as sweet as the desserts she made.

But ultimately, getting close to her wasn't good for either of them. He needed to keep things professional and keep his distance. So, he gave her a brisk nod and looked down at his phone rather than encouraging her to talk.

Landon had a feeling he was just one more person in her life who'd done that to her.

CHAPTER
FIVE

BY THE TIME they landed less than an hour later, Bethany was clutching that checklist in her hand again. After he'd shut down their friendly banter, she'd gone back to it. She hadn't freaked out anymore, but neither had she tried to engage him in conversation.

As soon as the plane stopped, she jumped to her feet and rushed toward the door. The attendant barely had time to get it open before Bethany hurried outside. He shrugged at the attendant and followed. Bethany was ready to work—as tense as she'd been before.

Landon could've helped her relax more on the plane and get her mind off it, but he hadn't.

Focus on the mission.

Bethany's emotional well-being and stress levels were not his problem. But it still went against his nature to see someone carry such a big burden on their own when he could help.

She was heading toward where the cargo was being unloaded when she was stopped by a woman waiting on the tarmac under an umbrella held by a man in a blue uniform. Her clothes seemed far too formal for island life.

"Bethany, darling," she called out.

Landon recognized her as the groom's mother from the files he'd studied. It paid to know as many faces and names as possible in a mission like this.

"I noticed your plane was scheduled for this morning. I thought I'd say hello." She walked over and blew air-kisses on either side of Bethany's cheeks.

"Hello, Patricia." Bethany's smile was forced, nothing like what he'd seen from her earlier, and she held out her arm toward him. "This is Landon, he's helping me. Landon, this is the groom's mother and a longtime family friend, Patricia Carter."

Landon held out his hand. "Pleased to meet you, ma'am."

She shook it with a limp wrist, then ignored him. He was the help, obviously not even worth speaking to. She turned back to Bethany.

"I'm so pleased you were able to find it in yourself to support the wedding, darling. You know I had hoped things would turn out differently, but it's so big of you, despite everything."

Bethany's smile got even stiffer but stayed in place. "Simon and I were never that close. So think nothing of it."

"I know." She grabbed Bethany's hand. "But it still has to be hard for you, Christiana being the younger sister and all."

This woman was just trying to stir the pot. Fortunately, Bethany recognized it too. "I promise I'll be fine. Now, I need to oversee the unloading of my supplies. You go have a nice drink for me. I'll see you at the brunch."

Patricia made a distressed face. "You're sure you'll have everything you need for the desserts you're providing? I would hate to think of anything going wrong. Accidentally or…otherwise."

Bethany stiffened, smile barely hanging on to her face. Patricia had basically accused her of sabotaging the event.

"Nothing is going to go wrong. I'm sure you'll be impressed, Patricia. I'll see you later."

Bethany turned and walked toward the back of the plane, leaving him standing with Patricia. The older woman was obviously not used to being dismissed. She glared at him, as if daring him to say something.

He was tempted. Lord, was he tempted. But the help didn't get the luxury of telling the uber-rich that they were fake and crass and that Bethany had more work integrity in her little finger than Patricia had ever had.

Patricia spun on her too-formal heels and walked toward the main building, the uniformed umbrella-holder struggling to keep up with her. Good riddance.

Landon needed to get to the resort's security building. Callum would be sending instructions on how to hack into the feed soon. But instead, he hustled over to catch up with Bethany.

She nodded at him as boxes were unloaded from the plane. "I'd prefer we'd carry these cakes ourselves. The crew can help with the other stuff, but the prebaked cakes are the most critical element. We have to get them in the freezer at the main lodge auxiliary kitchen."

She stepped up and took over from the hotel staff and jet crew members. They all fell in line with her commanding voice. He stood at her side, and when the cakes were uncovered, they moved them to a waiting, air-conditioned van.

"The fondant too," she muttered and pointed to another series of boxes. "It's too important to leave to just anyone."

He hurried over and began moving those boxes one at a time. The rest of the staff loaded the other items, and they had two vans full of cakes and supplies in no time.

They split up then, each of them riding in the passenger seat of the vans driven by men in hotel security uniforms. Landon watched out his window, getting his bearings against the map of the property he'd studied.

Santa Catalina wasn't very large, and the entire island was owned by the resort. The main lodge housed thirty rooms and suites, and cottages were scattered all over. The northern end of the island was higher, with cliff views of the Pacific. The southern half had been made into more traditional beaches… white sand with lots of beach chairs, umbrellas, and cabanas.

Some of the cottages had their own pools or hot tubs. Then outside the main lodge was a huge pool/hot tub combination with views of the ocean. It was the primary gathering place on the island and where the resort hosted most of their activities.

According to Callum, the entire main lodge and over half the cottages would be occupied with wedding guests. Thornton had gone ahead and rented the rest of the rooms for the week to ensure the only people on the island were either resort employees or guests who'd been invited.

And him.

As soon as he broke into the resort's security building and finished his tasks there, his first order of business would be to figure out where Vincent Frey was. Landon needed to get on that immediately. He knew how quickly a week would go by.

But damn it, first he had to help Bethany. There was no way he could just bail on her right now, despite his *focus on the mission* mantra bullshit.

The vans stopped at the back of a large building, in front of a cargo door. Bethany jumped out of the lead van and didn't even wait for the driver to open the back. She did it herself and began unloading.

The woman definitely wasn't afraid of hard work. And he was sure Patricia's comments suggesting sabotage were not helping Bethany's peace of mind.

He grabbed more cake and followed her inside. The cargo door opened into the main resort kitchen. She quickly found someone who directed them to the auxiliary kitchen where they'd be working that week, so he followed her.

She looked around as she walked it, taking stock of the equipment and space. She nodded. "This will work fine. I can do everything I need to here."

She set her box down on one of the metal counters then opened the door to the walk-in fridge.

"To the left." She pointed to a shelf with her elbow. "The resort's in-house catering company gets the right side."

"They didn't leave you much room."

"Yeah. The resort wasn't thrilled that Christiana was bringing in an outside vendor. This is one of their ways of making that known."

"We'll make it work. I'll be happy to start stacking some of their boxes somewhere else if you want me to." Landon looked closer at some of the labels. "Some of this doesn't even need to be refrigerated."

She shot me a smile even through her stress. "I like how you think. Let's see if we can make it all fit."

He went back out and got more boxes. When he came back in, she was checking that damned list of hers. "This one is for in here." She took the box from him and walked it into the non-refrigerated storage. "I've got them marked based on when we'll need them."

When they exited the storage room, a couple of young men and a young woman in a starched white uniform approached Bethany. They each had a box in their hands. "Ma'am, where do you want these?"

Bethany's face tightened. She'd only wanted them to handle these particular boxes. He expected a meltdown, but it didn't come.

"Thank you," she said. She sent one of the boxes into the refrigeration unit and the other two into the freezer.

"You stay here and supervise." Landon told her. "I'll grab the important stuff and try to direct the staff to non-critical elements."

It took over an hour to get everything unpacked and situated to Bethany's liking. She was polite to everyone, but more than once, he found her moving things herself because she didn't like where or how it had been positioned.

Once all the freezer and refrigerated items were placed, he thought she might relax a little. But then she started rearranging everything in the nonperishable storage room, once again checking things off against her precious list.

Landon couldn't wait any longer. He needed to get to the opposite side of the island. Bethany didn't need him anymore. He'd come back and work on the stands after he got his real job started.

The kitchen bustled around them. Guests had already arrived on the island, and multiple waiters were bringing out drinks and hors d'oeuvres to people lounging by the pool. That would give him the opportunity to—

A server, obviously not aware that they had occupied the auxiliary kitchen, decided to cut through on her way out to the pool. She looked away from where she was going and ran straight into Bethany—lurching forward, drinks flying off the tray. Orange juice and champagne soaked Bethany's white shirt.

And, even worse, ruined her list.

"No, I'm so sorry!" the server exclaimed, eyes big. "Oh no."

Bethany was staring at her ruined list as it lost its shape and folded over her hand. Now he'd get to see that rich-lady ire that was sure to come out of her.

But she kept her cool, wiping off the paper as best she could, before trying to do the same with her blouse so it wasn't clinging to her chest. His eyes shot to the lacy bra exposed by the liquid before quickly jerking back to her face.

Then, to his utter shock, she crouched down with the server to help pick up the larger pieces of glass. "Are you okay?"

The woman looked over at Bethany in shock, tears rolling

down her cheeks. "I'm fine. I'm so sorry. I'll get fired. They told us not to cut through here this week, but I forgot. They don't tolerate mistakes like this."

Bethany offered the younger woman a smile. "Then we'll tell them I ran into you. Accidents happen."

Landon belatedly realized he was standing there doing nothing, so he grabbed the broom from the closet. He reached down and offered Bethany a hand so she could stand. "You guys step out of the way. Let me sweep this."

Bethany gave me a grateful smile as she took his hand. The server was still in tears.

"Please don't worry on my account," Bethany said. "I've got plenty of shirts, and these drinks can be remade, okay? We're fine. Go get back to your work."

The poor server nodded and swiped away her tears. Landon finished sweeping and dumped the pieces. When he came back, Bethany was studying her ruined list, almost in her own tears.

He was going to get a special spot in heaven for not looking at her breasts, even knowing that lace—his second biggest weakness after sweets—was clearly visible.

He gently pried the list from her fingers. "This paper has done its job. You know you have what you need. You've planned well, everything is here, you know what you're doing."

"If the mission alters, I work the problems as they come," she repeated his words from the jet back to him.

His phone chimed in his pocket again, but this time, he ignored it. Mission be damned.

"Exactly." She bit that plump bottom lip, and *that* he couldn't keep his eyes from.

"You're right. I can do this." She tossed the paper in the trash. "Plus, I've got to get ready for the welcome reception."

Shit. "Are we baking for that?"

"No. It's the only wedding event I'm not doing any work

for. But I've got to change and get ready." She straightened her shoulders.

"Uh-oh. Family?"

She rubbed her eyes. "Yeah. Might as well take them all on at once. I guess you're free to get checked in and hang out. You have a room assigned, and really, there's nothing you need to do until later this afternoon to get ready for the welcome reception setup tonight."

His phone chimed in his pocket again.

She looked down at her shirt and realized its state. She quickly pulled it from her chest, cheeks burning. "I'll see you later. I can't go to the brunch looking like this. Thanks for your help."

She turned away, but Landon grabbed her elbow gently, immediately aware of her soft skin under his fingers. He didn't turn her to face him, but he stepped closer so he could lean down to speak softly into her ear. "How you treated that server a few minutes ago makes you richer than anyone else on this island. You don't forget that."

He was holding her way too close to be considered professional, but Landon didn't care. She was obviously about to go into the lion's den, and if he could offer her some support, he wanted to do so.

She nodded, and he let her go, watching as she walked briskly through the busy kitchen, making sure to keep out of everyone's way.

His phone dinged again, and he pulled it out of his pocket. Callum.

Change of plans. More details forthcoming. Proceed to security building.

He'd been on the ground less than an hour, and already things had changed. He shouldn't be surprised.

If the mission alters…work the problems as they come.

CHAPTER
SIX

THE RESORT on Santa Catalina had been developed for the famous and uber-rich. Every whim could be catered to for the right price, and the security on the island reflected the clientele that visited here.

Landon strolled along the path of the guest section, nodding and smiling at other people who were walking with drinks in their hands. Once past them, he took a sharp turn to the north, along a road obviously not meant for guests.

As soon as he did, he dropped all pretense of leisurely wandering and began a fast jog toward the north side of the island. Half a mile later, he cut back into the treed section and made his way toward the resort's security building.

He came at the building from the east, stopping so he could observe. There were staff everywhere at the resort, but none of them carried semiautomatic weapons like the man guarding this building. Not to mention the other two guys, not in the resort security uniforms, standing over to the side, who also were carrying. Those had to be Frey's men.

He definitely wasn't going to be able to walk through the front door. Even playing lost tourist wouldn't work—he didn't want to do anything that was going to make him more memorable to security.

Despite his *change of plans* message, Landon knew Callum would be providing instructions soon. He hoped they would be pretty thorough. He'd spent his pre-mission time memorizing the info in the file rather than worrying about getting into this building—leaving that to him.

But now, looking at the security measures surrounding Fort Knox here, it seemed like the whole mission could be over before it started. From here, he couldn't see a single entry point.

A message came through on his phone, but not from Callum. It was an unlisted number.

Present for you at the bottom of the south side cliff.

He hoped it was a bazooka or a full SEAL team because that's what it was going to take to get Landon inside that building.

He eased back from his observation post and headed down to the bottom of the south side cliff as instructed. What awaited him there wasn't what he'd wished for, but it was close enough.

"You lost, sailor?"

Tristan Zimmerman grinned up at him from where he was removing objects from a waterproof bag at the bottom of the cliff-side wall. His hair was dripping, and a wet suit was piled on the ground next to him.

"What are you even doing here, Pisces?"

Tristan was the head of the Zodiac Tactical Guardian Unit, leading the bodyguarding and protection jobs. He worked out of Los Angeles.

He was taking rappelling equipment out of his bag. So that was going to be their plan. They would go up this cliff no one in their right mind would try.

"Callum sent me," Tristan said. "Evidently, the mole situation in his office took a turn for the worse yesterday, and he is not sure if he can trust anyone. He didn't want to have any more contact with you while this was going down in case it tipped off the mole. Ian had to leave to take care of some stuff with Wavy."

Landon nodded. Wavy still sometimes struggled with what Mosaic had done to her and then what she had done to him in the process.

"I had a couple days off," Tristan continued. "So, I volunteered to help sit on the beach, drinking mai tais and eating cake. Sadly, getting you into this building was the closest Callum could come up with."

"Looks like I'm going to need all the help I can get. Security at the front door is no joke."

"From the water too. Evidently, the Santa Catalina resort monitors all ships, no matter how small, that come closer than two miles." He grinned at him. "Couple-mile swim hauling gear through icy waters reminded me of the good old days at Coronado."

Landon chuckled. The BUD/S training he was referring to was considered the *good old days* by absolutely no one who'd done it. They were mostly glad to have just survived the Navy SEAL conditioning. "Your code name is Pisces, so you can be forgiven for loving the water so much."

He winked at him. "What's not to love?"

Tristan was in nearly as good of shape now as he'd been when he was a SEAL. As with everyone at Zodiac, just because they weren't active duty anymore didn't mean they weren't in fighting form.

Or, in Landon's case, attempting to get back to it.

"Thanks for taking a break from your job of babysitting the rich and famous to help me out."

They both knew that wasn't anywhere close to what his job was like. Heading a security team involved a lot of long, uncomfortable hours and focus, often for people not much fun to be around. Glamorous, it was not. But Tristan was one of the best in the business.

And he'd trust him with his back any day.

"What's the plan?" he set out rings, anchors, and carabiners.

"I'll free-climb up and set up the rappelling equipment, in case a fast getaway is necessary. Then once you're up, we'll both go in through the ventilation system at the back of the building."

Landon looked up at the cliff wall. He was glad he wasn't free-climbing that. Unlike Tristan, he hadn't grown up in the mountains of Wyoming, and he didn't have nearly the experience he did.

"Please don't die. I don't want to have to make a trip to the Wyoming governor's office to explain."

He grinned over at him. "Dad is used to my shit. Or, if I'm taking a break from giving him more gray hairs, Andrew or Gavin take over."

Yeah, the Zimmerman brothers were...*active* when it came to danger. Even baby sister Lyn had nearly gotten herself killed a couple times.

"Just don't cut yourself. That'll draw the sharks on the swim back out." he was only half kidding.

He grimaced and handed Landon a comm device so they could communicate. He slipped it in his ear.

"Once I'm up and we're through the vents, I'll tranq the guard in the observation room. When he's out, you can hack the feed from the server room and get everything set up. Instructions are on your phone, study them while I'm playing Spider-Man."

"Roger that. Be careful."

He winked. "Catch me if I fall."

"Uh, no can do, buddy. You may have heard Callum got down on one knee with me the other day."

"Damn it, missed my chance." He laughed and took off up

the cliff wall like he had, in fact, been bitten by a radioactive spider and had the superpowers to show for it.

Landon watched him for a few seconds before turning to his phone to study what he needed to do once he was in the server room. Tristan would make it. He needed to be ready for his part once he did.

"I'm up." Tristan's voice came through the comm device a few minutes later. "Give me a second to secure the anchor, then you'll have your ride."

It wasn't long before the rappelling rope lowered down to Landon. He clipped himself in and started hoisting himself up. A *ride* it definitely wasn't. But this was why he'd pushed himself well beyond what his doctors and physical therapists had wanted him to over the past few months.

So that when the time came, he'd be ready.

Granted, hoisting himself up a cliff wall on an island that catered to extravagantly rich people hadn't been what he'd been envisioning when he'd worked himself to exhaustion in the gym so many nights.

Regardless, he made it. A little more winded than he wanted to be, but within acceptable limits.

Tristan and Landon crawled into the vent and scooted themselves forward silently. Their shoulders barely fit in the square metal tube, making progress slow. He was glad Ian wasn't there with them. This would play hell with his claustrophobia.

He'd force it down and inch his way forward with them, but it would definitely take a toll. He'd earned his phobia the hard way, and sometimes even riding in an elevator was difficult for him.

By the time they made it to the server room, he and Tristan were both sweaty. Landon used a battery-powered screwdriver to remove the vent covering to the room and lowered himself into it.

"Watch your time," Tristan said from above him. "Window is pretty narrow. I'll tranq the guard, which will buy us about five minutes before he wakes up, thinking he fell asleep in his chair. But if you're in the system for more than ninety seconds, it'll set off alarms."

"Roger."

Tristan took off farther into the vent, and he dashed through the server room to find the panel he needed.

Tristan and Landon would have to time this perfectly in order for it to work. They'd both have to trust each other to do their parts, or it would all be for naught.

And it felt fucking good to be part of a team again. This part of him had definitely been dormant for far too long.

Landon used his screwdriver again to release the computer panel from the wall of servers. The resort here truly did take its security seriously to have so much in place. Hosting its own server room meant no one could hack into it from off-site.

And would have to do some pretty death-defying feats to hack it from on-site. Like, climb up a cliff wall and muscle through ventilation shafts.

"Guard is night-night." Tristan's voice came through the comm in his ear a few minutes later. "You're clear, Libra."

"Starting now. Count me down."

"Roger. Ninety seconds."

He blew out a breath and focused on steadying his hands and connecting the wires he needed in order to break in to their system. This override would allow Tristan to monitor the resort's internal system.

Once the wires were attached, Landon hooked up his portable keyboard and followed the instructions he'd been given to link the resort's system with theirs.

"System patch complete," he muttered.

"Roger. Thirty-five seconds remaining."

"Going in for security camera override." He glanced at his phone for the info he needed then typed rapidly on the keyboard. Once that was done, no one would have any proof he'd been there, even if they came back to look at the security footage afterward.

The first override attempt failed, so he switched to the second.

"Twenty seconds."

Shit. He was running out of time.

Landon typed in the code, but a shaky hand caused him to enter one of the digits incorrectly. If this didn't work, the mission would be over before it even started. He needed to pull himself together.

He closed his eyes, sucked in a breath, then blew it back out.

Focus, Black.

"Ten seconds. Shut it down, Landon. We'll find another way."

He ignored Tristan and typed the code a second time. This was it. If he screwed up here, he'd not only fail to override the security cameras, he'd be sending out a red flag that someone was in their server room.

"Five, four..."

Landon finished the code, hit enter, and yanked the wire so the panel was no longer attached to his keyboard.

"I'm out."

"Hold for confirmation."

He packed the equipment back into the small backpack then jumped up to the air vent, grabbing the edge and pulling himself up. Regardless of whether the patch was successful or not, he had to get out. The guard monitoring the room would be awake before he could try it again.

Now they would see if his fuckup had blown the whole mission.

Maybe Callum should've sent someone else.

"Patch successful. We're a go," Tristan said. "Nice work, Libra."

"Roger that."

Landon lay back in the vent shaft and blew out a breath. He just hoped he didn't screw up the rest of the mission like he nearly had this.

CHAPTER
SEVEN

BETHANY CHECKED into her room and rushed to get cleaned up before the brunch. She'd spent so much time making sure her supplies were organized she had no time now to take a shower.

Of course, she hadn't expected to be wearing mimosas and what smelled like gin and tonics. Her curly hair needed a lot of love after being washed, so showering would have to wait.

She wiped off her chest, cringing at the sight of her bra shining proudly through her now-transparent blouse. Great. She'd been standing in front of Landon half naked.

After getting as much stickiness off her as possible, she changed into a knee-length dusty-blue chiffon cocktail dress the porters had delivered to the room and hung while she was getting her supplies situated. Looking in the mirror, she realized the sleeveless cut of the dress probably wasn't the best look for her pudgy arms. But she liked its cascading ruffles, so she was going to wear it.

Twenty bucks said Mother pointed out how her arms looked. Or that she offered to send Bethany her personal trainer or something.

Her hair… she grimaced. It was relatively decent in her messy bun, so she wasn't about to fool with it. She'd be getting it straightened at the resort salon for the wedding itself, but until then, it would do its own thing, as always.

She blew out a breath as she stared at her reflection. "You can do this."

She wasn't sure if she was talking about the brunch, the catering, or spending the whole week working with her charming, gorgeous new assistant.

Probably D, all of the above.

But right now, she would concentrate on the brunch. It was the only wedding event at which she wasn't responsible for providing any desserts. The hotel was taking care of this one since she was arriving today. She'd offered, but Mother had put her foot down, arguing she wouldn't have enough time. That she would be too rushed getting in and trying to get everything ready.

Her phone buzzed on the counter.

Where are you?

Mother. She'd been right; Bethany wouldn't have had enough time to set up anything for the brunch. She was already late. This was going to give her more ammunition.

She brushed on a little lip gloss then rushed out the door, not worrying about anything else. No amount of makeup was going to turn her into someone who looked like Christiana, so why bother trying?

She left her one-bedroom suite then cut through the lobby, taking a right as she got outside. She was glad she was already familiar with the resort. They'd spent multiple vacations there as she was growing up. She'd wanted to go to Disneyland, but Dad had said that place was a nightmare.

It wasn't until Bethany was in college that she realized he'd meant *security* nightmare. And that some of the people Dad worked with were quite a bit less than upstanding.

That knowledge had made the choice of separating herself

from the family and starting her own business easier to make. Mother had acted like she'd joined some sort of cult that sacrificed kittens on a regular basis. Dad hadn't supported her, but he hadn't been that upset either. Christiana had done what she was told—cut her off. That had hurt most of all.

But she was here now. That was all that mattered.

As she passed the resort's massive pool, Bethany half expected to see Landon lounging and chatting, all easy smile and laughter. He didn't seem like the type to stay in his room if there were people he could charm, just by his very presence.

He was good with his hands. Good with people. Landon Black was a pretty dangerous package.

And heck if *package* didn't send her mind spiraling in all sorts of salacious directions.

With a sigh, she turned and cut over to the glass-enclosed conservatory where the family brunch was being held. She wanted to stop for a moment, take a breath, get herself together. But she knew another more-frantic text would be hitting her phone any moment if she wasted more time.

Her mother spotted her the moment she walked in. She hurried over, smile on her face but eyes traveling up and down the length of her body. "Bethany, dear, there you are! Are you sure you won't need a light sweater or shawl?"

In eighty-five-degree weather? Probably not.

Bethany owed herself twenty dollars.

"No, Mother, I'll be fine. Thank you."

She leaned in and pressed her cheek to Bethany's. "It's wonderful to see you, sweetheart."

She meant well. She just couldn't help criticizing with one breath as she gave affection with the other. She'd done it all her life. At least it wasn't reserved for only her. Christiana got it just as much.

"You should've let me hire someone else so you could enjoy yourself this week. You deserve a break." She fiddled with Bethany's hair. Bethany took the opportunity to study her mother's face. It was as unlined as she ever remembered it. She'd probably had more Botox.

She said it all as if they were the perfect mother and daughter. As if they hadn't barely talked to each other for the past two years. Appearances were everything to her mother.

"I didn't want a break. I wanted the job," Bethany said through a forced smile.

"Oh, you and your little cake shop." She waved her hand in dismissal of her *silly hobby*. "I'll never understand why you can't use your talents for charity work or to make a husband happy."

Bethany nearly bit off her tongue in an effort not to respond. This was not the time to get into it with her again. Her mother had never worked a day in her life. She'd been wealthy before she got married and even more so afterward.

She turned and hooked an arm in hers. "Come on, you were supposed to be here early to help us greet the guests. This brunch is for close friends and family only."

Fantastic. All the people who would feel close enough to Bethany to comment on her life, flabby arms, and lack of a date. Maybe she'd get lucky and a tidal wave would hit the island.

"Well, you at least could've opened your shop in Beverly Hills instead of all the way out in the boonies of Carpinteria. You might as well be in Minnesota," she complained.

Right. Because an hour outside of LA was the same as being halfway across the country. Actually, to her mother, that was probably true.

"And where is your boyfriend?" she continued. "I told everyone you were bringing him. I was hoping he would be here for the brunch."

Bethany stiffened, about to explain, when Christiana and Simon made their way around one of the huge hanging flower arrangements, and she was able to see them for the first time.

Patricia was beside her son, but he stared down at Christiana as if the sun and stars aligned for her very pleasure.

She hadn't seen them together much while they'd dated. Mother had been so upset about the bakery that it had been easier to ignore Christiana also. She'd chosen Mother and Father over her.

It had hurt, but she shouldn't have let it come between them. Christiana was younger than Bethany, only twenty-two. And she'd only ever wanted this life. She wanted the charity work and luncheons with friends.

And just like she wished her family had not rejected her choices, she should not have rejected Christiana's. She was her sister, and she loved her.

And Simon did too. The devotion on his face made something click inside her. He and Bethany, in the short time they'd dated, had never had anything close to the feelings he had for Christiana now.

Christiana turned to respond to whatever he'd said, and her face changed when she looked at him. It softened, and her mouth tipped up in a smile. She could be as much of an ice queen bitch as Mother when she wanted to, but this was the *real* Christiana.

She loved him just as much as he did her.

Bethany was happy for her. So, so happy.

She was still a little concerned that the desserts she would provide wouldn't be perfect, and that people were going to pity her because she and Simon had history. Her not having a date was going to add fuel to that fire. And everyone always noticed that Mother and Christiana were a size two and Bethany was more than quadruple that.

But her sister was marrying the man she loved, and ultimately, that was the most important thing. Tears welled in Bethany's eyes.

Her mother grabbed her hand. "Are you all right? I thought you were okay with Christiana marrying Simon."

"I am. Even more so seeing them together right now." Bethany turned to her. "I want you to help me squash any rumors. There was never anything serious between Simon and me, and if you hear anyone try to make that a thing, you shut it down. I know you can."

She tucked an escaped curl behind her ear. "I will."

Bethany smiled at her. She and her mother were always going to have their differences, and until she learned to accept Slice of Heaven as part of her, they were never going to be close. But Bethany knew she had her back on this.

Her shoulders slumped in relief as Christiana's voice interrupted them. If her mother said she'd take care of it, she'd take care of it.

"Bethie!" Christiana exclaimed. "I'm so happy to see you." She rushed over, and she pulled her in for a hug. Bethany was a little surprised she was showing this much emotion in front of everyone, but then decided she didn't care and wrapped her arms around her tighter.

"Simon," Bethany said when she pulled back. "Congratulations."

She gave him a genuine hug with one hand still in Christiana's. She beamed at them over Simon's shoulder.

"I'm so happy for you both," she whispered to her friend.

"I'm glad to hear that," he said. "I was worried it would be awkward."

"Not at all." Bethany pulled back, stiffening as his mother joined them. "Hello again, Patricia. Good to see you."

"Darling." Completely inauthentic air-kisses. "You look... pretty. Did you get your...work finished?"

Her pauses said so much more than her actual words. Bethany kept a smile plastered on her face. "I did. Thank you for asking."

A member of the hotel staff came to ask Patricia and

Mother a question just as Simon was called across the room by his cousin, leaving her a few precious moments alone with her sister.

Christiana still clutched her hand tightly. Bethany gave her a concerned look. "What is it?"

She shook her head. "Nothing. Just nerves."

"You don't want to marry Simon?"

Her eyes shot over to him, and she gave a soft smile. "No, I definitely want to marry Simon."

"But the rest of it?" Bethany asked.

She blanched. "Wedding jitters. That's the problem."

Bethany laughed and put her arm around her sister. "I'm sorry I didn't check in on you these last few months. I could've helped more."

Christiana bumped the side of her head to Bethany's. "No, stop it. You've been working at your amazing bakery. I'm the one who should've been more supportive of you. I'm just no good at standing up to Mother."

Bethany kissed her forehead. "Don't you worry about it. Especially not this week. You focus on getting married."

She looked over at Mother and Patricia, who were both speaking in low, angry tones to the staff member who'd requested an audience. She felt sorry for the woman. "I'm just worried about everything going perfectly this week. Normal Bridezilla stuff."

Bethany snorted. "Don't pretend it's not Mother who's the Bridezilla."

"Patricia isn't helping. The two of them are such frenemies. Always wanting to outdo each other, but also willing to help the other tear someone else apart."

They walked toward the table of mimosas. "It means so much to me that you hired Sime for the desserts. It's going to do wonders for my business. Plus, I can't wait to show you what I can do."

"I know, Bethie, but..." Christiana's hand shook as she reached for a flute.

"What?"

"Patricia thinks you're going to sabotage the wedding. You know how Mother was upset when she found out I'd hired you? Patricia was so much worse. She's convinced you took the job to ruin this week and the wedding."

"Because you're marrying Simon? That seems like overkill."

Christiana shrugged both shoulders. "That. The fact that the family cut you off financially when you opened the bakery. The fact that I'm getting married even though I'm younger."

Bethany rubbed her eyes. "You realize how ridiculous and paranoid that sounds."

"Yes. *I* do."

But not Patricia. She loved drama.

She grabbed a mimosa and sucked half of it down in just a few seconds. Definitely tasted better than wearing it. "What about Mother? Does she think I'm out to sabotage?"

Christiana took a glass and sipped it at a much more appropriate rate. "I'm not sure. She never really contradicted Patricia, but she didn't agree that you would try to make trouble. Don't get me wrong, she still didn't want me to hire you. But for her, I think it was a status thing."

"Didn't want me to sully the family name by having a blue-collar job?"

Christiana gave her a sheepish look and shrugged one delicate shoulder. "You know Mother."

"Well, don't worry." Bethany drank down the rest of her mimosa, before placing the flute on a well-trained waiter's tray as he came by. "I have no plans whatsoever to sabotage any part of your wedding. I'm truly happy for you two."

She wanted to grab another drink, but resisted. As soon as this event was over, she had work to do to get desserts ready for the welcome reception tonight. It would be her first chance to prove what Slice of Heaven could do.

But she had to survive this brunch first.

She shouldn't have been surprised Patricia wanted someone else as the dessert caterer. If anything, the Carter family had even more money than theirs. She would've wanted someone who had catered for celebrities so she could boast about it.

But to think Bethany would sabotage the wedding? She'd known their family for over a decade. That was pretty low, even for her.

Christiana slipped her arm through hers. "I know you would never do something like that. I'm so excited to taste your treats. I know they'll be wonderful!"

Mother and Patricia joined them and grabbed glasses of their own before she could respond. Both of them were looking quite pleased with themselves. Meanwhile, the staff member they'd been talking with looked close to tears.

"Darling, when is that handsome boyfriend of yours going to join us?" Patricia asked her. "Your mother showed us your pictures on social media. It's so nice that you...have someone."

That fucking pause again.

Worse, as Simon rejoined them along with some of his extended family, Bethany realized everyone was staring at her, waiting for her response.

She couldn't do it. No matter how strongly she believed a woman didn't need a man to complete her, and that it was a practical and even noble choice not to pursue a relationship while getting a business off the ground, she could not stand there and make that announcement in front of everyone.

Patricia would probably suggest if Bethany had worn a light sweater over her chubby arms, she'd probably still have a boyfriend. Mother would nod and say she was always welcome back at home where she belonged.

Every second she stood in silence, the worse it got.

"Oh, he's going to—" she cut herself off and grabbed her phone out of her clutch as if she'd felt it vibrate. "Oh dear."

Bethany stepped back a little so no one could see it and looked down, pretending to have a message. "I'm so sorry. I've got to deal with this. Work emergency. It's about the icing. I'll see everyone later at the welcome reception."

She kissed Christiana on the cheek, gave everyone else an awkward little wave, and hurried for the door.

She didn't move fast enough to miss Patricia's words. "See, Angelique? I told you you should've insisted on using another bakery. The...*problems* are starting already."

She didn't stop walking, but she strained to hear how Mother would respond.

"I'm sure it will be fine," she said. "But I did put the hotel on alert. So don't worry, we have a backup."

Bethany's heart sank. Mother didn't trust her to do the job. Maybe even thought she was sabotaging also.

She blinked back tears as she reached the door and pushed into the warmer air outside.

According to these people, she was the pitiful, unmarried elder sister of the bride.

She was the hired help who probably couldn't be trusted.

And she was the guest who'd RSVP'd plus-one, but wouldn't have a date. There was no way in hell that would go unnoticed, even when she made up some excuse why her boyfriend wasn't there.

Bethany straightened her shoulders. She'd walked away from this life because it wasn't what she wanted. And although she couldn't deny that what they thought of her mattered, she wasn't going to let it derail her.

They might think she was personally pitiful, but by the end of this week, they would damned well know, professionally, she was someone to take seriously.

CHAPTER
EIGHT

THIRTY MINUTES after sending Tristan back out into the Pacific, Landon was at the main pool area of the resort. He'd sprinted back, then gotten checked in. He needed to blend in with everyone else.

The hotel security feeds were no longer an issue. If things went sideways and someone from the Frey Cartel decided to search the hotel security footage from any of the public areas or hallways, they'd get nothing. His face wouldn't be traceable, and more importantly, they wouldn't be able to connect him to Bethany in any way.

But things weren't going to go sideways.

He'd wanted to be in the lobby to make sure he saw Frey and his entourage enter. He'd barely made it since he'd been roped into helping some woman carry items to her room, even after explaining he wasn't hotel staff.

Frey had arrived with three security guards, his personal assistant Landon could identify from Callum's photographs, and his girlfriend.

Not his wife. Interesting. The file had a picture of both women. He would've thought the wife would accompany him to a society wedding like this.

He already knew which suite the hotel had placed Frey in since Tristan now had a direct feed into their computer system. He'd be providing Landon any intel updates if things changed. But he still took the next elevator up after he did. If he were in charge of Frey's security, he would've checked him in to one room, then actually placed him in another under a different name even the resort wasn't aware of.

Seeing if that was the case would give him a better understanding of what he was up against. But when his elevator opened on his floor, Frey was entering the room he'd been assigned. Landon took one look around and got back on the elevator.

"Oops. Wrong floor." He chuckled and studied his keycard. "I'm up one more." Both guards with Frey gave him a bored look. Only one even stiffened in the slightest.

Looked like Callum had been right; being on a tropical island for a wedding had everyone relaxing their guard.

After getting off on his floor, he went into his room and changed clothes, then headed back down toward the pool to look for the third guard who'd been missing from the hallway. He'd probably been sent to scope out the outside area to look for anything suspicious.

Landon smiled as he found him sitting at one of the smaller side bars, already nursing a beer. Maybe Frey kept his employees on a pretty loose leash and allowed them to drink on the job. But even if so, the beer in the security team member's hand told Landon things about him, just like what had happened earlier in the hallway.

Mainly that this security team wasn't in top form.

Landon slid into the seat two down from his and focused his attention on the game on the screen behind the bartender. When she turned her attention his way, he ordered the same brand beer the guard had in his hand but didn't otherwise acknowledge him at all. Then he waited.

When he cursed about a missed basket, he followed suit more quietly, but he noticed. "You a fan?"

"Yeah. I was stationed at a base for several months not far from there." That was true. He'd learned with undercover work to always provide as much truth as he could to his lies. He held out his hand. "Landon. Nice to meet you."

"Adams." He pointed at his drink. "Lemme buy you another."

Landon shook his head. "Naw, I'm technically on the clock. Just got away from my boss for a few."

"Security?"

"Sort of jack-of-all-trades for the bride's sister."

Adams nodded and looked back up at the screen. "This is a pretty sweet gig. Resort security takes care of most of our problems."

"I'm not complaining, that's for sure."

He knew not to rush. Fishing for info would only make Adams suspicious. Maybe after he got another drink in him, he could figure out a way to be chummier.

But he'd barely finished the one he had before catching something over Landon's shoulder and stiffening. "Damn it. Fucking newbie."

Landon followed his gaze to see one of the two men who'd been assisting Frey into the hotel room when he'd been in the elevator. *Newbie* was also information he could use. He turned back to the TV and pretended not to be interested in their conversation.

"What is it, Fanshawe?" Adams asked the other man tersely. "What part of stay upstairs and guard the door did you not understand?"

Out of the corner of his eye, he caught how Fanshawe's jaw tightened. He didn't like how Adams was talking to him. Landon didn't blame him. Fanshawe might be new, but he wasn't young. Early forties. Big guy—six feet, weighed probably two ten.

"Brammer and I were confused about Mr. Frey's schedule." Fanshawe crossed his arms over his chest. "Are we supposed to wake him up for the welcome event tonight?"

Shit. The event Landon still needed to get cake stands together for.

"By wake up, you mean pull him off his girlfriend?" Adams winked over at him. "I'll come up and go over it one more time with you, seeing as you couldn't quite get it right."

Fanshawe stiffened again. He might be the weak link… frustrated at being at the bottom. Adams treating him with disrespect wasn't helping. Adams himself was another option. He'd been around longer, but he was complacent and ran his mouth.

Maybe he could even pit both men against each other. Wouldn't take much. And while they were focused on each other, he would get closer to Frey's phone.

Adams stood from his stool and threw a twenty on the table. "Keep the change," he called to the bartender. "And I'm buying his." He clapped Landon on the shoulder as he walked away. "Good luck with your boss."

"Yeah, you too. And, uh"—he jerked his chin toward Fanshawe—"the rest of your headaches."

He stayed on his stool until he was sure they were gone. He hadn't even taken a sip of his beer. Drinking wasn't going to happen on this mission, not when he had to look for every possible available opening to get the transmitter placed.

Bethany caught his eye. She stormed out of a set of doors and took off across the other side of the pool. That wasn't good. She should still be at her brunch. And he didn't like how her arms were wrapped around herself protectively.

Definitely not good.

Landon threw a five on the bar for the bartender and high-tailed it after her. He thought he might lose her if she went to her room, but he saw her turn toward the auxiliary kitchen.

By the time he caught up to her, she was already wearing

an apron over a blue dress and was securing her hair more firmly in a ponytail. She muttered to herself with her back to him as she started wiping down the metal preparation counter, but he couldn't quite make out the words.

"Everything okay?" He asked.

She whirled around, eyes narrowed at him. "Why wouldn't everything be okay? I'm starting the prep work for tonight's sweets. Something wrong with that?"

This was not his first day around women. Landon stuffed his hands in his pockets. "Absolutely not."

"I guess you think I'm an idiot for doing my work in my dress and heels."

Wasn't his second day around women either. "I think you should do your work in whatever you're most comfortable in."

"Damned right I should. Because I've built this business from the ground up, and I would never do anything to jeopardize it." She flung the cloth she'd been wiping with toward the sink. "I make desserts that are absolutely fantastic, no matter how unmarried, older, or flabby-armed I am."

Obviously, something had happened at the brunch. This conversation was a minefield. "Your desserts *are* fantastic, from what I've tasted."

"Damned right they are." She turned back toward the counter. "And now, if you'll excuse me, I have to make sure everything is absolutely perfect for tonight. There is no room for error."

She spun back around toward him so quickly his body tensed in preparation for an attack. "Speaking of error, have you got the dessert stands set up? That's what you're here for, not sitting around the bar looking sexy."

Landon raised an eyebrow. He'd skip the sexy comment altogether. "It should take about an hour to set up tonight's stands. I have two hours blocked off from three to five just in case more time is needed. If I set them up this early, they would be in the way of everyone else attempting to work."

Her jaw tightened at both his logic and reasonable tone. "Fine." She spun back around.

She needed…something, but he didn't know how to help her. Maybe the most help he could provide would be to get out of her way.

"I'll check back in with you later to see if you need any assistance."

"Yeah, do that."

This had been more the attitude he'd been expecting from her from the beginning. Maybe he'd been wrong and the kind Bethany was an act. He turned for the door.

"Landon, wait." He stopped but didn't turn back around.

"I'm sorry," she continued. "The brunch…didn't go so well. Like I explained on the plane, my relationship with my family is complicated. Some of it, I can't do anything about. The only thing I feel like I have control over is making these desserts awesome."

He turned. "Let me help. It'll give you more time, and you can make sure everything is exactly the way you want."

She rubbed her eyes. "You're only being paid for the carpentry and construction. And honestly, I can't afford much more than that."

Landon grinned and walked back toward her, hands held in front of him. "You get Mr. September's hands for free."

She let out a pained laugh. "I had hoped you didn't hear that."

He had heard it when she said it back at Slice of Heaven yesterday, and it had thrown him for a little loop since his code name at Zodiac Tactical was Libra. For just a second, he'd thought she'd somehow figured him out.

"Tell me what I can do."

"Are you sure? I did a bunch of the prep work at the

bakery so that I would be able to handle everything here by myself. Wouldn't you rather go back out to the bar?"

It might have been smarter, but he'd honestly rather be in here helping her. "I was only out there to escape this lady who kept trying to put me to work carrying her bags. It was all very awkward."

Some of the tension fell from Bethany's face as she laughed and shook her head. "Lord. It was probably my mother."

"She said she was the groom's cousin. Lena or something?" He pretended to be confused, but he knew her name and profile from the file.

"Mina." Her eyes narrowed. "Yeah, I know her."

Landon grabbed an apron and put it on. "Put me to work."

"Wash your hands then start unloading those cupcakes onto the prep table. I'll start icing them." She handed him a box. "Thank you."

As they worked, she told him more about Mina. Definitely no love lost there, and based on Mina's behavior earlier, he wasn't surprised.

"Mina is an acquired taste. She and I have never gotten along. I usually avoid her as much as possible. I'm sorry she made you do more work."

It wasn't even so much that as the fact that she'd hit on him the moment he'd brought her cases into her room. He appreciated a beautiful woman as much as the next guy, but this had been completely inappropriate and almost distasteful. He hadn't made a scene, but he'd gotten out of there as quickly as possible.

But he wasn't about to tell Bethany about that. He started unpacking the cupcakes. "No worries. I handled her."

Bethany laughed. "She hit on you, didn't she? Or flirted, at least."

Landon looked at her over his shoulder and raised his eyebrows. "How'd you know?"

"Mina is constantly on the lookout for her next fling. Always wants to be able to show off that she can get the best-looking guys. Has so much money that usually she's successful." She looked him up and down, waggling her eyebrows. "It's a miracle you made it out alive."

"It was touch and go there for a while," he said in a gravely serious voice. "Thought I might have to pull out some old Navy moves."

Her laugh filled the small prep kitchen and made him smile as he carefully lined up cupcake after cupcake.

Once she started icing, he probably could've run around naked and she wouldn't have noticed. She was completely focused on the tiny cakes in front of her.

When her phone beeped and lit up where it leaned against the wall the first time, she ignored it. When it happened again a half dozen more times, she cursed under her breath.

"Need to get that?"

She let out a sigh. "It's my mother. Or Patricia. Or at this point, maybe even my sister Christiana."

"Do they need you?"

"They're probably wondering if they need to get Plan B going. Evidently, Mother has the resort on standby to provide desserts just in case I can't get my shit together and I'm frantically icing cupcakes while still in a dress and heels as if it's my first day on the job."

She said it lightly like it was something she could laugh off, but he knew it stung.

Landon put his hand over hers on the icing bag and had her place it on the counter, then turned her toward him. "Hey. Stop for a second and look at what you've created here. We're surrounded by wildflowers."

And they were. She'd precut wraps for the cupcakes that

resembled the paper that went around bunches of flowers. After attaching them, she'd begun icing the treats with tiny tips that made the tops look like flowers.

Each cupcake resembled a small, squat bouquet of wildflowers. It was elegant and quirky at the same time. When they were put together on the display structures, they would be stunning.

"Yeah. Christiana was always fascinated by wildflowers when we were young, much to Mother's dismay. She called them weeds."

He grinned down at her and winked. "Then I think this is a particularly nice, yet subtle, *fuck you* to your mom."

He couldn't help it; he tucked one of her wayward curls behind her ear. So soft. Her hair, her skin, this woman in general. His fingers trailed down her cheek of their own accord. "They're beautiful, Wildflower."

Those big green eyes stared up at him, and even though he knew he shouldn't, he wanted a taste of those sweet, plump lips.

That damned phone buzzed again and broke the moment. Landon dropped his hand from her cheek, and they both stepped back.

"Text whoever it is back and tell them you've more than got it under control. In a few hours, they'll see what Slice of Heaven is truly about."

A smile brightened her face, and she nodded enthusiastically. "Damned right they will."

He kissed her forehead, unable to help himself, unable to stop cursing himself. She was just so fucking genuine. Landon wanted to bring a smile to her face as often and in as many ways as possible. Smiling was meant to be her natural state.

But he couldn't. He stepped even farther back. "I'm going to get the display stands together. Everything is going to be perfect."

Everything except for the fact that Landon needed to get his priorities straight and away from this woman who was way too distracting.

Slice of Heaven, indeed.

CHAPTER
NINE

BECAUSE OF LANDON'S HELP, or maybe more because he'd kept Bethany from hurtling herself off the nearest cliff, she'd not only gotten the cupcakes finished on time, she'd had the opportunity to pamper herself a little while getting ready for tonight.

A soak in the tub and extra time to spend on her hair and makeup had Bethany much more relaxed than she'd been at the brunch this morning.

Landon was right. People were about to get a taste—literally and figuratively—of what Slice of Heaven was about. The cupcakes looked fantastic, and their flavors were even better. The stand Landon had put together had worked perfectly. The finished product looked like a bouquet of cascading wildflowers.

Exactly how she'd planned.

Tonight's welcome reception wasn't a formal event. It was a chance for everyone to say hello, reconnect, make informal plans. The island was available for the entire week. Many of the people Christiana and Simon had invited were making use of that and staying the whole time. Others would be coming in closer to the wedding itself.

So tonight, there would be no sit-down dinner or assigned seating like at the actual reception after the wedding. Yet another reason why both wildflowers and cupcakes worked—casual and people could serve themselves. And hopefully be the source of smiles.

Everyone was walking around chatting when Bethany arrived. Her mother and father were in conversation with some guests. Christiana and Simon were talking to some people they'd known at their private, exclusive high school.

And guests were already gathered around the elaborate cupcake display, studying and discussing it. It was all she could do to not break out in some sort of celebratory dance right there in the middle of the room.

Probably wouldn't go well with the gentle melodies coming from the string quartet in the corner.

Bethany couldn't help herself; she walked toward the group. She wanted to hear what they were saying. At this point, almost no one would associate her with Slice of Heaven. So she could eavesdrop without being obvious.

She briefly greeted extended family members and business associates of her father's as she inched toward the display. But as soon as she got close enough to hear the comments, Bethany wished she'd stayed away. It wasn't the words; it was the primary speaker: *Mina.*

As she'd told Landon earlier that afternoon, there had never been any love lost between her and Mina. They'd known each other in high school before Bethany and Simon had dated. She hadn't liked him and her together, but they'd ended it before that could become an issue.

The fact that she hadn't wanted her to be a couple with Simon irritated Bethany much less than the fact that she'd hit on Landon today. That was messed up on multiple levels she wasn't even going to think about now.

Mina's posse was hanging on her every word, just as they

had in high school. Hell, some of them probably were the same girls from high school.

This was not a group she wanted to engage with. She turned to make her escape before they saw her but didn't get that lucky.

"Well hello, Bethany." The posse member who had outed her—Daniela? Desiree? She'd definitely gone to high school with them, but she couldn't remember her name—announced her presence with glee.

All five of the women turned in unison to face her.

"Bethany!" Mina blew air-kisses toward her face with as much practice as her aunt Patricia. "You over here to eavesdrop?"

Totally busted.

Bethany forced a smile onto her face. "No, of course not. Just wanted to make sure everything was still looking as it should. I didn't realize it was you over here." *Because she would've lit herself on fire rather than come over if she had.*

"We were just discussing how you were providing the desserts this week with your little business. What is it called again? Slice of Pie?"

"Slice of Heaven."

Mina's laugh was high-pitched and nasal. "Right. Slice of Heaven. See, Diane? I told you it was something clever."

Diane. That was the woman's name. She muttered something about it not being so clever under her breath, but Bethany ignored her, keeping her eyes on Mina. It was instinctual, like her body was aware that Mina was the most dangerous and taking her eyes off her would be a mistake.

"I see your sister hired you to make her…" She waved vaguely toward the dessert stand. "Cupcakes? So quaint. It's like a princess's birthday party."

Mina's posse did a poor job of smothering their snickers.

Her balance shifted from one foot to the other as she tried to figure out what to say. She didn't want to justify her reasoning behind this particular dessert when she knew Mina didn't really care.

She went on before Bethany could say anything anyway. "I mean, I like it. You've obviously got an artistic talent. These are lovely."

That was the thing with Mina; like Patricia and even Mother, she could offer such a blend of compliment and insult that the two were almost interchangeable.

This sort of social repartee was not her forte. It never had been, much to Mother's dismay. Bethany hated playing these games. So she wouldn't.

"Thank you," she said simply. "I'm very proud of them."

Mina's eyes narrowed. She didn't like it when someone didn't do what she wanted, and she wanted them to fight. She forced a smile on her face.

"But the truth is in the taste, isn't it? We'll just have to see. Later, of course. Not while you're in front of everyone. Not trying to put you in the spotlight."

Maybe she did like to play the game a little bit. She couldn't resist this challenge. "Why don't you have one now?"

Bethany knew she was taking a chance, that Mina might spit it out and call it disgusting here in front of everyone. But then she'd make herself a liar because she knew the cupcakes were good. *Better* than good.

Her lips pursed. "Since you insist."

She turned and picked out a cupcake. By this time, they had drawn in a small crowd. She hoped this didn't detonate in her face.

Bethany gritted her teeth when she saw that, instead of choosing a cupcake on an edge where it would have minimal effect on the overall presentation, Mina picked one right in the middle of the arrangement, leaving a small gap.

Bitch. She forced her smile not to slip.

Mina giggled and dipped her finger into the icing before

placing it in her mouth delicately, sucking the small bit off the tip.

Her eyebrows went up. "Oh, that's delicious."

Damned right it is. "Take a bite."

She did, and a small moan of pleasure escaped before she realized it and stopped herself. But it was too late.

Now Bethany's smile was big and genuine. She knew her dark chocolate cupcakes with salted caramel frosting were, in fact, moan-worthy.

"Quite tasty," she said, placing the rest of the cupcake down on the small plate.

She knew that was all the positive she would get out of her. "Thank you."

Now she could leave.

"I'm not surprised," Mina said. "Truly. I mean, look at you. You can tell you're an excellent cook by looking at you."

Bethany froze. She was already well aware that she was the only one in her entire circle who wore a size with two digits. Not fat, no. But not a size two either.

She put a friendly hand on her arm. "It's totally understandable, you putting on the pounds. With all that baking stuff, how could you not? You know, the best trainers in LA will make house calls."

Bethany felt her face flush, and she jerked her arm out of Mina's grasp. "I haven't gained weight."

And it was true. She hadn't. She was very careful with what she ate and how much she exercised. She'd been that size before starting Slice of Heaven.

Once again, choked smirks surrounded them.

"You're right," she soothed. "I should never have insinuated otherwise. I just meant that your treats are so good, we may all be just as fat by the end of the week."

Bethany stood there staring at her. Goddammit, why could she not think of a comeback? Where was her mother with all her venom when she needed her?

"But let's not talk about that." Mina had the audacity to link her arm through hers. "Where is this handsome boyfriend Aunt Patricia has been telling us all about? The one who reassures us you're not pining away after Simon."

Silence fell around them. Not just the posse but the crowd they'd drawn.

"Mina, stop this. This isn't the time," Bethany said in a low voice, trying to keep the conversation private.

"We just want to meet him. He wasn't at the brunch this morning. But I know he's got to be here tonight." She made a big show of looking around.

She should've been honest that morning. As painful as that might have seemed, nothing could be as bad as having to admit this publicly. She spun back toward the cupcakes, trying to figure out anything she could do or say.

"He… We…"

Mina chuckled and swiped another bit of icing off her cupcake before slipping her finger into her mouth. "You what?"

"There you are, sweetheart. I've been looking all over for you." Bethany turned toward Landon's voice behind her.

He looked amazing, in a well-tailored deep-blue suit that fit his physique perfectly and played to every advantage he had. Which were *a lot*.

"I didn't think to look over here," he continued. "You promised me no working tonight—that you were going to enjoy yourself."

The crowd, when they realized Landon was talking to her, parted like the Red Sea. She tried not to let her jaw drop as he walked forward and put his hand on her waist, then bent to press a kiss to her cheek. "I'm sorry, I got held up on a phone call with the office," he said. "What did I miss?"

He looked around at the crowd expectantly, shooting that gorgeous smile—dimples out in full attack mode. Mina was the closest guest to her, so he held out his hand to her.

"Landon Black. We met a little earlier today, I think? You mistook me for a hotel employee."

"You mistook *him* for a hotel employee?" Diane whispered a little too loudly. People chuckled, and Mina's back went ramrod straight.

"He was hanging out in the lobby like he was one." She crossed her arms over her chest. "You're Bethany's boyfriend?"

Each word of her question had a higher lilt, as if she couldn't figure out which word was most important to emphasize as ridiculous: *you're*, *Bethany's*, or *boyfriend*.

Hell, all of them worked.

"Bethany," Patricia chimed in as she walked over. "This isn't the man we saw on your social media a few weeks ago."

She felt like her face had frozen into that laugh-with-sweat-pooling-on-the-forehead emoji. "No, this is Landon, not Brad."

Landon shrugged and pulled her closer. "She and Brad broke up a while ago. He's old and tired news."

Mina was looking Landon up and down. Everyone was looking at him that way. He ignored them, smiling down at Bethany.

She stared at his dimples to keep from hyperventilating.

Patricia finally spoke. "I thought you worked for Bethany."

"It's hard to be around Bethany without getting inspired by her work ethic. When her normal carpenter had a family emergency, how could I not offer to stand in as her Man Friday?" He chuckled and straightened his tie. "It makes a man feel good to work with his hands, if you know what I mean."

She couldn't get a word out. She wasn't sure if she was ever going to have the ability to speak again. But evidently, he didn't need her backup to continue this charade.

"Now, if you'll excuse me, I'd like to drag my sexy woman

away from her work. Although, if you're all smart, you'll start with dessert. It's the best thing you'll have all night." Landon winked down at her. "I always like to start with dessert. And finish with it too."

The words dripped with sexual yumminess. Which, okay, wasn't a word, but Lord, nobody had any doubt what he was talking about.

He kept her pinned to his side with his arm around her waist as they walked away. "Want a drink?" he asked. "Or a hand grenade to lob over your shoulder? Though, it would be a shame to mess up your gorgeous display."

Bethany tried to swallow past the huge lump in her throat, but it didn't work, so she just nodded—she wanted both. He steered them toward one of the less crowded bars and got her a white wine. After a few sips, she was finally able to speak.

"What just happened?"

"Sorry, I could not stand by and let Mina and her bot crew do that to you. I probably could've handled it differently. Sorry," he repeated.

"Please don't apologize. You saved me."

"I know you would've preferred to keep things more low profile. This was the most direct way, but not the most subtle."

People were glancing at them in that *don't want to stare but want to get a closer look* sort of way. A few were sneaking cupcakes. That was good, at least.

Patricia and Mina had their heads together, phones in front of them. She was sure they were trying to find any details on Landon they could.

"Hope you don't have a wife or something on Instagram."

He chuckled. "No wife or girlfriend, don't worry. And no social media profiles at all."

Bethany took another sip of her drink. "Smart."

People were still looking at them. Landon's hand still rested over hers. "You going to be okay?"

"Yeah. By tomorrow, they won't be talking about us anymore. Gossip will have blown over, and we can come up with excuses why you're not attending events or hanging out with me. Work emergencies or something."

He shifted slightly closer. "I don't mind attending, unless that's weird for you."

"No, it'll be great. Keep everyone off my back so I can focus on my desserts and the wedding itself. As long as you're sure you don't mind."

He smiled, but somehow, it didn't quite reach his eyes. "I'm happy to. It'll give me something to do. I can mingle with the guests."

It unsettled something inside her to see an inauthentic smile on his face. She stepped in closer and placed a hand on his chest, telling herself it was to sell the role.

"Are you sure? This goes way beyond the carpentry work and cake stand setup. I'm sure Harley sold you on helping me by telling you it was an easy week on a tropical island."

His hand covered hers, and he moved it in gentle circles, almost as if he were soothing a pain there. "I'm sure I want to be at as many events as possible. Now, how about if we go sell this little charade of ours?"

He stayed by her side for the next hour as they circulated. She saw Mother side-eyeing them as they talked to various people, but evidently, the gossip hadn't hit her yet. She would know when it did.

After her challenge to Mina to try the cupcakes, others had followed suit. Now Bethany didn't have to eavesdrop to know what people thought. They were coming directly to her and telling her.

It was perfect.

Right up to the point when her mother tapped her on the shoulder. She knew immediately she'd heard the gossip and was not happy about it. Her father stood by her side, not looking terribly pleased either. They'd waited until Landon had gone to get them drinks at one of the bars.

"How could you?" her mother hissed softly. "I can't believe you would do this!"

Her voice was low so no one could overhear. She kept hers low too. "Do what, Mother?"

She glared over at Landon.

Bethany rolled her eyes. "You mean, bring a date?"

"It sounds like he's much more than just your date, isn't he?"

"Fine. Yes, he's my boyfriend, but I don't think that's any reason to get upset. I'm sure you'll like Landon once you get to know him."

Why was she defending her imaginary boyfriend? Once they left this island, Mother would never see him again. Hell, *she* would never see him again.

If anything, her mother's stare got icier. "Boyfriend?"

Was this because she thought Landon was a carpenter? This was the last straw. Bethany was about to tear into her mother when Landon joined them.

"Mr. and Mrs. Thornton," he said with one of his smiles as he handed her a glass of wine. "I'm sorry we're meeting this way. I'm Landon Black."

He shook her mother's hand then her father's.

"I hear congratulations are in order," Dad said.

Oh sweet Jesus. "I don't think dating really calls for congratulations." She tried to laugh lightly, but it came out pretty choked.

"No need to keep it a secret," Dad whispered. "We know."

"Know what?"

Mina stepped out from behind Bethany's father. "Oops, I might have let the truth slip. Sorry!"

There was nothing sorry in anything about her. If she were a cat, a canary would've been half hanging out of her mouth.

Bethany narrowed her eyes at her. "You let the truth slip about Landon and me dating?"

Her smile got bigger. "About you two being secretly *engaged*."

She stiffened, forcing herself not to fling the chardonnay in Mina's face. This was too far, even for her. She was deliberately trying to make Landon run for cover and publicly humiliate her.

Bethany had no idea what to say. She could feel all the eyes on her.

Landon took it all in stride. "How did you know? It was supposed to be a secret."

Mina's face went from triumphant to shocked. Realizing Bethany's probably mirrored her expression, she tucked her face against his chest. His arm came around her, keeping her close.

Oh, bless him. She'd keep him in cupcakes for the rest of his life. He'd said something about cinnamon. Maybe she'd keep him in cinnamon rolls. Whatever he wanted.

Mina recovered quickly. "Well, show us the ring, you two lovebirds."

"We didn't even bring the ring. Bethany didn't want to take the focus away from Christiana and Simon." Landon pressed a kiss to the side of her head. "You're such a good sister, sweetheart."

For a second, all the drama around her disappeared, and she wanted that kiss to have been real. There was something truly special about kisses on the hair or forehead. They were a level of intimacy that transcended lust and moved into passion and true affection.

Bethany wanted hair and forehead kisses. Every woman wanted hair and forehead kisses.

Too bad it was all a big lie, even if Landon had saved her from embarrassment twice in one night.

There were handshakes and hugs before she insisted they

not discuss the engagement more. This was Christiana's week. Watching Mina skulk away, foiled, was the best part of this whole situation.

The worst part? Knowing she was eventually going to have to unravel this huge knot she was creating.

But that could wait until after this week. Right now, Bethany was going to revel in the fact that her desserts were being enjoyed by everyone and her mother was actually beaming at her in approval for once.

She was going to float on a gorgeous, attentive man's arm. She was going to smile up at him and pretend the sexy winks he gave her were real.

When they left the island after the wedding, she and Landon would have some dramatic breakup. She'd make Mother understand.

But for right now, she would pretend he was hers.

CHAPTER
TEN

BEING Bethany's *significant other* opened way more doors for his mission last night than Landon could've opened on his own. He was grateful seduction hadn't been the plan ahead of time because he wasn't sure he could've done it.

Not because Landon wasn't attracted to Bethany, but because she was trusting him so completely.

Every time those pretty green eyes smiled up at him last night, he felt like shit. All he could do was keep repeating to himself that this fake-fiancé situation worked in Bethany's favor just as much as it did his.

After Mina's little bombshell, they'd agreed with Bethany's parents to keep the *fiancé* thing under wraps. For this week, he'd merely be Bethany's boyfriend, so they weren't taking away from the bride and groom.

Fiancé or boyfriend didn't matter in terms of the mission. Instead of having to find a way to be invited to the events where Frey would be present, he'd been instantly included in the inner circle.

Hell, Thornton had even introduced Landon to Frey. He hadn't spent much time talking to him, not wanting to be too memorable. But he'd tried to gather as much detail as possible.

Frey was dressed casually—no jacket, just a black dress shirt with black tailored pants. As much as he didn't go around looking at other men's packages, Landon could tell his phone was in his front right pocket.

But knowing where his phone was didn't make it any more accessible. If he made a dive for that front pocket, he was going to get himself killed.

Bethany knew Frey by name but didn't seem any closer to him than she was with any of her father's business associates. He wanted to press her for any details she had—anything could give him an advantage—but knew that would seem odd. So instead, he kept his questions broad—asking about everyone, redirecting to Frey when he could.

Bethany may not have associated much with this crowd in the last couple of years, but her upbringing in wealthy circles was still evident. She could work a room like the best of them—conversing, smiling, remembering names and faces.

But even as she did it, she was totally different from most. She wasn't trying to impress anyone or get one up on them. She wasn't concerned with how they could help her climb the social ladder. She was authentically friendly. Most people were drawn to her for it.

That, and wanting to know a little more about the woman who had made such amazing cupcakes.

When anyone asked about him, he'd tried to keep with as much truth as possible. Landon told them he was former Navy—leaving out the SEAL part. He'd told them he'd wanted to be a carpenter as a kid, which made him perfect to help his sweet girlfriend with her cake stands.

All in all, being on Bethany's arm had been a great way to establish himself and make him less suspicious.

Now, to use it to his advantage.

Landon was back out at the pool. He had kept an eye on the area from his room, waiting for a chance to make a move.

When Fanshawe, Frey's pissed-off newbie security guard from yesterday, showed up at the bar, he had what he'd been waiting for.

He was alone at the same bar where Landon had talked to Adams yesterday. Again, as he'd done with his boss, he sat one seat down and ignored him. This time, there was no television on, so Landon turned around to observe the hotel lobby.

Wedding guests milled about, enjoying the pool and beach. He hadn't seen Bethany since last night. She was supposed to be spending today with her sister and mother at the spa. She deserved to relax. There were no events today requiring effort from her.

Plus, her being at the spa meant Landon had uninterrupted time to work. After a few minutes, his plan worked. Fanshawe turned around and people watched alongside him.

"You're the guy who was talking to Adams yesterday," he finally said.

He glanced over. "Yeah, kind of. We were both watching the game. You work for him, right?"

His jaw got hard. "No, I work for Mr. Frey. Adams may act like I work for him, but I don't."

That's right, buddy. Get yourself wound up. "Sorry, man. That's hard to deal with."

He whistled to himself as a group of women walked up from the beach on the other side of the pool. Mina and her posse. She was leading them, as always.

"I wouldn't mind dealing hard with that one. Not an ounce of bounce anywhere on that body."

Landon didn't want to spend even one more second with this asshole, but that wasn't an option. "I prefer them with meat, myself."

He chuckled. "You're with the bride's sister, aren't you?"

He grunted. Landon wasn't sure how much he knew.

"She's definitely got some junk in the trunk."

Squaring his jaw, Landon looked over at him. "Careful. She's not just a job to me."

Hell if that wasn't becoming more and more true.

"Yeah, I heard you guys were together." He held up his hands. "I was just making an observation."

Landon reached over and slapped him on the arm even though he wanted to punch him in the face. "Just fucking with you. No harm." After clapping him on the bicep, he held out the same hand. "Name's Landon."

"Fanshawe." He shook his hand firmly, gripping too hard. Trying to prove something.

"Outside of people not giving you the respect you deserve, how's this gig going for you?" He asked him. "At least you're getting a little time off to enjoy yourself."

He rolled his eyes. "I mostly get shitty shifts off. You know, five a.m. to nine a.m. or something like that. Midafternoon like today. Nothing when there's any action."

"That sucks. Frey like to do anything interesting?"

"He likes to fuck his girlfriend and lie to his wife. Does that count as interesting?"

Making his chuckle sound authentic was tricky. "Anything that doesn't require you to guard his door?" Finding out Frey went for a dawn swim every morning would be nice. Or that he liked to go work out at two a.m.

"I wish. So far, it's either been at the room or standing near a table while he works. Fucking boring, especially here."

Dude was not going to make it long in security work. A lot of it wasn't interesting at all. It required you to stay focused and disciplined and ready for when the true action did happen.

Fanshawe would never be ready for real danger because he wasn't willing to put in the boring hours. They never would've hired him at Zodiac Tactical, no matter how big the guy was.

"Yeah, boring," Landon muttered.

"You would think they'd give me a little more respect, you know? This isn't my first job. I may be new with Mr. Frey, but I've got experience in the security world. Adams shouldn't be treating me like I'm some peon."

He started complaining about Adams again, but he cut off when Frey himself walked down to the bar and sat in a booth not far from them. He made no motion to join them or invite either of them to join him, but he was too close for Fanshawe to continue to speak freely.

He'd made his connection with Fanshawe, so Landon turned around in hopes of Frey saying something or doing something that would help.

He had one of the nano transmitters in his pocket. Maybe he'd get really lucky and Frey would go to the bathroom and leave his phone on the table.

Yeah, right.

He spent the better part of two hours sitting at that damn bar, listening while Fanshawe made obnoxiously sexist comments under his breath and Frey nursed a couple of drinks and read through papers. His other guards and personal assistant came and went, and the man didn't say or do anything that would help him.

When Frey left, Adams motioned to Fanshawe he needed to come too. Good. Let Adams continue to piss him off. Hopefully that could work to Landon's advantage. But honestly, he didn't see Fanshawe remaining in Frey's employ for long.

He paid for the two drinks he hadn't done anything but swirl in his glass and stood.

"Here all alone? Where's your fiancée?"

Landon turned to find Mina right behind him.

"She's enjoying a spa day. She deserves it."

"Because she works so hard with her job. True." Her eyes

narrowed. "I haven't been able to find much out about you. I'm somewhat of an expert at cybersleuthing. You don't seem very big on social media."

Because he worked for one of the best security companies on the planet and knew what a personal information sieve social media could be. "I'm not big on computers. If you'll excuse me, I've got to get going."

She didn't move. "I know you and Bethany aren't really together."

"Why would you say that?" Landon leaned his elbows back on the bar. The most important part about being undercover was not giving too much away.

She took a step closer, and he straightened. He didn't want this woman in his personal space. "Because someone like you doesn't go for someone like Bethany."

"Someone like *me*? Someone like *Bethany*?" He narrowed his eyes. "Do you know how elitist and conceited you sound right now?"

She shrugged one small shoulder. "I prefer the term realistic. And I'm not necessarily talking about her weight or her looks. Bethany has never really fit in."

"That doesn't necessarily seem like a bad thing, given what I've seen." He stepped farther to the side, away from her.

"I used to think Bethany thought she was too good for us. Then I thought she wasn't aware of how our world worked. When she opened the bakery, her parents were shocked, but it made sense to me. Her mind had always been focused on different things than what we thought were important." She stepped closer. "But actually, it's neither. She doesn't care. Our opinions don't matter to her."

Landon wasn't going to discuss Bethany and her fears with Mina; that would only give the woman more ammunition.

"I think Bethany wants to enjoy her sister's wedding and

provide the best desserts she can. Not a damned thing wrong with that."

"And what about you, Landon? What do you want?"

He straightened. "To help my fiancée in whatever way I can."

"That may be true, but that's not all. You're looking for something more than her. I can see it. Your focus is not fully on Bethany."

Shit. Mina had seen what everyone else had missed. She was misattributing the fact that his focus wasn't solely resting on Bethany, but she'd still seen it.

Mina placed her hand on his chest. "I can give you what you're looking for."

Oh, hell no. He picked her hand off his chest. "There is not any situation where you can give me what I'm looking for. And believe me, I would never choose you over Bethany. So, back off."

This conversation wasn't his normal way of dealing with people. Landon always tried for charm over rudeness. But this woman was a viper in very expensive clothing, and he wanted nothing to do with her.

He dropped her wrist and walked away. People like Mina didn't know how to handle the word no. She would either get pissy or take it as a challenge to further try to hit on him. He wasn't going to stick around to find out which.

He headed to the main lodge and got to his room. It was getting dark, and after spending the afternoon with Fanshawe and Mina, he needed a fucking shower.

Landon let out a curse when the keycard didn't work. He tried it again, but nothing. Gritting his teeth, he walked back to the lobby.

"How can I help you?"

His smile was forced even though the man at the counter was friendly and professional. "I'm Landon Black, room 306. My keycard isn't working, and I can't get into my room."

The guy's face brightened. "Mr. Black, oh yes. You've been moved into a suite. As per orders, the porter has already collected your belongings, and they should be at the new suite momentarily."

He stiffened. He'd gotten that corner room on purpose since it allowed him to see both the pool area and beach. Not to mention, it offered a second exit via fire escape if he needed it.

Did someone suspect he was undercover? He'd swept his room for any transmitting devices, and Tristan had eyes on the resort's security system. He would've notified Landon if something was off.

No news was good news, but someone had packed up his stuff. His weapons were hidden within his belongings, but if someone had searched systematically, they'd probably find them.

He shot the desk attendant a friendly smile. "I don't think I want to be upgraded. Any way I can get my previous room back?"

The guy's face crumpled like he was really upset. "The suite is a very nice one. Has an absolutely stunning view of the sunset from the balcony. As a matter of fact, the champagne should be delivered any moment."

"Champagne?"

"Mrs. Thornton was insistent that a bottle be delivered every night at sunset."

"The Thorntons are the ones who upgraded me?"

The guy's head bobbed up and down. "Yes! I'm sorry, she made it seem like you'd already agreed. I think she felt bad that their other daughter's"—his voice dipped lower, like he was in on the secret—"*fiancé* was in one of our smaller rooms. The suite is much nicer. So, she had us move your things."

Landon relaxed. He would still sweep the new room to make sure it wasn't under surveillance, but Angelique and Oliver upgrading him was much less suspicious.

"Yeah, she must've forgotten to mention it."

The guy programmed a new keycard and handed it to him. "I hope you enjoy yourself."

"I will. Thanks."

The suite was farther away from Frey's room, but that didn't matter much now. Fanshawe was his best bet. It was just a matter of figuring out how to use him.

Landon's keycard worked fine at the new door. But as soon as it clicked, he froze. Someone was inside; he could hear voices. He reached down to his ankle holster and got his weapon as he slid the door silently open.

CHAPTER ELEVEN

"SO BASICALLY, EVERYBODY LOVED THEM."

Bethany was curled up on the deep couch in her room, dressed in the fluffy white robe the spa had provided for Mother, Christiana, and herself during their treatments today. This had been the first chance she'd had to check in with Michele since arriving on the island.

"And the tree motif worked like we planned? Landon didn't have any problem setting it up?"

"No, no problem. Landon has been...amazing." She winced at her pause, hoping Michele wouldn't pick up on it. She rushed on. "Everything going okay there? Any problems?"

"No, solid business for early week. Don't worry, Captain, your ship is sailing just fine without you. Now, let's go back to Landon being—dramatic pause—*amazing*. I know that means at more than building cake stands. Spill, sister."

Busted.

"He's been super supportive. Helped me defuse the whole dateless situation with my family." She wrapped one of her curls around her finger.

Mom and Christiana had asked her all sorts of questions

about him today, but she'd deflected. Talking about him made it feel too real.

Bethany had spent the day reminding herself that none of this was real. Not the dimples, not the charm, not the forehead kisses.

Not. Real.

Fake.

Fake was a very clear term.

She just needed to remember it.

"Yay! See, I knew this would work out better than Harley. What did Landon do, pretend to be your boyfriend?"

Damn it. Bethany's silence answered her.

"He did!" She had to hold the phone away from her ear to keep from going deaf from Michele's squeal. "Oh my God, he pretended to be your boyfriend!"

She let out a sigh. "Even worse, when Simon's cousin tried to make it awkward, he told everyone he was my fiancé."

She had to hold the phone farther away.

"I love it! Did you kiss him? Lawd, I'll bet he's a good kisser."

She'd had the same thoughts herself. "No, I didn't kiss him. But I appreciate him helping me out."

"Girrrrl." Michele dragged out the r to an annoying length. "You need to run with this. Get as much out of this fake engagement as you can. Is he there with you in your room?"

Bethany rolled her eyes. "Of course not, dumbass. First of all, I wouldn't be talking about him if he were here, and second, *fake* engagement. *Faaaaaake.*"

She let out a dramatic sigh. "Whatever. I'm not saying the engagement needs to be real. I'm saying you need to get you some of those dimples since he offered and all. Invite him over. Make up an excuse to get him in your room and then jump his sexy bones."

She had to laugh. "I don't see that happening, but if he shows up, I'll see what I can do."

"Yeah, you do that. I don't want to hear that you—"

She heard the door rattle.

"Michele, hang on. Someone's at the door. Mother told me she was sending me a gift, so I guess it's arrived."

Bethany stood and waited for the knock but didn't hear it. Then realized the door was *opening*. Oh shit.

Why hadn't she put the latch on? Who was trying to get into her room without announcing themselves? What should she do?

"Michele," she whispered. "I think someone is breaking in to my room."

"What? I can—"

She took a step toward the door as it opened farther, then let out a breath in relief when she saw it was Landon. Her hand flew to her chest.

"Landon, oh my gosh, you scared me. What are you doing here?"

"Landon?" Michele screeched in her ear. "Landon is there? You just said if he showed up, you'd jump his bones. Get some! You—"

"I'll call you tomorrow." She was still making suggestions on what she should do with Landon when she ended the call.

Landon crouched down, messing with the hem of his pants then tying his shoe. Bethany took the opportunity to make sure her robe was securely tied.

"How'd you get a key to my room?" She asked once he stood and they were facing each other

"*Your* room. Of course it is." He scrubbed a hand down his face. "My key didn't work for my room, so I went to the lobby, where they notified me I'd been upgraded to a suite."

Oh God. "My mother."

He shrugged, face wry. "Yeah, seems that way. I guess she thought we should be together since we're...*together.*"

Bethany nodded, big awkward smile on her face. Him sleeping in there was not a good idea, despite the fact that she could hear Michele screaming the opposite all the way from the mainland.

Her suite had a bedroom and a living area with a couch, but still, it was too much. She didn't want him to have to sleep on a couch, and she didn't want him sleeping in the bed with her.

Even if she could still feel those kisses on the top of her head and forehead from last night.

"Let me call the front desk and sort this out."

Here she'd thought Mother was on her best behavior today at the spa. That she was actually honoring her wishes by not talking much about Landon, and keeping the conversation focused on Christiana.

Bethany should've known she was up to something.

She picked up the phone by the bed that connected her to the front desk. "Hello, this is Bethany Thornton. My mother moved my fiancé into my room, but we'd actually prefer to keep separate rooms. Can we get one for him?"

"Sure," the receptionist said brightly. "One second."

She heard the sound of clacking keys on a keyboard, then he came back. "I'm sorry, Ms. Thornton, but all the rooms are booked."

"That's not possible," she said. "We haven't used all the rooms in this resort. Perhaps you can discuss it with your supervisor, if that's okay. He or she may have insight you and I don't have."

"Of course. Hold one moment and let me get Ms. Hebron."

Jeez. She hated being the snob asking to talk to the manager, but what else could she do? Bethany shot Landon an awkward smile as she waited.

He smiled back—not awkward. He never seemed awkward.

"Ms. Thornton, this is Nicola Hebron, resort manager. I am so sorry to say this, but Gregory was actually correct, we do not have any other rooms available."

"Are you sure?" She rubbed the tension building in the middle of her forehead. "I know my parents booked the whole island, but we don't have that many people attending."

"Right, that is correct." She said it with the practiced ease of someone used to customer service. "But the agreement the resort made with your parents was to give them a discount if they allowed us to do renovations on any unused rooms."

"I see." She rubbed her head harder. That made sense. Her family had significant money, but renting out this entire island for a week was an extravagant event for them, especially when they were only using two-thirds of the rooms available.

"When your fiancé's room opened up, we were able to give it to one of the guests who had originally requested a second room for their teenagers. So, all of the available rooms are full."

"I see." She was aware she was repeating herself, but she wasn't sure what else to say.

She paused, then continued. "Your parents' suite does have an extra bedroom if one of you wanted to see about staying with them?"

It took all of Bethany's willpower not to laugh in the poor woman's ear. Staying with her parents wasn't an option. She'd sleep on the patio chairs first.

"No, that's not necessary. Thank you for your time." She put the phone receiver back on the base much more gently than she wanted to.

"No luck?"

Bethany turned to face him with a shrug. "Doesn't look like it."

The knock on the door made her jump.

"Probably my stuff," Landon said then turned to answer it.

Sure enough, the porter pushed in a cart with Landon's duffel and hanging bag. "Mr. Black, I'll put these in the bedroom closet if it's okay?"

Landon looked over at her.

"Sure," she whispered.

The man worked quickly and efficiently, hanging Landon's shirts and pants next to hers, then setting up a suitcase rack and placing his case on it. He started to organize the contents of the duffel, but Landon stopped him.

"I've got it from here, man. Thanks." He tipped the porter as he left.

She was still staring at Landon's things next to hers in the closet. It was so domesticated. She'd never lived with a man, so it was a bit of a shock to her system.

Oh shit. Bethany could feel panic bubbling up inside her.

"Okay, then," she said, trying to get herself under control. Perfect. Wittiest line since *I carried a watermelon.*

Landon walked back over from where he'd shut the door behind the porter. "You okay? Listen, why don't I go talk to the front desk? Nobody is working on the empty rooms at night. I can sleep on the floor."

Bethany rubbed her hand over her eyes. "No. I'm being ridiculous. There's plenty of room for you to stay here. It's fine."

Her phone buzzed in her hand, and she looked at the text from Michele.

Jump his sexy bones! Bow-chicka-wow-wow

Followed by what looked to be five hundred kissy emojis and a couple of highly inappropriate gifs.

The laugh that escaped her was tinged with hysteria.

He stepped toward her, concern evident in those hazel eyes. "It'll be okay. I'll sleep on the couch. We can make up a bathroom schedule."

He was still smiling. He obviously was not worried about the forced proximity like she was.

Because this relationship of theirs wasn't real. She wasn't sure how many times she was going to need to remind herself of that. He obviously didn't need the reminder. He knew.

Not. Real.

Those dimples of his were staring her down like they wanted to start a fight. "We can do this, Wildflower."

Wildflower.

She snapped. "How can you be so calm?"

"About sleeping on a couch? I was in the Navy for over ten years. I've slept in much worse—"

"About it all! About my mother casually moving you in here without your consent! About pretending to be my boyfriend then my fiancé without even blinking an eye!" She walked over to the closet and gestured to the clothes. "About your clothes hanging right next to mine!"

He ran a hand through his brown hair, walking toward her. "Hey…"

"Why are you so calm? Why are you willing to do all this? Why don't you tell me and my family to go jump in a lake?"

"Calm is my superpower. That's how I operate. And thus far, nothing has happened that's too stressful. Pretending to be close to you is no hardship, Bethany. You're a beautiful person, inside and out."

She rolled her eyes. "You don't have to say stuff like that. There's nobody here to hear you."

He was next to her so fast she blinked. She'd never seen him move at anything more than a casual stroll.

"You're here to hear it, and you're who I'm talking to. You're beautiful."

Bethany shook her head. "I know what I bring to the table. I'm smart and driven. But you don't have to look around this island for more than ten seconds to know that I'm not of the same caliber as them. You don't have to pretend to be attracted to me when we're in—"

His lips crashed against hers. Scorched air fled her lungs as he slid one of his hands into her hair at her neck to hold her in place as his lips devoured hers.

Holy hell, Michele had been right. Landon could kiss. His mouth was hot and wet and open against hers, and she was drawn under his spell. She wrapped her arms around him as he pulled her closer.

Then he slowed down, his teeth starting to nibble her lips, tease her tongue with his.

All she could do was hold on.

They were both breathing heavily by the time they pulled away. Her fingers moved up to touch her lips of their own accord. His eyes flared a little as he watched.

"I'll have to pretend a lot of things while we're on this island, but being attracted to you isn't one of them. Get that straight."

"Okay," she whispered.

"Now, why don't you shower, or whatever, in the bathroom. I'll get the couch ready for me to sleep on."

She nodded, not sure whether to be disappointed or relieved. But she couldn't deny the heat in his eyes.

Fake had just become a lot more blurry.

LANDON HAD NEVER BEEN a good sleeper. Home life for him as a kid hadn't been the greatest. Alcoholic dad with a temper meant he'd learned to sleep light. Or not at all.

His ability to cope with insomnia from an early age had given him a leg up when it came to SEAL training hell week. It was surprising how many guys rung out because of the exhaustion. Big, tough guys who could bench three hundred plus pounds without breaking a sweat cracked because their minds weren't tough enough to handle what lack of sleep did.

Hell, it was why it was such an effective torture method.

After getting out of the Navy a few years ago, his sleeping patterns had gotten a little better. Until he took that bullet to the chest. Almost dying had somehow thrown him neck-deep back into insomnia. He hadn't slept for more than a couple hours at a time in months.

Landon had hidden it pretty well from his coworkers. Only those people closest to him—Ian, in particular—had recognized the symptoms and his coping mechanisms.

Insomnia was different for everyone, but for him, the key was not letting it get the best of him. He rarely lay awake in his bed, allowing his mind to wander. He got up and put his sleepless hours to good use: physical workouts, planning missions, research.

Not last night. Not after that kiss with Bethany. He shouldn't have done it, should never have given in to that instinct to cover those full lips with his.

But not kissing her hadn't been an option.

She'd been standing there saying he wasn't attracted to her, and every instinct he'd ever had demanded he prove that wrong in the most visceral way possible.

It had only been through years of discipline and focus that he'd been able to pull himself back from what his body had really wanted to do—lay her down on that bed and fill her until they didn't know where one body ended and the other began.

Instead, Landon had managed to get himself under control and say something non-caveman-like, although hell if he could remember what. She'd gone to bed, and he'd lain on that sofa, staring up at the ceiling.

He could've gotten out of the room without waking her. Hit the extensive resort gym or, hell, just walked the beach. He could've studied files he had on his laptop.

But this time when sleep wouldn't come, he'd let his mind wander. Straight to Bethany Thornton.

Everything about the woman was soft. In his line of work, soft was considered a weakness or insult. But her soft was a thing of beauty.

Soft lips, soft curves, soft soul.

And all he wanted to do was get as close as he could to that softness. Damn the mission.

He'd had respect for her before their lips touched. He'd been impressed by her work ethic, her kindness to others, the way she hadn't been hardened like the inner circle surrounding her seemed to be. He'd known she was attractive—big smile, riotous curls, cute freckles. And to be honest, he'd liked being her knight in shining armor. Being able to help her out by pretending to be her significant other made up for using her for the mission.

He'd *liked* her, but it had been in a sort of distanced way. Distance was necessary for undercover work.

But the moment their lips touched, that distance had been blown to hell.

It had been all Landon could do to stop. He had wanted nothing more than to place her on that bed and forget about everything else happening on this island.

But he couldn't. There was too much at stake. But when he hadn't been able to sleep, instead of getting up and doing something productive, he'd let his mind imagine all the things he'd like to do with Bethany. *To* her.

He hadn't held back—he'd put his insomnia to good use and given his mind free rein. Positions, locations—kissing every inch of her from the crown of her head to the soles of her feet.

Knowing she was only a few feet away had been a beautiful sort of hell. Knowing that fantasizing about laying her out on that bed until she was crying his name was as close as he was ever going to get to being with Bethany was a *not-beautiful* sort of hell.

But Landon wasn't going to let this situation get out of control while on an active mission. No matter how much he wanted her.

No more mind-blowing kisses.

Focus on the mission.

———

Just before dawn, he'd cleared out of the room—not wanting to be there when Bethany woke up. If she wanted to talk about their kiss, he wouldn't shut her down, but there was so much he couldn't say that he wanted to avoid it.

But she didn't bring it up when they'd both found themselves working side by side in the auxiliary kitchen. They'd both had a lot to do to prepare for the luau tonight. She'd spent the day putting together the various tropical-themed sweets being served. He'd gotten the stands set up and placed, then spent the afternoon trying to find a way close to Frey.

It was already Wednesday. He was running out of time. He needed to make a move tonight.

Tonight's theme was a luau, and everyone was dressed casually—sundresses for the women, khakis and Hawaiian shirts for the men. The drinks were mostly fruity, and a DJ was playing tropical-island-themed music.

Landon was on Bethany's arm again, doing boyfriend duty, when he spotted Frey at one of the bars. He was wearing a blazer tonight. He shifted, and he saw the outline of a shoulder holster.

Immediately, he went on high alert. No other time that he'd seen Frey had he had a shoulder holster. Why would he now?

Bethany was talking with one of the hotel staff who would be in charge of serving her desserts. Landon turned to excuse himself with a gentle squeeze at her waist. He wasn't sure what his plan was, but he needed to figure out what had changed that caused Frey to feel like he needed more security than just his team.

Before the words left his mouth, Bethany's father joined Frey at the bar. Oliver's features were pinched and body language stiffer than he'd seen that whole week.

Damn it, he needed to be over there for that conversation.

"I'm going to grab a drink. Want anything?" He whispered the words into Bethany's hair during a pause in her conversation. He tried to ignore the smell of it that made him want to pull her closer.

She looked up at him. "I'm sorry. I'm boring you."

He kissed her nose before he thought better of it. Damn it. "Not at all. I'll be right back."

By the time Landon made his way to the bar, Oliver was already leading Frey toward a man standing on the outskirts of the party near the shadows. *Fuck.* He couldn't go over there without being completely conspicuous.

Who was the man in the shadows? He continued to the bar then pulled out his phone, keeping it low, but pointing it in their direction, rapidly snapping pictures without looking like he was.

Oliver looked like he was introducing the two men, although neither of them offered to shake hands. He glanced down at his camera. One of his shots had gotten the mystery man's face.

He fired off a text to Tristan.

New guest at the party. Made Frey nervous enough to carry.

He tucked his phone back into his pocket as Oliver headed in his direction. He came to the bar next to Landon and ordered a scotch, neat. He drank it without saying anything then placed the glass back down for another.

"Everything okay, Mr. Thornton?"

He looked over at him like he wasn't sure who he was for a moment, then nodded slowly. "Landon. Yes. Had an unexpected guest for the wedding."

"A friend of Mr. Frey's?"

Oliver's eyes narrowed. "You know Frey?"

"Met him here, making the rounds." Landon took a sip of his drink, hoping he hadn't made an error.

"Frey is part of a group of people I don't associate with much anymore. Evidently, he had some contacts with the groom's family, and that's how he got an invite. I would've vetoed if I'd known."

He was glad to hear that, if only for Bethany's sake.

"And the unexpected guest?"

Oliver took another sip of his drink. "Martinez is even worse than Frey."

Martinez. That didn't ring any bells for him.

"Do you want me to get resort security? If these people weren't invited, I'm sure security will escort them off the island."

Oliver shook his head rapidly. "No. No, just leave them be. Whatever is happening, I don't want to know. It has nothing to do with us."

"If you say so."

He turned more fully to Landon. "Look, I made some poor choices trying to get ahead when the girls were younger. I've spent a lot of time unraveling myself from people I should've never been connected with in the first place."

He sounded authentic. He leaned a little closer to him. "You were a soldier, so you may not understand, but the best way I can protect the people I love is to let those two men do whatever it is they're going to do and keep out of it."

He'd been in enough battles and fights to know that sometimes the only way to win was to walk away. So he respected what Oliver was attempting to do.

But he sure as hell wasn't going to stay out of it. Whoever Martinez was, he was scarier than Frey.

"I'll be sure to keep Bethany away from them." That was the truth.

"Thank you." Oliver seemed to relax just a little. "You're good for her. She smiles more when you're around."

Now he was back to feeling like shit. "She deserves to have every reason to smile." Truth again.

"I agree. I let Angelique convince me that not supporting Bethany in her business endeavor was the best thing. That was definitely incorrect, and I plan to rectify it. Those desserts of hers are amazing."

"Damned straight they are. And I'm sure she would

appreciate your business advice so she can concentrate more on the aspects she's passionate about."

He finished the last of his drink and slid the glass to the side. "I plan to be as big a part of her business as she'll let me."

Landon snuck a look over at Martinez and Frey. They were still in the shadows closer to the beach. Adams and Fanshawe were staying discreetly to the sides. He spotted at least two other men who were probably Martinez's.

He looked back over at Oliver. "I think she would like that."

"Let me go find my wife before she hunts me down. Why aren't you with Bethany?"

"She was talking business with one of the hotel staff. I'll head back over in a second."

He slapped Landon on the shoulder and walked away just as his phone buzzed. Tristan.

"Can you talk?" he said without greeting.

"I'm here at a luau with about three hundred of my closest friends, Mom." He smiled at the bartender who'd glanced in his direction.

"Fine, then just listen. I talked to Callum. That guy in the picture with Frey is Joaquin Martinez. He's pretty high in a terrorist organization that operates out of South America. Callum had no idea he'd be there."

"I'm pretty sure that's the case all the way around."

"You still have all three transmitters?"

"Yep, Mom. Sure do." Another couple came to stand at the bar. He gave them a friendly wave.

"Whatever Frey and Martinez are meeting about can't be good. Callum nearly wet himself at the thought of getting a transmitter on Martinez. Said it would be even more helpful than Frey. You can get it on his phone, computer, anything electronic."

"Sounds great, Mom. I'll do my best."

"Be careful. This Martinez guy sounds like bad news. Don't forget that you've got no safety net. I'm still only two miles offshore, but that's not going to help you if things get ugly. No transmitter is worth your life, Libra."

"Yeah, I love you too." He disconnected the call. There was only so long he could pretend to talk to his mother before it became weird. And he had the information he needed.

Landon's mission had become twice as hard.

"Were you talking to your mom?"

Shit, Bethany. He forced a smile on his face as he turned toward her. "She doesn't always have the best timing."

Worry puckered her brow. "Is everything okay with her?"

He wrapped an arm around her shoulder. "Yeah, she gets a little worried sometimes. I might need to put a call in to her later." Better to go ahead and set up that excuse. He was going to need it soon. Having to call Mom was as good a reason as any to escape the party.

Bethany dipped her head against his chest. "You're a good son. A good man."

Landon gritted his teeth to keep his smile on his face. Then to make matters worse, Angelique spotted them and came fluttering their way.

"Speaking of mothers... Incoming," he whispered.

"Okay, you two. We're about to have family dances. You need to be out on the floor as a couple."

Bethany peeked up at him. "Is that okay?"

"Of course it's okay," Angelique interjected. "Why wouldn't it be okay? You do dance, don't you, Landon?"

"I do." But damn it, he didn't want to now when he needed to get closer to Martinez and Frey.

"Then it's settled." She grabbed his arm and urged them out to the floor.

CHAPTER
THIRTEEN

BETHANY COULDN'T REMEMBER the last time she felt this free.

She was two for two when it came to the desserts. Her tropical-themed goodies had been just as much of a success as the cupcakes had at the welcome reception. People were specifically starting to ask about the bakery. She'd given out over a dozen of her cards so far tonight. She wasn't sure things could be going better professionally.

Personally… Well, personally seemed to be going just as well.

She was dancing under the beautiful lights, surrounded by the crisp ocean breeze, in her fiancé's arms. She hadn't talked to him much today. She'd been busy making sure everything was ready for tonight. And besides, she wasn't sure what to say anyway. Despite Michele's three dozen texts asking for an update and coaching her—in unnerving detail —into putting the moves on Landon, she wasn't sure if that was what she really wanted. After all, what did she really know about him?

His thumb brushed down the middle of her forehead. "What's got you thinking so hard?" he asked.

Bethany shrugged. Might as well be honest. "I don't know much about you. I've been fortunate so far that I've been able to deflect any questions."

He stiffened just slightly before relaxing. "What do you want to know?" he asked as they swayed to the music. He looked off to the side, but then back at her.

"You were just talking to your mom on the phone. Are you guys close? Do you have any siblings? Where are you from?"

He chuckled. "My mom and I are reasonably close. She's a recovering alcoholic, so we've become closer since she's gotten sober."

"Oh, I'm sorry."

"No, don't be. I'm happy for her. She is living a much better life than she did when I was a kid."

"Is your dad around?"

He shook his head. "No, he died when I was young."

"I'm sorry," she said again.

He looked like he was about to say more but stopped himself. "Thank you. My dad and I weren't close before he died."

Better to change the subject. "How about siblings?"

"None. It was just me. Well, that's not true, I guess," he continued. "I picked up quite a few brothers in the Navy. They may not be blood related to me, but I know they have my back and I have theirs no matter what."

He meant it. Sincerity was all but pouring from his hazel eyes.

"That's good," she said. "I believe in found families also. How long were you in the Navy?"

"I joined just after my seventeenth birthday. Forged my mom's signature. I was in for thirteen years then got out when some of my best friends did."

"How long ago was that?" She wasn't even sure how old he was.

"A while," he finally responded.

"I should stop prying." He obviously didn't want to talk about this.

"No, you're not prying." He pulled her in a little closer. "I have a friend—Ian. He came into some money and started a business once he got out of the Navy. It's a sort of jack-of-all-trades company. We do lots of different things."

"Like carpentry?" She asked.

"Yeah, there's definitely some work like that involved. Ian hired a bunch of us that were in the Navy with him, so each of us takes on jobs based on whatever our strengths are. So, like this, with you, building the stands. That sort of mechanical work was right up my alley."

"And you like working for your friend?"

He nodded. "I never thought I would find a place where I fit in like I did in the Navy, but Ian's business, it's my home."

"That's good. I know some people struggle with finding their way once they get out of the service."

"Yes, definitely true," he responded.

Bethany still felt like she was missing part of the information, but she really didn't want to pry.

"And truly, this gig with you has been great," Landon continued. "When I was growing up, I loved carpentry, loved to build things. I had a shed a couple miles from my house that was off on an empty lot, and I used to build all sorts of things in there. I'd forgotten how much I loved it until being back here with you. So, thank you."

He was *thanking* her. All she'd done was pay him a fair wage for good work. He'd done so much more. "I'm glad it worked out for both of us."

The song shifted into something new, but Landon didn't miss a beat. They kept dancing.

"Now, let's talk about something important, like what do you do for fun?"

He was trying to get out of talking more about himself,

but she would allow it. It was nice to have him focused on her.

"I'm not sure that I have done anything fun since I opened the bakery. It has taken up all my time. But I don't mean that in a bad way. I knew going in it would require all my time and effort to get the business off the ground. And I feel like we're almost there, especially after this week. If things go the way I expect, we'll need to hire a couple more full-time employees. Maybe then I'll get to take a day off."

His arm came a little more tightly around her waist. "What about if you took advantage of being on this island? You don't have any desserts you have to provide tomorrow, do you?"

She shook her head. "No, I don't have anything due now until the rehearsal dinner on Friday, so nothing tomorrow. But I'm not very good at relaxing." There was always so much to do even when she wasn't actively baking. Catching up on bills, emails, promotions.

He smiled, those dimples out in full force. "What if I help you with that? What if we spend part of the day tomorrow at the pool—relaxing, enjoying ourselves. Maybe a walk on the beach?"

Bethany narrowed her eyes at him. "You don't have to babysit me."

His face turned wry. "Don't insult either of us. It would be my pleasure to spend time with you."

She stared down at his chest, not wanting to meet his eyes. She wasn't sure what was real and what was the part of him playing the role of her fiancé.

"Okay," she finally said, "the pool sounds great."

The DJ announced the end of the family dances, and the beat of the music picked up. Landon smiled at her as they broke away from each other.

"Okay, it's a date for tomorrow." He glanced at something over her shoulder and his brows pulled together, but Christiana rushed over and grabbed her arm before she could turn to see what it was.

"Can I borrow my sister?" She smiled at Landon.

"Absolutely." He gave her a little bow. "I'll grab a drink and entertain myself. Back in a few minutes."

Bethany hooked arms with Christiana and walked in the other direction from Landon—he seemed to be going toward the ocean. She didn't think there was a bar in that direction, but he'd figure it out.

"You doing okay?" Yesterday at the spa, she'd seemed relaxed and perky, but now, her pinched features were back full force.

"Yeah, I just needed to escape Mom and Patricia. They made another hotel employee cry tonight because some of the seafood on the buffet tasted a little iffy."

Bethany made a face. "The last thing we want is anyone getting sick from spoiled food."

She rolled her eyes. "It wasn't spoiled. They wanted something to complain about. I saw Patricia and Mina circling your desserts earlier. But I don't think they could find anything wrong with them, so Patricia moved on to easier targets."

"I'm sorry, sweetie." She bumped Christiana with her hip. "But more sorry that you're marrying into that family."

"Don't remind me. I'm glad Simon's not like that."

She wrapped her arm around her shoulder. "Mom and Patricia aren't usually this bad either. It's how they handle stress. Some people drink, some people exercise, Mom and Patricia make themselves feel big by making other people feel small."

"God, it sounds so awful when you say it out loud like that."

Bethany shrugged. "The best we can do is not follow in their footsteps."

She breathed in deeply and let it out before turning and grabbing both her arms. "Then don't assume I'm being like them when I ask you this. You're sure everything is good for Friday and the wedding, right?"

She kept her patience. Christiana was under a lot of stress. If it were any other bride freaking out a few days before her wedding, wanting reassurance she had everything under control, she wouldn't falter. She needed to treat Christiana with the same courtesy.

Bethany tucked a strand of her sister's hair back over her shoulders. Her hair was as curly as hers if she left it natural, but no one would ever know that. She kept it straight or, at best, in a gentle wave.

She smiled at her. "The groom's cake at the gala on Friday has so much chocolate, people might go into a coma. And your wedding cakes will be so beautiful, you might get mad that people are looking at them instead of you."

She let out a laugh that was more like a blubber. "We wouldn't want that."

She pulled her in for a hug. "I promise your wedding cakes will be absolutely perfect. You focus on getting through the ceremony, and don't worry about that at all."

"Okay. I wish Patricia would stop making offhanded suggestions that there might be problems."

Bethany gritted her teeth. "What did she say?"

"Nothing to me directly, I overheard her. She found out Mother canceled having the hotel on standby as a backup since everything you've provided so far has been stellar. Patricia thought that was a bad idea, and the people she was talking with agreed."

People she was talking with. She rolled her eyes. "Let me guess. Mina."

Christiana bit her lip. "She was one of them. Suggested that if you were planning to make waves, you wouldn't do it at the beginning of the week. You'd wait until the end."

Bethany cupped her sister's face with her hands. "You know I would never do that. Although, if I could figure how to make sure only Mina and Patricia would eat it, I'd been tempted to put a ton of laxatives in their cake."

She smiled and leaned her forehead against hers. "I'm crazy. I'm sorry."

"Don't be sorry. But don't let them drive you insane. I can personally promise everything will be fine." There was no way she wasn't going to keep that promise.

"Thank you."

"Now, go find your fiancé and dance with him."

"Only if you promise to find yours and do the same."

Bethany grimaced. "You heard?"

"You know how rumors fly. Once I get back from my honeymoon, I'm going to expect a full report."

By then, Landon would be out of her life. That made her sadder than it should. At that point, maybe she'd tell Christiana the whole truth. It could be something that bonded them—keeping the secret from Mother. "Full story once you get back. It's a deal."

She hugged her and rushed over to Simon, who immediately whisked her out onto the dance floor. Bethany didn't see Landon anywhere around, so she went to check on the desserts. Everything looked fine; the serving staff was doing a good job. Her babies were looking sexy and delicious as they should.

Speaking of sexy and delicious…

"Lose your fiancé?"

She didn't even justify Mina's comment with a response.

"I saw him leave right after you started talking to your sister. If I'm not mistaken, he was following a cute little blonde who started chatting with him. Just wanted to let you know he's not around, so you're not standing over here looking all pathetic."

Bethany crossed her arms. "I know he left."

She didn't know he'd left. But it looked as if Mina was right. Landon was nowhere to be seen.

Why did that hurt? He didn't have to check in with her. He'd gone above and beyond with everything he'd done. Hell, even if he was flirting—or more—with some other woman, that shouldn't bother her.

Not. Real.

But somehow, it did hurt.

"Oh, and look, there's your mother and Aunt Patricia talking with another hotel employee."

"So?" She hoped they weren't about to make her cry.

"Oh, wait," Mina said with a smile. "I see who that is now. It's the pastry director for the resort. I wonder what they could possibly be talking about?"

As if Mina had choreographed the whole thing, at that very moment, Bethany's mother looked over at her, guilt blanketing her features. She turned and ushered the pastry director and Patricia in the opposite direction.

Mina bunched up her nose. "Yeah, that definitely has nothing to do with you."

She didn't know how to respond. It obviously did have something to do with her.

"Anyway, I'll leave you alone." She shot me a smile and turned. "That's your default setting when we strip it all down to the truth, isn't it? You being alone?"

Suddenly the lights and breeze she'd found so charming felt empty. Mina might be a bitch, but that didn't mean she was wrong.

Bethany was alone.

CHAPTER
FOURTEEN

LANDON LEFT Bethany at the luau without a word. He felt like shit, but when he saw Frey and Martinez leave, he couldn't miss the chance.

They were using the wedding as an excuse for a face-to-face meeting. He might not be able to get the transmitter on them tonight, but he could at least try to gather as much intel as possible.

They'd headed toward the beach like they were going on a damned lovers' stroll, so he went in that direction too.

He never thought he'd use any of the tracking measures he'd learned in the SEALs while on a vacation island wearing a tropical-themed shirt and loafers. He'd much rather be attempting that in his camo and boots.

And with weapons and backup.

Good news was, Frey and Martinez and their teams weren't concerned about not leaving tracks. They didn't expect anyone to be following them. Why would anybody be when there was a great party going on?

And they had their guards, who wouldn't hesitate to put a bullet in his brain if they found him and realized he was undercover.

They'd walked far enough away from the festivities, so they were at the cliff beaches rather than the sandy ones. At some point, they'd cut uphill, still easy enough to follow since at least one of them was smoking. Once he pinpointed exactly where they were, he circled around so he was coming at them from the cliff side. Hopefully the guards would be paying more attention to the main path.

Landon had to lie flat just off the secondary path near the edge of the cliff to be able to hear Frey and Martinez at all. But the waves hitting against the rocks meant he was only able to capture every few words. He couldn't get any closer without them discovering him.

"…handoff is still a go for next week."

That was Frey. Whatever else he said was lost by the waves.

He pulled out his phone and opened the recording app. It was more sensitive than his hearing and would allow him to send the entire recorded conversation to Tristan. He could get it to Callum.

He kept the phone pointed at them from his awkward angle. The more he caught of the conversation, the more concerning it became. They were talking about deliveries and packages. He thought they were discussing drugs at first. Then maybe weapons.

Finally, Landon realized the *shipments* they were referring to were people.

Zodiac Tactical had already had a very up close and personal run-in with scumbags attempting human trafficking. Hell, that bullet wound in his chest was an indirect result of that.

Frey was on Callum's radar because of his connection with Mosaic, the above-mentioned scumbags. He shouldn't be surprised Frey and Martinez would be conducting similar sick business.

But it did make getting the nano transmitters placed even

more critical. People's lives were at stake. If he wasn't able to—

A hand on his shoulder blew adrenaline through his body. "What are you—"

Landon reacted instinctively, not waiting for the whispered sentence to be completed. Reaching behind him, he yanked on the arm and twisted the person so that they'd be on the ground and he'd have the upper hand. If it was one of the guards, he had to get their weapon away from them and fast.

But as soon as he yanked the intruder down, he realized the body against him was soft, small.

Bethany.

Shit. *Shit.*

His brain raced. How not to blow his cover with her waged war with how not to get them both killed. Had they been heard?

Bethany's green eyes were huge in the soft moonlight. He placed a finger over her lips. He looked up and through the bushes, praying the guards hadn't noticed.

"Quiet," he mouthed. Her brows furrowed, but she nodded. Landon put his phone in his pocket and grabbed her hand, pulling her back along the cliff path. If he could get her out of this, he'd make up some story about a wild animal he hadn't wanted to interrupt.

They only made it a few yards before Landon realized they'd heard them. Frey and Martinez weren't talking anymore, and the guards were now all on high alert, barking quietly at each other. It wouldn't take long before they found them.

He needed a plan, right fucking now.

He stopped walking and yanked Bethany to him, wrapping one arm around her hips, the other cupping her nape. His mouth covered hers.

She stiffened. "Landon?"

He didn't let up. His lips nipped at hers and she opened them with a gasp, and he slipped his tongue inside, coaxing her, demanding a response.

She gave it. He felt the second she stopped fighting her confusion and gave herself over to the kiss.

God, she was so damned soft, so warm and giving. There was nothing he wanted more than for this to be real, for them to be alone where he could continue kissing her until neither of them could breathe.

Mission.

Landon forced the thought into his lust-hazed brain. This wasn't about a kiss; this was about preserving his cover—and getting them both out of there alive.

He didn't have long. Sweet Bethany didn't resist as he lowered them both to the ground, never moving his lips from hers. Her arms slipped around his neck, their tongues continuing to duel, as he laid her underneath him.

He slid his hand down the base of her thigh, coaxing it to wrap around his hips. The groan that escaped him as that lined up their bodies perfectly was only half fake. If it weren't for the clothes between them, he'd be sliding inside that delectable body.

Mission.

Landon moved his lips down to her neck, drawing a soft gasp from her. His hand covered her breast. Those guards were going to be on them any second. They had to believe that they were so wrapped up in each other that they'd decided to have a quickie right there in the sand.

Convincing his body that wasn't what was about to happen was pretty damned difficult. This might be a ploy, but he was rock hard against Bethany's soft curves.

And she was pressing up against him. Grinding. Low moans escaping her throat. Holy hell.

"What are you doing here?"

He heard Adams's voice and felt the muzzle of a gun

pressed against the back of his neck. He immediately froze. A soft gasp left Bethany's lips.

Landon prayed his acting chops were enough to get them out of this.

"What the fuck, man? Do you have a gun to my head?" He wanted to roll off Bethany, but he didn't want that gun getting any closer to her. "Is a quickie under the stars a capital offense on this island?"

"Landon?" Adams took a step back, pulling his weapon with him. "You should not be out here. Neither of you."

He glanced at Bethany's face as he slid off her and stood, keeping himself between Adams and her. She looked well-kissed, disheveled, confused, scared. She was selling their cover story whether she wanted to or not. Thankfully, she kept quiet.

"Dude, we wanted a little alone time. I was showing her the cliffs."

Fanshawe came rushing into the clearing. "Everything okay? Mr. Frey wants a repor—" He saw Landon. "What are you doing here?"

Adams put his weapon away, but Fanshawe had his out. He was leering at Bethany where she still sat on the ground. He wanted to break the guy's nose.

"It's fine," Adams said.

"Oh, I see. Landon was getting himself some." Fanshawe's grin was greasy. "Daddy's princess likes the wildlife, huh?"

"Shut the fuck up, Fanshawe." Adams pushed at the other man, able to see what Fanshawe couldn't.

That Landon was about to throw his ass over the side of the cliff.

"This isn't a good place to be, Landon," Adams continued. "You need to stay closer to the resort."

"Roger that. I didn't realize these paths were…off-limits. We'll head back to our room."

Adams and Fanshawe turned and walked away, Fanshawe humming obnoxious porn music. What an asshole.

They were safe, but he had no doubt Frey and Martinez were gone for the night and would now be much more careful. They wouldn't have any more open meetings like this. Hopefully Callum would be able to make something of what he'd recorded.

He turned to Bethany. She was pale, eyes big from where she still sat on the ground. "Did those guys have guns?"

"Yes, they were security team members." Security for criminals, but that was immaterial for this conversation.

"Why were you even out here?"

Landon scrubbed his hand down his face. "The party got a little much for me, so I decided to go for a walk. I accidentally stumbled onto these guys and was about to go back the way I'd come when you tapped me on my shoulder."

Her face said she couldn't decide whether to believe him. She looked out toward the cliff edge then back at him. "Did you make out with me because you knew the guards were coming?"

"Bethany—"

"The truth, if you don't mind."

He crouched down beside her so they were eye to eye. "Earlier tonight when I was at the bar, I saw Vincent Frey had a gun under his blazer. I know you've mentioned your father has had some contact with criminals in the past. I wasn't sure if Frey was one of those criminals. If he was, I didn't want him to think we were spying on him or something."

"So, you did what you had to do."

"Yes, exactly. I wanted to keep you safe."

Her face fell carefully blank. "Well, I'm safe now. So, no need to pretend anymore."

Her tone was as blank as her features. That wasn't good.

"Bethany, look—"

She moved to stand up. He offered her his hand, but she didn't take it.

"Thanks for the rescue. Again. Goodnight, Landon."

Shit. That phrase could've come straight from her mother's mouth it was so dismissive and cold.

Landon wanted to chase after her, wanted to explain that it had been a cover, but that hadn't been *all* it was.

And then prove it to her in a way that ended with both of them naked and him buried deep inside her.

So he forced himself to stay where he was as she walked away. Because that couldn't happen.

He followed her from a distance back to the resort to make sure she got back to the room safely. *Their* room. For once, he could be thankful for his insomnia. Staying out of the room wouldn't be that difficult.

Once she was inside, he turned back toward the ocean. He needed to get this recording sent to Tristan, then find out what he could about Martinez, including his room number.

Mostly, he needed to figure out a real plan to get these transmitters planted.

He was running out of time in more ways than one.

CHAPTER
FIFTEEN

LANDON DIDN'T EVEN TRY to stop Bethany from walking away. Didn't offer to get her back to the room safely. Didn't attempt to convince her that lying down on top of her and kissing her senseless had any elements of real attraction to it.

She supposed she should be thankful he was so quick-thinking. She knew some of the people Dad associated with were criminals, but she didn't think he would invite them to the wedding. But she believed Landon when he said he saw Vincent Frey carrying a gun.

Bethany didn't think he or his men would've shot them over running into him while on a walk, so the whole make-out session was probably overkill.

Did Landon think she was an idiot for the way she had responded?

She thought she was an idiot for the way she had responded.

Worse, her body was still tingly and heated where his had pressed up against hers when he'd hiked her leg over his hip. She could still feel the phantom touch of his hand on her breast and his lips on her neck.

She *wanted* him.

And once again, it was all just an act for him. Not. Real.

Bethany wasn't sure when he was coming back to the room, and she definitely didn't want to discuss anything that had happened tonight, so she rushed into the shower. He still wasn't there when she got out. Still wasn't there when she got into the bed and turned off the light.

When she finally fell asleep and woke late the next morning after a pretty fitful sleep, it didn't look like he'd been there at all.

She hugged one of the pillows from her big bed and stared at the sofa. There was no folded-up blanket, no pillow. Evidently, Landon had preferred not sleeping at all to being in the same room as her.

She guessed that meant their date at the pool was canceled too.

Bethany clamped down on the disappointment trying to well up inside her. Landon had made that offer as part of his act. It all was part of an act he took ever so seriously for whatever reason. There was no need to be disappointed just because they were taking a break from the ruse.

She'd work on business stuff instead. She certainly had enough to do. A small business owner's work was never done, and she was behind on paperwork.

She called to order coffee and breakfast delivered, got dressed, and sat down on the couch to get to work. Concentrating wasn't as easy as it normally was—with her balcony door open, she could hear people laughing and splashing outside in the pool—but she wasn't going to let it derail her.

She'd had to re-add the figures in one column three times to figure out how much she owed one of their vendors when the knock came on the door. Good. Maybe coffee would set her straight.

It was the blessed nectar of the gods at her door. But

Landon was holding it. Beside him was a cart with her breakfast plate.

She raised an eyebrow. "You working for the resort now?"

"I told the waiter maybe this could help get me out of the doghouse. And I tipped him twenty dollars." He handed the coffee mug to her.

Bethany took a sip. It had cream but no sugar, just as she preferred it. Landon had been paying attention at some point when she drank coffee and had made note of how she liked it.

That was something, but not enough.

"You didn't sleep in here last night."

"No. I didn't sleep at all."

"Really? Why?"

He took a breath and blew it out. "I actually don't sleep a lot in general. Chronic insomnia since I was a kid."

"Oh." She stepped out of the way so he could come in. He wheeled in the cart. "I'm sorry."

He shrugged one shoulder. "It's been a fact of life for me for so long, I've learned to cope and work my way around it pretty well."

"So, what did you do last night?"

He took the top off the tray of food and gestured for her to sit, then wheeled the cart over in front of her. Eggs, bacon, toast. She grabbed a piece of bacon and nibbled on it as he sat in the armchair.

"I worked out. Sent some emails. Stared up at the moon and pondered…things."

She wanted to ask if what happened between them was one of the things he pondered but was too chicken. "What causes your insomnia?"

"Navy shrink says a combination of childhood trauma, genetic makeup, and stubbornness. The last mostly because I refuse to take medication."

Bethany placed her bacon back down on the plate. "Childhood trauma. Your dad?"

Landon shrugged. "He was a drunk and he was mean, and I learned from an early age to sleep lightly, or even better, not sleep at all, if I didn't want a fist catching me unawares."

"I'm sorry." The words seemed woefully inadequate.

"Don't be. It's actually helped me some in my adult life. They thought I was a superhero in the Navy—could function on less sleep than everyone else combined. I've learned to cope."

"Do you need to sleep now? I can clear out."

"Nope." Dimples. "I'm hoping I still have a lovely date for the pool."

She grabbed her bacon again. "Landon, there's no need. I get it—it's all an act. And while I'd appreciate it if you'd be willing to keep it up a few more days while we're in public and, of course"—she threw him a forced smile—"if we're about to get shot by bad guys, there's no need to waste your time with me."

Before she could blink, he'd moved from his chair to next to her on the couch. He'd moved that fast last night when she'd come up on him unawares. He was so damned fast when he wanted to be.

"Time spent with you is not a waste." His face was close to hers. She could smell his own coffee on his breath. She just wanted to get closer.

No. She needed to keep her distance. "You don't have to pretend when it's only us. I shouldn't have gotten upset about what happened last night. I just felt stupid."

"Why?"

Because she'd been willing to have sex with him right then, and he'd merely been putting on a show? She shook her head. "It wasn't real. I get it. You were protecting us."

She leaned back from him and put the bacon back on the plate. The thought of eating now curled her stomach.

He ran a hand through his hair. "I was trying to protect us.

And I won't lie, I did kiss you and pull you to the ground so they wouldn't get suspicious."

"I know." Her voice was small. She couldn't even look at him. She thought about her moans last night, about grinding up against him.

"But that didn't mean I was unaffected, Wildflower. Don't think that you were the only one aware of the heat between us."

Now Bethany looked at him. "Really?"

He shook his head with a wry grin. "Oh, believe me, yes."

He seemed authentic.

"I don't want to let things get out of hand," he continued. "Or take advantage of an unorthodox situation and make it more complicated. But don't think I wasn't affected by what happened between us last night."

If she told him she wanted him to take advantage of her, or vice versa, would he let her talk him into it? She could hear Michele screaming internally at her to find out, but she was too much of a coward. So she merely nodded.

"But I would very much like to keep our pool date today if you'd agree. You deserve a chance to relax."

He looked like he wanted to say more, and she knew there was a lot more she wanted to say, but both of them stared.

Finally, she nodded. "Pool date sounds great."

"Good. Don't bring your computer. This is an afternoon off."

She couldn't meet his eyes. "I wouldn't do that."

"Tablet either."

Damn it. She definitely would've slipped her tablet into her bag. "Fine."

He grinned and winked at her, and parts of her body flushed all over. "Let's have some fun, Wildflower."

CHAPTER
SIXTEEN

BETHANY HAD THROWN her bathing suit into her suitcase at the last minute. She hadn't expected to be spending much time lounging by the pool or frolicking in the ocean on this trip.

Definitely hadn't planned on having someone who looked like Landon by her side as she did those things.

She put on her bathing suit and looked at herself critically. Definitely wasn't going to be confused with a size two, but overall, she wasn't upset with how she looked. Her one-piece was modest but cut out in places that gave it a sexy vibe rather than matronly. At least, she hoped.

She threw on a sheer cover-up and grabbed her beach bag, pre-packed with a book, sunglasses, and sunscreen.

They made it down to the pool early when there weren't many people there, so they snagged two loungers close together under an umbrella. Even though she had no reason to feel any embarrassment about what her body looked like, she felt a twinge of shyness as she pulled off her cover-up and her body was more exposed than it had been.

Hell, the cover-up was sheer to begin with. It wasn't like she'd stripped from a turtleneck and jeans into the buff.

But Landon's eyes went to her body and lingered there a few seconds longer than they had to. Definitely appreciative. She sat quickly and put on her sunglasses to hide her blush.

Then he took off his shirt.

Holy bathing suit gods. His trunks were plain navy blue. Nothing notable. But the sculpted abs he revealed under his shirt were notable and then some.

"Come on, Wildflower." Landon grinned at her. "Let's swim."

He jumped up and ran for the water at full blast. She laughed as he dove in because he totally messed up his dive, belly-flopping with a resounding smack. His glorious abs were going to be super-bright red.

Maybe that would give her an excuse for staring.

Bethany shook her head as she walked at a much more reasonable pace toward the pool.

He swam back to the edge. "Was that funny?"

She crouched down next to him. "Sure was. I wouldn't keep admitting to being former Navy with that dive, *sailor.*"

That speed of his again. He reached up and grabbed her upper arms, pushing himself off the pool wall as he yanked. With a screech, she fell face first into the water.

"Still funny?" he asked.

She shrieked and lunged for him. She hadn't planned on getting so far in that she ruined her hair and makeup, but now she was soaked from stem to stern. She laughed. Nothing she could do about it now, except take him down in revenge.

Of course, Mr. Hotbod got away from her easily. They played a game of cat and mouse for a while as the pool and surrounding chairs filled up with guests.

Bethany came up for air and whirled, looking for Landon. She was ready to splash him as soon as he materialized. Even though the pool was crystal clear, he was so sneaky that he'd startled her several times.

And he managed it one more time as she spotted her mother and Christiana walking toward the pool, both of them looking like swimsuit models on a photo shoot.

Landon burst from the water and tackled her. She barely had time to gulp in a breath to hold before going under.

She did, however, have time to see her mother roll her eyes. Of course. She'd look down on such frivolous behavior. But Bethany didn't care. This was the most fun she'd had in as long as she could remember.

Sinking to the bottom of the pool, she peeked her eyes open and ignored the burn of the chlorine, trying to find Landon.

Bubbles erupted from her mouth when she realized he was underwater too, on the bottom of the pool with her, staring right at her. She squealed and pushed off the bottom to get away from him.

When her head broke the surface of the water and she sucked in a deep breath, she swam for all she was worth, but still, when she grabbed the side of the pool and looked around, he was right beside her.

"You can't beat me," he said smugly. "I'm a seal."

Bethany didn't care what sort of water animal he was. She gave no warning as she pushed off the side of the pool and sprinted her way across the water to the other side. She heard his splashes, but she wiggled her body, kicked her feet, and swung her arms harder than she had before in an attempt to beat him. Even though they were both laughing so hard every time they came up for air she was surprised they didn't drown.

This was what she wanted. To have fun with a man who legitimately seemed to be having fun with her right back.

Water stung her eyes, so she glanced quickly at how much farther she had to go and closed her eyes for the last push. But she'd misjudged the distance or something because instead of slapping her hand on the side of the pool, she slapped it onto the hard muscles of a chest. She gasped and sucked in water.

Sputtering, Bethany came up for air. Landon's strong arms circled her and held her upright as she wiped droplets from her eyes and caught her breath. Her feet floated off the bottom of the pool as her legs pressed against his.

Oh goodness.

The laughter in her chest fizzled out as she raised her eyes to meet his. His gaze was glued to her lips. Then she couldn't help but stare at his.

The sun beat down on their heads as their lips touched. After the way they'd teased each other in the pool, back and forth, racing, tickling, dunking, her body was overly ready to rub against his as his mouth pressed against hers.

Bethany didn't want the moment to end. She wanted to push it further, grind against him or let her legs lift in the water and wrap around his waist. To feel all that muscle and hardness against her again like last night.

Somebody cleared their throat, bringing her back to reality. They were in a public pool. She opened her eyes, easing back from Landon.

He looked just as dazed as she felt.

And that made Bethany smile.

When he saw it, he wrapped his arm back around her waist and pulled her closer. Almost as if he couldn't help himself.

One of her arms resumed its place around his neck, and she slid her other hand up his chest. She looked down as her fingers traced over a scar on his pec she hadn't noticed before. Puffy, round.

"What's that from? Somebody shoot you?" she asked.

It was the wrong thing to say. Bethany watched as the Landon she'd been playing with for the past half hour disappeared and someone else took his place.

Someone with razor focus and almost palpable determination. His features hadn't turned exactly *hard*, but they were crisp in a way they hadn't been a few seconds ago.

Charming, laughing Landon was sexy, but this Landon… He was so much more. He was compelling, dangerous even.

But then dangerous Landon disappeared, and charming Landon was back. He placed his hand over hers. "Yeah, bullet wound. The list of people who want to shoot me is impressively long. Come on, I'll race you to the other side again."

He shot off then spun back around and splashed her, trying to get her to chase him.

Trying to avoid talking about that scar.

She'd been joking when she'd suggested it was from a gun, but now, she honestly wasn't sure.

They raced to the other end again, and she only won by cheating, pulling him back by the leg and using the momentum to propel herself forward. They were both laughing and out of breath as they leaned up against the wall.

"Ready to get out for a while?" he asked.

Her stomach growled loud enough to be a reply, and they both burst out laughing. "How about lunch?" she asked.

"Sure," he said. "I'm going to use the restroom first."

"I'll order us some burgers." She floated on her back, kicking her feet to propel toward the pool stairs as he walked beside her.

"Sounds great." He shoved her head underwater with a grin, and by the time she slung her hair out of the way and wiped her eyes, he was out of the pool and headed toward the outdoor restrooms near the entrance to the gardens.

Bethany grabbed one of the fluffy white towels from a stack and dried her face and arms, so she didn't drip all over the counter at the pool bar.

"What can I get you?" The bartender smiled and cocked her head at her, then typed onto a tablet screen as she rattled off Landon's order, then her own. She spread the towel over the seat of the barstool to keep it from scalding her legs and perched on it. She knew she had a stupid grin on her face, but she couldn't seem to stop.

Her grin faded when she sensed someone standing close behind her. Turning to her left, she was blinded by the sun, so she didn't recognize the man at first. When she shaded her eyes and squinted, she realized it was one of the guards from last night. The one who'd been so obnoxious when he found them.

"You looked like you wanted some company," he said. His gaze was glued to her breasts, and she wished she'd wrapped the towel around herself instead of using it on the stool.

The bartender set her iced tea on the counter. She hoped she'd stay, but she walked back to the other side of the bar to take someone's order.

"No, I don't want company. I'm waiting for my fiancé."

His smile was more of a leer than anything else. "Sorry we interrupted you last night. Hope you don't hold that against me."

His pinkie touched her arm on the bar, and she yanked it away. She didn't want to make a scene, especially since this jerk seemed like the type to announce to everyone that he'd stumbled across her and Landon making out.

"I don't hold it against you." Snatching up her tea, Bethany slipped off the stool and walked in the opposite direction, around the side of the bar.

As soon as she got there, she realized she'd made a mistake. The bartender had gone to deliver some food, and of course, slimeball guy followed her. They were secluded.

"Smart. Now, we'll have some privacy. I like it." He stepped closer.

She held up her hand. "No," she said in a firm, strong voice. "I do not want privacy with you. Please leave. Now."

His face changed from suggestive to angry in an instant. "You seemed okay with being pretty public in your affections last night on the beach. Almost like you wanted us to see you."

Bethany gritted her teeth. "I'm the sister of the bride, and if you don't walk away this instant, I'll have you removed from the island."

Her words fell on deaf ears as the man closed in on her further. "No need to be like that. I promise I can show you an even better time than your fiancé. You won't have to put on a show if you've got a real man to keep you happy."

She could not believe this was even happening. If she screamed, she could get rid of him, but she knew that would draw everyone's attention at the pool. Patricia and Mina would have a field day.

"Back off, asshole."

He sneered at her. "I don't think so. I think if you really wanted me to back off, you would've let somebody know by now. It's okay to want a man to take it from you. I know how to play that game."

Bethany wasn't going to try to hit him; he was a trained security guard. Creating a scene was going to be her only option. She opened her mouth to yell for help, knowing it was going to cause as many problems as it solved. But she wasn't going to stay there and be molested by this guy.

Landon's voice stopped her. "How about if you and I play a game instead, Fanshawe?"

She spun to look at him, so relieved. But she froze as she saw his face. This wasn't friendly, grinning Landon. This was the man she'd caught a glimpse of a few minutes ago in the pool.

Dangerous Landon was back.

CHAPTER
SEVENTEEN

LANDON KNEW something was wrong by the look on Bethany's face as he headed back toward the pool area. She looked scared and pissed at the same time, off to the side of the bar, but he couldn't tell who she was looking at.

He suspected Mina, but when he rounded the bar, it was fucking Fanshawe. He already owed him from his obnoxious shit last night.

As he took in the scene, he stepped forward again, his body language menacing. He was so big next to Bethany.

Neither of them noticed Landon heading their way. As he got closer, Bethany's eyes darted around, searching for a way to bolt.

He moved faster, catching the guard's words to her. "...it's okay to want a man to take it from you. I know how to play that game."

Landon could feel fury bubbling up inside him like a goddamn fountain. He'd thought he'd been propositioning her, which was bad enough. But this was outright threatening.

"How about if you and I play a game instead, Fanshawe?" He closed the rest of the distance as Bethany spun toward him, relief and some sort of surprise evident in those green eyes.

Landon stepped past him and put his arm around Bethany. She trembled once, her skin cool from the pool water drying on it. He knew she wasn't cold, though. He'd gotten to her. He wanted to rip his face off.

He forced himself to pull back the rage. Fanshawe was still his best shot at getting to Frey. Putting him in a coma wasn't going to help.

He sneered at him. "I was just trying to be friendly with your fiancée here, and she's ordered me to leave and says she's going to have me fired."

Even with Landon standing in front of him, obviously willing to protect Bethany, he still glared at her and clenched his fists.

This guy was definitely not suited for security work.

"I'm sure it was a misunderstanding," he said. As much as Landon wanted to break his hands, he didn't touch him, just forced a smile onto his face. And he needed Bethany not to have Fanshawe fired. "Let's all calm down." Landon turned and squeezed Bethany's shoulder. "I'm sure if we avoid each other the rest of the week, there's no reason for anyone to be fired."

He hated saying the words. Fanshawe deserved to be fired. Moreover, he deserved to have the shit kicked out of him. But that wasn't a viable option at the moment.

"Yeah, right," Fanshawe drawled. "This bitch is going to go running to Mommy and Daddy the minute my back is turned."

He took his arm off Bethany's shoulders and held up his hands. "Hey, man. I'm trying to say let's let bygones be bygones, whatever happened. There's no need for you to call her names."

Fanshawe laughed in his face. "You're so pussy-whipped you can't see what a slut you're marrying."

And he'd just crossed a line Landon wasn't going to back down from, mission or not.

"Watch your fucking mouth." His voice dropped in volume, but he had no doubt he heard him.

"Or what?" He stepped forward and squared off his shoulders.

Bethany plucked at his arm. "Come on, Landon. Let's go. This asshole isn't worth it."

She was right. They should walk away and have her father make sure Fanshawe was removed from the island.

"Who are you calling asshole?" Fanshawe lunged at Bethany in that threatening, shoulders-first way that cowards did when they wanted to appear menacing. He wasn't actually trying to grab her. It was nothing more than a dick move to get her to flinch. And it worked.

She flinched.

Landon had had enough.

He stepped in front of Bethany so she couldn't see clearly what he was doing. With three jabs of his hand, Fanshawe was laid over the bar, unconscious.

He probably had him on brute strength, but when it came to speed and actual knowledge of how to incapacitate someone, he'd beat someone like him every time. He could've just as easily killed him, so he should consider himself lucky.

"Landon," Bethany gasped. She hadn't seen exactly what he'd done, but she knew he'd done something. "Is—is he dead?"

"No." Sadly.

She had one hand over her mouth and the other on his arm again. "You barely moved. How did you know how to do that?"

She didn't look scared, just shocked. He wasn't sure how he was going to explain this to her. Giving her as much of the truth as possible seemed like the best option. "You know how I was in the Navy?"

"Yeah. They teach you that sort of stuff?"

"They do if you're a SEAL."

She stared at him. "You said seal in the pool, but I thought you meant the animal."

Fanshawe began to stir. He'd known he wouldn't be down long. The blows hadn't been meant to render him completely unconscious, just stop him in his tracks and give him a hell of a headache.

"Adams, get Fanshawe out of here." Landon grimaced at Vincent Frey's voice behind them.

"With pleasure." Adams walked forward and grabbed Fanshawe by the back of the collar, straightening him as he blinked and moaned.

Frey sighed. "I apologize for my employee's lack of respect, Miss Thornton. It won't happen again."

Bethany gave him a little nod.

He needed to smooth things over if he had any chance of getting near Frey again. "Mr. Frey, I'm sorry I hit your man. He—"

Frey held out his hand. "Fanshawe has been a problem more than once. I don't hold you responsible for doing what you had to do. I'm glad you were here to take care of it."

Fanshawe was fully awake now and livid at being pushed around by Adams. "That bitch came on to me, then when her boyfriend showed up, she changed her tune, tried to act like she hadn't been trying to get some good dick."

That fucker truly didn't know when to keep his mouth shut.

"Fanshawe," Frey said sharply. "I left my phone in my room. Go get it. I'll use it to set up your removal from the island."

Fanshawe—*a total fucking dumbass*—opened his mouth to argue with Frey, completely oblivious that no one was believing his lies and that anything he said would just get him in more trouble.

"Now!" Frey's tone brooked no argument.

With one last nasty look at Bethany, Fanshawe whirled and stalked toward the hotel.

Frey and Adams turned and went back to their cabana by the pool.

Shit. This was the best chance he'd had all week to get his hands on Frey's phone.

But it meant leaving Bethany alone.

Landon took her arm. "Come on, let's get you back to our loungers until the food comes."

She was a little unsteady as they walked. He was sure adrenaline was playing havoc with her system.

"That was crazy," she whispered.

"It sure was." He helped her into one of the loungers. He grabbed the towel he'd wrapped around his stuff…including the transmitters in his wallet. "Whole thing gave me a bit of a headache. Do you mind if I run up to the room and grab some ibuprofen?"

She didn't want him to go. She didn't say it outright, but he could tell. And rightfully so. After what had just happened to her, what she needed most was for someone to sit with her, let her system settle.

Landon had to harden himself not to be the person who gave her what she needed. He was tempted to let this opportunity pass and hope for another one. But he was out of time.

"Yeah," she said, voice shaky. "I might need some too."

He shot her a smile, forcing himself not to drown in those green eyes taking up half her pale face. "Be right back."

Landon walked at regular speed until he was out of sight. As soon as he hit the cool interior of the hotel, he sprinted toward the stairs.

He took them two at a time up to Frey's floor. When the door opened, Fanshawe stood in front of Frey's room with a cell phone in his hand.

They both stared at each other.

Shit. There was only one way for him to play this.

"You need to stay away from her, asshole," Landon snarled and exited the stairs, advancing on him. He didn't budge. He crossed his arms over his chest and glared at him.

Landon shoved him. He took the bait and swung at him.

He ducked his fist with ease, but while doing so, Landon threw his arm out and hit the one holding Frey's phone. It went flying down the hall, landing several feet away. Good.

He slammed his fist into Fanshawe gut, doubling him over, before cracking him on the side of the head with his elbow.

As he reeled from Landon's blow, he pulled the transmitter out of his pocket. He shoved him back toward the phone on the carpet. He tripped and hit the floor.

He rolled to the side, away from the phone and onto his knees, trying to get up. Before he could see his movements, he pulled the transmitter off the clear backing and, in one swoop, stuck it on the back of the black case. It was tiny, not much bigger than a speck of dust.

It was done.

Landon got up and backed away from the older man.

"Enough, Fanshawe. Leave Bethany alone, and I'll have no problem with you." He needed him to get that phone back to Frey.

He turned and walked toward the elevator. The muted sound of Fanshawe's footfalls on the thick carpet alerted him to the fact that he was rushing him from behind. Landon didn't move until the last second, then shifted his weight, stepping to the side and catching his arm as he lunged for him.

With one fast move, Landon yanked him over his shoulder. He flew through the air and landed with a thud in front of the elevator, just as it opened.

Adams was there, staring at Fanshawe on the floor, in shock. "What the fuck is going on?"

He held up his hands. "I was on my way up for ibuprofen for Bethany when the elevator stopped here. He attacked."

"Bullshit," Fanshawe croaked. "He came to find me."

Adams looked back at Landon to see if he would refute. All Landon did was raise his eyebrows and shake his head. Sometimes less was more.

Adams bought it. He turned back to Fanshawe. "Yeah, I don't think so. Mr. Frey sent me up here to find you. Go pack your shit. You'll be on the next flight out."

Adams grabbed the phone and pocketed it without noticing anything amiss.

Couldn't be any more perfect than that.

"Sorry for the drama, man," Adams said to me as he once again grabbed Fanshawe by the collar and hoisted him up. Fanshawe was still whining about his innocence as Adams led him down the hall.

"No worries." He turned and got in the elevator, but he took it up rather than back down to the pool. He needed to get in touch with Tristan right now to make sure the transmitter worked.

Landon took the elevator all the way up to the rooftop balcony then walked over to a corner away from the few people who were out there.

Original cake is in the oven. Need confirmation that the recipe was good.

Tristan's reply came in seconds. *Hold.*

Landon knew he needed to test the transmitter to make sure it was working correctly. And he knew sometimes that wasn't a quick process. But every minute that passed was another minute Bethany was down at that pool, wondering what the hell he was doing.

Cursing down at his phone wasn't going to help, but that was what he did anyway. It was another ten minutes before Tristan finally replied.

Cake looks like it's going to taste wonderful.

The transmitter was working. Landon bolted toward the elevator without responding, trying to think of what he'd say to Bethany. Should he go get ibuprofen? She had some in the bathroom. But that would take more time.

He would tell her Fanshawe jumped him. That would match what Adams thought had happened and explain Landon taking so long and not having the painkillers.

She would buy that. His step was lighter as he came out of the elevator. One transmitter down, one to go. Getting close to Martinez would be even more difficult, but at least he was all Landon needed to focus on now.

And Bethany. He wanted to make sure she was all right after her scare with Fanshawe. At least he could assure her she wouldn't have to worry about him anymore.

He wanted to spend time with her, talk her into swimming some more with him in the pool. He liked having her lush curves pressed up against him in the water. He liked spending time with her on multiple different levels.

He wanted to make her smile. Wanted to confirm she was okay. He'd get a couple of drinks in her and make sure she could laugh it all off by later this afternoon.

But when Landon got back to the lounger, it was empty. Bethany had taken her stuff and left.

CHAPTER
EIGHTEEN

WHEN LANDON DIDN'T RETURN by the time Bethany had eaten her meal, she got worried. She went to the room to find him, but he wasn't there.

But the ibuprofen was. So, wherever he'd gone, it hadn't been to the room to get the pain medication.

She looked at herself in the mirror. Her eyes were still a little too big, her hands shaky. She might not have been in actual danger with that guy Fanshawe at the bar, but evidently, her mind and body hadn't gotten the message.

She'd needed a hug. Specifically, she'd needed Landon's strong arms around her, assuring her everything was okay.

But he'd disappeared, right when she'd needed him most.

Not tonight, honey. I've got a headache.

Bethany would admit, it stung. As the minutes passed and she tried to sort out her own shaky feelings and body parts, she kept expecting him to return to help her. But he hadn't.

Then she'd had to add crushing disappointment to the list of emotions coursing through her body. She didn't want to be a diva, but what could possibly be more important to Landon than being with her when she was so shaken?

Because: *not real.* Once again, she didn't seem to be able to understand that simple fact. Although the playing in the pool had felt real. Or at least like they were friends and he cared what happened to her.

But the truth was, she didn't understand anything about her *fiancé*. Didn't understand how he jumped from hot to cold so quickly. Didn't understand how he authentically seemed to care, then disappeared without warning.

Didn't understand how a Navy SEAL was working as a part-time carpenter.

But SEAL explained a lot of things about him. How he sometimes moved so quickly. How he'd been able to take down Fanshawe without hardly moving.

A Navy SEAL. Hell, maybe that really was a bullet wound on his chest.

Despite their kisses, despite their talks, despite the fact that Bethany was desperately attracted to him, she really didn't know Landon Black at all.

She needed to get out of her own head and get her wobbly body under control. The best way to do that was to dive into work and put Landon and what had nearly happened at the bar out of her mind. She changed clothes and headed toward the auxiliary kitchen.

The rehearsal dinner was tomorrow, so it was time to pull out those cake pieces anyway. They needed icing and then decorating, which could be done tomorrow, but starting today would give her the extra peace of mind of knowing she was ahead.

Bethany was still pretty shaky even as she put herself back into the world her mind and body understood. This was a world she controlled, rather than being thrown around by what others did. She needed to focus on it.

When she pulled the cakes out of the refrigerator, she discovered one had an enormous crack. Normally she'd be irritated, but today, she smiled. Even better that she was prepping a day early. She could've hidden the cake's flaw with icing, but this would give her a chance to rebake it. Maybe that was what she needed.

Bethany put on some soft music on her phone and got busy. Her body still didn't feel exactly right as she measured and combined ingredients, but this at least allowed her to push everything else from her mind.

The groom's cake was going to be an absolute masterpiece. Christiana wanted it at the rehearsal gala so it wouldn't detract from the beautiful wedding cake itself at the reception.

The gala tomorrow night was taking the place of a traditional rehearsal dinner. Christiana and Simon had decided not to have any attendants as part of their ceremony—they'd just be saying their vows to each other on the beach—so they didn't need an actual rehearsal. But, of course, they hadn't wanted to miss a chance to include one more party in this week's affairs.

Tomorrow's gala was fashioned after Carnevale in Venice. Everyone would be wearing elaborate ball gowns, tuxedos, and masks. The whole thing was a little over the top for her tastes, but she'd made sure the decadent chocolate groom's cake would fit right in.

The multitiered cake—each layer a different type of chocolate and surrounded by various fruits—would wind up and around a chocolate fountain. It was the most elaborate cake stand of the entire week.

She put the cake mixture in the oven and stared at the stove. Could she trust Landon to get it built?

Yes, he would get the job done. He might run hot and cold when it came to the two of them, but he had yet to be anything but thorough and professional when it came to the stands.

Thinking about Landon had tension pounding through her body again. It was almost as if she was dealing with two people when it came to him—one so considerate and attentive, one distracted and not interested in her.

Bethany cleaned up her working area and got the other cakes out of the walk-in and the decorating materials out of the pantry closet.

No thinking about Landon allowed. No thinking about the kiss two nights ago or their fake make-out session last night. No thinking about what his hands had felt like on her in the pool.

No thinking about Fanshawe at the bar or that Landon had disappeared when she'd really needed him.

The door slammed open behind her, and she spun, heart racing. Two young waitstaff stood there giggling and holding hands.

"Oh crap," the girl muttered. "We're sorry."

The boy was backing out, pulling his girlfriend with him. "We forgot they'd assigned this room for use. Sorry."

They backed the rest of the way out, muttering apologies. Obviously, this was their normal make-out room. At any other time, she would've thought it was cute. But this one last shock to her system had hurled her over some sort of edge.

Bethany couldn't stop her hands from shaking. Couldn't seem to get her pulse down to a normal level. Couldn't get the tears out of her eyes.

She tried to push through. Her somewhat-shaky hands hadn't made much difference when she was remaking the cake, but now that she was trying to decorate it, they made a huge difference.

She managed to get the first layer of frosting on, but attempting to add the delicate piping of the royal icing was nearly impossible. More than once, she had to start over completely.

She worked for hours. At some points, her hands were steady; at others, the shakiness returned. She forced herself to keep going even when that happened.

Bethany couldn't let today derail her completely. She couldn't let Landon or Fanshawe or anything steal the joy of what she loved to do.

"You're not supposed to be in here." Landon's sexy, deep voice pulled her from her work. "Today's supposed to be your day off."

She laid down the piping bag without turning to him. Just as well anyway. Once again, her shaky hands had messed up the intricate design she'd been attempting. She rubbed her eyes. Normally, elaborate icing was her forte.

And why was he even here?

"I decided to come in here and get some of tomorrow's work done. Not that it's doing much good."

He walked over to stand next to her, but she still didn't look at him. "Are you okay?"

Bethany didn't want to admit how badly her body and psyche were responding to the past twenty-four hours. It wasn't like anything had actually happened.

"I'm fine." Now she looked at him. "Ever get your ibuprofen?"

He winced. "I ran into Fanshawe as I was on my way back to the room. He was still pretty pissed and tried to start something. Took a while to get it sorted out, and by the time I got back, you were gone."

The fact that he hadn't left her for no reason made her feel a little bit better. "He didn't hurt you, did he?"

"No, he didn't get a hit in. For a guy who works in security, he broadcasts his punches pretty loudly."

She tilted her head as she looked at him. "You being a former member of one of the country's most highly trained military forces helps out too."

He stiffened just slightly. "It does."

"Why didn't you tell me you were a former SEAL?"

"I wasn't trying to keep it from you. I just generally don't mention it unless it comes up. It can have various effects on people. Not always good."

"Like what?"

He shrugged and turned so he was leaning back against the counter, studying her. "Some people are normal. A 'thank you for your service' or generic questions about how long I was in, stuff like that. Some people are nosy, want to know if I ever almost died or killed someone else. I don't generally answer, unless it's someone I know well."

"Yeah, I can see why that would be off-putting for you." Bethany cringed as she thought of herself asking about that wound on his chest. She hadn't thought she was overstepping a boundary at the time.

"People are curious. I don't give them details, but I at least understand their reasoning behind asking. They're definitely not the worst."

"What's the worst?"

"There are women—and men—who are SEAL groupies. Bag 'n taggers, we call them. Willing to sleep with anyone who has ever been a SEAL."

"Oh." Mina's face immediately came to mind. She'd been all over Landon and hadn't even known he was a SEAL.

"And then there are the guys who take it as some sort of badge of honor to pick a fight with a SEAL. Hoping for bragging rights or some such shit."

"So, it's easier to keep mum about it from the beginning."

He nodded. "Yes. My service is a big part of who I am, but it's not the only identifying factor about me. Just like being a fabulous baker isn't the only identifying factor about you."

She took a large spatula and scraped icing off the layer of cake she'd been attempting to decorate. It was definitely subpar.

"Being a baker isn't even going to be a single identifying factor about me if I don't get my shit together," she muttered.

"Things not going right?"

Bethany rubbed her eyes again. "I want tomorrow's cakes to be as good and as beautiful as what people have tasted the other nights." And she wanted her body to cooperate with her to get it done.

"If I go ahead and get the cake stand together, would that help?"

"Yeah, sure." Although it probably wouldn't.

They worked for a couple more hours, not necessarily talking much, but not in awkward silence either.

She couldn't worry too much about talking with him. She had to restart what she was doing more than once, but she tried not to let it show.

Though by the time she had to redo the decorations on the same cake for the third time, she was ready to fling it against the wall. She was even more frustrated at the tears leaking out of her eyes. This shouldn't be a problem. She was safe; she was fine. Creating the flowers and geometric shapes was nothing she hadn't done a hundred times before.

Bethany needed to get out of there before Landon realized what a mess she was.

"Hey, what's going on?"

Too late.

He covered her shoulders with his hands, pulling her back against his chest. She couldn't help but lean against his strength.

"I can't seem to get this decorating right, even though I should be able to do it in my sleep. I've been like this all day."

"Is there something wrong with the ingredients or the gear you're using?"

"No, it's me. My hands are shaky. My head is spinning. I feel like I should go run five miles, and I don't even like running."

He tightened his fingers on her shoulders. "It's from what happened earlier with Fanshawe. Your body can't figure out what to do with the stress."

Bethany spun so she was facing him, which she immediately realized was a mistake. They were way too close. She was caught between him and the prep counter.

"That's just it. Nothing happened. You stopped him before he did anything."

He tucked a curl back behind her ear. "Your body recognizes the danger it was in. Combine that with what happened last night—hell, this entire week of having to constantly watch your back? The shakes and spinning head are your body's way of dealing with compiling stress and threats of harm."

"So, I do need to go out and run five miles, that's what you're saying?" Lord, she'd have a heart attack. "Because if I can't get these cakes decorated by the gala tomorrow night, then I'll basically be proving everyone who said I would fail completely ri—"

He kissed her.

His tongue buried itself in her mouth as their bodies melded against each other like he couldn't bear for there to be space between them. She expected him to ease back after a few moments like he had in the room when they kissed.

But he didn't. He moved closer, one hand wrapping around her hip, the other grasping her at the back of the neck. His lips moved from hers, nipping down her jaw.

"I should've come back sooner today." His lips continued to work their way down to her throat, tilting her neck with his hand so he could have the access he wanted. "I could've helped you work through this earlier. Gotten it out of your system and mind before it spiraled. I shouldn't have left you to deal with it alone."

Bethany could barely make sense of his words. She wanted to focus on the apology that meant so much to her, but she was drowning in what his lips were doing to her neck. She strained closer.

He slid his hand up from her hip to cup her breast, rolling

her nipple in a motion just short of pain. She moaned and lifted on her tiptoes to get closer. Yes, this was what she wanted.

His lips moved away from her, but before she could let out a moan of disapproval, he dipped down and slipped his arm behind her knees and lifted her into his arms.

"Landon!" Her voice came out as a shriek. She wrapped her arms around his neck. "I'm too heavy. Put me down."

He shot those dimples at her full force. "Nothing about you is too heavy. And what I want to do to you can't be done on this food prep table."

Bethany was pretty sure her eyes were bugging out of her head. "Oh," she managed. "And what's that?"

"I want to taste you, Wildflower."

He walked with no problem—honest to God, as if she weighed no more than a tray of cookies—into the storage closet and set her on the table in there. His lips met hers again as his hands reached down and made their way slowly up the outsides of her thighs, catching the edge of her skirt and hiking it up until it was bunched at her hips.

He was staring at her black panties, the heat in his eyes unmistakable. He'd seen her in less earlier today at the pool, but she still felt exposed.

He gripped the sides of her underwear, easing them over her hips and all the way down one leg until they were hanging off the ankle of her other. Then he started kissing his way back up her calves, moving back and forth between both legs.

When he got to her knees, he wrapped his hands around them and opened her wide.

Maybe she should've been embarrassed at the dimples in her thighs and the looseness in the muscle tone. But she couldn't be with him looking at her like she was the sexiest thing he'd ever seen.

His eyes met hers before sweeping back down her body. "So beautiful."

He kissed his way up her thighs and covered her with his mouth, his tongue moving in a swirling motion that had her sobbing his name in just seconds. He played her, alternating between jabs that teased and long, steady strokes that had her gasping for breath.

Bethany gripped his hair with her fingers and kept him pulled to her, not that he seemed to want to be anywhere but there. She looked down her body at them. This strong, sexy man between her sprawled legs that he held open, her skimpy panties still hanging off her ankle. It was nothing less than decadent.

All she could do was moan. And feel. And dissolve into nothing.

His hazel eyes locked on hers as he thrust his tongue deeper, and new waves of fire rolled up her body. And he didn't stop. Not until ecstasy crashed over her in swells and she sobbed his name.

Only then did he slow, easing her down from the orgasm, her body boneless.

Those dimples were back as he helped slide her panties back up her legs and smoothed her skirt down so she was decent. She was still trying to pull her world back into one coherent whole.

"What about you?" She finally got out. "I—"

He shook his head. "No. This was about you and what you needed." He jumped up onto the table next to her and pulled her into his lap.

And with the beat of his heart against her ear, she realized the extra adrenaline was gone.

No more shaking.

CHAPTER NINETEEN

THE KEY to undercover work was not to just stand and stare. That drew too much attention. Made people nervous.

Do something and stare instead.

So here Landon was playing cornhole—the nicest set he'd ever seen—by himself at the edge of the beach.

1. Toss a sparkly silver beanbag. 2. Look for Joaquin Martinez. 3. Repeat.

Actually, it was more like: 1. Toss a sparkly silver beanbag. 2. Look for Joaquin Martinez. 3. Think about how fucking fantastic Bethany had tasted yesterday and how amazing it was to hear her crying out his name. 4. Shift shorts so it wouldn't be so obvious he was becoming aroused. 5. Repeat.

He never should've left her yesterday at the pool. Not that he'd had an option. But she wasn't a warrior, didn't have the mind-set or coping skills to talk her body down from the ledge stress had driven her up.

Unfocused adrenaline was like quicksand. You never knew what step was going to cause you to sink.

There had been times after missions when he'd had to spar or work out for hours in order to get himself to the point where he wasn't buzzing.

He couldn't imagine trying to do something as intricate as decorating cakes with that extra energy coursing through him. She'd attempted it for hours.

No wonder she'd been about to completely fall apart by the time he got there. Even though she'd tried to hide it.

There had been other ways he could've helped her deal with the stress: a run, a swim, even some self-defense moves he could've taught her.

Who the hell was he kidding? As soon as he kissed her, he knew he wasn't leaving there without getting a full taste of her sweet body.

He drew the line at having sex while on an active mission where he was using her as his in. But evidently, draping her gorgeous thighs over his shoulders wasn't over the line.

Adjust shorts.

Toss beanbag.

Afterward, he'd known her crash was coming. He'd helped her get the kitchen into some semblance of clean, then gotten her back to the room.

She was shy, even a little embarrassed at what had happened. That brought out every protective instinct he had. While she'd brushed her teeth, he'd gotten her one of his shirts to sleep in since he didn't know what she normally wore. He'd helped her into it and tucked her in bed, getting in next to her.

She was asleep almost as soon as her head hit the pillow. He'd planned to move to the couch as soon as she did, but hell if he didn't fall asleep for a few hours holding her.

Landon threw the beanbag way too hard.

This woman was all up under his skin.

After all the shit he'd given Ian and Sarge for falling so hard and fast for their women, this was karma coming around to bite him in the ass. Here he was, unable to get Bethany off his mind, even in the middle of a critical mission.

This job needed to conclude so that he could move on

with his life. But now, he wanted to find some way that his post-mission life could include her.

Shit.

That was going to take some unraveling of a lot of half-truths, and he wasn't sure she was ever going to forgive him.

His phone buzzed in his pocket. Tristan.

"What's up, honey?"

"Had your fill of eating Bethany's sweets yet?"

His eyes bulged out of his head. How did Tristan know that? *"What?"*

"I'm going to laugh when you come home weighing twenty pounds more. I've been reading up on how good Slice of Heaven is."

Bethany's sweets. Not Bethany's *sweets*.

"Right. Yes. She's a very talented baker."

"You lucky bastard."

He didn't know the half of it. "Believe it."

"How's it going with Martinez?"

"Haven't seen him at all since that recording I sent you. He doesn't hang out at the pool like Frey."

"We know he's still on the island, so be ready."

He tossed the beanbag again. "I'm thinking his computer might be easier. Lifting someone's phone involves getting up close and extremely personal."

"Be careful, brother. Bad guys don't like strangers getting personal."

"Given what's at stake, it's worth the risk. Find out anything more about the *shipments* Martinez and Frey were talking about?"

"Callum is on it. Definitely human trafficking."

Lives were at stake. "Then I'm definitely going to do whatever I need to do to get the transmitter on Martinez."

He tossed one more beanbag, not coming anywhere near the hole he was aiming for. But it didn't matter. Martinez and his two guards walked across to the café where breakfast was being served.

There was no chance of getting to his phone but maybe his computer, which would still be in his room.

"Gotta run, T. Going to try a break-in."

"Roger that. Watch your six."

He disconnected the call and walked toward the lobby, being careful not to make any eye contact with Martinez or his guys.

He went to the lobby phone and dialed the front desk.

"Guest services," a polite voice said.

"Yes, Mr. Martinez asked me to have housekeeping come by while he was at breakfast, if you don't mind."

"Of course, sir. I'll send someone up right away."

After thanking her, Landon headed to the stairs and up to Martinez's floor, watching through the door until the elevator opened and the maid rolled a cart out. As soon as she opened the suite door, he walked out of the stairwell and headed straight for Martinez's door.

"Morning," he said. "Sorry to interrupt, I forgot something. I'll be out of your hair in just a moment." He swiped his keycard in the open door to prove the room was his but positioned his body so the maid couldn't see the light flash red when it didn't work.

He shot her a smile. She nodded and smiled back. "It's okay, sir. I can start in the bathroom."

As soon as she disappeared through the bathroom door, Landon rushed over to the desk. No computer. Nothing on the couch or coffee table. He went into the bedroom, but he didn't see one lying around either. He glanced over at the safe. Shit. If he'd put it in there, he wouldn't be able to get to it.

Hell, maybe he hadn't brought one at all.

He grabbed Martinez's suitcase and rifled through it as

neatly as he could. He hissed a small sigh of relief as he found the laptop nestled in the back.

A noise behind him had him glancing over his shoulder to find the small woman in the kitchen area, wiping down the counters. Her attention wasn't on him, but he was running out of time.

He peeled the plastic off the back of the transmitter and stuck it to the bottom of the laptop.

"Mr. Martinez?" the maid asked. She looked at a piece of paper in her hands. "Can I help you with anything?"

She was getting suspicious. He needed to get out of there right away. "No, I forgot my hat. Got it." He grabbed the Dodgers cap at the top of the suitcase and put it on his head. "But thank you."

He left without making any more eye contact, pulling the door closed as he went.

The elevator doors opened seconds after he called it. He pressed the button for the lobby and breathed a sigh of relief when the door shut without further incident. He slipped the hat off his head.

He'd done it. The transmitters were both placed. Martinez's computer might not be as ideal as his phone, but hopefully it would get Callum the intel he needed to stop whatever human trafficking plans Frey's and Martinez's organizations had. He needed to let Tristan know so he could get the info to Callum.

Landon was barely out of the elevator in the lobby when he spotted Martinez walking from the café toward the elevator. Shit. It had taken too long for housekeeping to get to the room, and evidently, Martinez hadn't been enjoying a full breakfast.

If he went up to the room, the housekeeper was going to know there was a problem. It wouldn't take much for her to remember it was him rummaging around in Martinez's room.

He had the hat. It had the slightest bit of suntan lotion

smell. It had been used recently out in the sun, which gave me an idea.

It was a Hail Mary, and he prayed it would work.

He plastered a huge grin on his face and brought the hat up in front of his face so he was looking at it as he walked. He stayed in the middle of the foyer so Martinez couldn't help but notice him.

"This is it," he said to the hat as Martinez and his men got closer, heading toward the elevator. "This is a sign that you guys are going all the way this year. Don't let me down."

Landon's eccentric behavior worked. Martinez stopped to talk to him. "You a Dodgers fan?"

"Every year. Win or lose. But this is going to be a winning year. This hat proves it." He blew a kiss toward the hat. "You a fan too?"

"Yeah, although sometimes I'm tempted to give up on them." Martinez shot him an indulgent smile. "I have a hat just like that, and unfortunately, it has never meant that they had a winning season."

"I was sitting out by the pool, thinking about how last year was a rebuilding season and they should reap the benefits this year, and then I found this hat." Landon grinned over at him. "It's a sign, I tell you."

He didn't follow baseball much. He hoped Martinez didn't start talking about specific players.

But mostly, Landon hoped he stayed here and talked to him.

"You said you found that hat at the pool?"

When Martinez didn't see the cap in his room, he was going to know right away that Landon had it. How Landon answered now would affect whether he believed he'd accidentally left it somewhere.

But if Martinez hadn't been at the pool yesterday and Landon said he'd found it there, he'd know Landon was lying.

He shot Martinez a sheepish look. "Actually, some employee had it. He'd found it somewhere, and I told him it was mine. Do you think it's yours?"

He held it out to him, and he looked inside it before handing it back. "Probably."

Landon made his face fall. "Sorry, man. I wasn't trying to steal your stuff or anything. I figured it was about to go in a lost and found basket somewhere, and I thought I'd keep it. Put it with my shrine."

"Why don't you go ahead and do that?"

He shook his head and held the hat back out to him. "No, it's yours. Like I said, I wasn't trying to pull anything over on anyone."

Martinez was a few inches shorter than Landon's 6'2". Midfifties, dressed in tailored trousers and a collared white shirt. Nothing about the man screamed *bad guy*. If you didn't know he was terrorist scum who dabbled in human trafficking, you'd probably label him as nonthreatening. Friendly, even.

He was more dangerous because he'd made sure not to make himself look that way.

He gave Landon a smile. "If you really think you being in possession of that hat will make the Dodgers win this season, then I will gladly donate it to the cause."

His men had been standing to the side, out of the conversation, but as he turned toward the elevator, they took a step forward also.

"Hey, can I buy you"—Landon looked around like he wasn't quite sure what his security team was—"and your friends a drink? We can talk team stuff. I'm bored with wedding shit."

All three men chuckled.

"While I can understand that boredom, I'm afraid I can't join you right now."

"Are you sure?" He asked. "It's the least I can do for

giving me your hat and making sure we have a winning season."

"No, but thanks for the offer."

He couldn't push any more. The last thing he wanted was for Martinez to think he was stalling him. Hopefully, he'd bought enough time for the housekeeper to be finished with his room.

"No problem, another time. When the boys go all the way this year, you remember—we did it together! If you change your mind, I'll be at the bar."

Landon turned and walked the rest of the way through the foyer, hat in hand. He sat at the bar, choosing a seat where he could see the doors. He crossed his leg casually so he'd have easy reach of his ankle holster and waited to see if Martinez sent one of his men to get him.

Landon relaxed after twenty minutes. Housekeeping must have already been gone by the time Martinez got to his room. He wasn't coming after him.

He paid for his drink and stood. He shot off a text to Tristan about having gotten the transmitter on the computer.

His steps were lighter than they'd been all week, and he knew very clearly why.

The mission was over. Now there was no reason he couldn't concentrate completely on Bethany.

WHEN LANDON MADE it back to the suite, Bethany was already gone from the bed. His disappointment was tangible. He had wanted nothing more than to wake her up and not leave the bed for the entire day.

The mission was over. If she wanted him and he wanted her, then there was nothing to stop them from enjoying the hell out of each other.

He knew exactly where she was. And when he walked into the auxiliary kitchen, she was back at the counter, working on the decorations she didn't get through yesterday.

The smile she shot him over her shoulder when he came in took his breath away.

"Look, no shaky hands."

Landon came up behind her and kissed her nape, exposed by the curls tucked up in a messy bun. "Good." He liked how she shuddered and goose bumps broke out on her skin.

"Watch it, buddy. I can't afford to have to start over again on these after the time I lost yesterday."

"How about if we have a repeat of yesterday, but in a bed where I can drive you crazy for hours?"

Those green eyes got big as she looked up at me. "Really?"

"Do you not want to?"

She put down her decorating tools then spun around to face him. "I would very much like to…continue last night's activities. But I wasn't sure you did. Despite yesterday, I wasn't sure that you were interested in me that way."

He shouldn't be surprised she'd picked up on his reluctance, although it had been for an entirely different reason than what she thought.

Landon wrapped his hands around her soft waist. "Never not interested in you. Only not interested in making a complicated situation more complicated."

Her smile stole his breath once again. "Then let me get everything finished up here."

The next hour was filled with laughs and touches and her feeding him bits of cake and icing. And as good as that tasted, it still wasn't anywhere near as sweet as her.

The air was charged with the knowledge of what was to come.

He should've known it was going too well. The hotel staff had come to get the cakes and they were closing up the auxiliary kitchen with four hours left before they needed to be at the gala, when she got the text. His hands were on her hips once again—since he couldn't seem to keep them off her—and he felt her stiffen.

"Everything okay?"

"It's Christiana. She's having a bride moment. Wants me to come get ready for the gala with her."

Disappointment crashed through his system with surprising force. It still didn't stop his words. "You should go."

Bethany's face scrunched up into the most adorable little pout. "I don't wanna." She ran her hands up his chest. "I want to stay with you."

Landon kissed her forehead. "How about if we make up

for it later? If you don't go to your sister now when she needs you, you'll regret it."

She muttered something about having the worst luck ever and responded to the text. He cupped her cheeks and kissed her.

"I'll see you tonight."

———

The only thing that made rich people seem richer was when they dressed up for a masquerade ball. This entire thing reminded him of something out of *Phantom of the Opera*.

The men were in tuxedos, the women in formal dresses. Everyone in masks of some sort, either the kind held by a stick or tied behind their heads. Unlike the luau two nights before, where the DJ had played upbeat and contemporary music, tonight's classical strains were provided by a chamber ensemble orchestra.

Bethany's chocolate decadence fit right in with the feel of the evening.

She and her family hadn't arrived yet, but he'd already spotted both Martinez and Frey. Martinez hadn't bothered with a mask at all, and Frey kept taking his off since it didn't fit perfectly around his pudgy face.

When they started talking with each other, everything inside him itched to get closer and find out what details he could. Landon had to force himself not to. He'd placed both transmitters, and now the best thing he could do was to keep the hell away from them and not make them suspicious.

He wanted to take them down right there and then, but he couldn't. Law enforcement had to make their move, and what he'd done on this island was probably only the first step. And it would all be out of his hands.

That sucked.

He removed his mask a few minutes later when Frey

walked over to his perch at the bar. Adams was just a couple paces behind him.

"Landon, right? That's your name?" Frey asked.

He kept his face as neutral as possible. "That's right."

"I want to thank you again for handling the situation with Fanshawe yesterday. It really could've turned into some unwanted attention, and I appreciate you stopping it before it got to that point."

Landon relaxed. He wasn't suspicious of him. "That guy is an asshole."

"Agreed. And he's no longer in my employ. No longer around at all."

Shit. He wasn't sure if that meant Fanshawe had been escorted off the island or if they'd buried him somewhere. He made a mental note to have Callum's team check. He hadn't been trying to get the man killed, asshole or not.

"I'm glad to hear that Bethany doesn't have to worry about him harassing her."

Frey nodded. "It was a mistake to bring him here. I apologize."

"Apology accepted."

He shook the man's outstretched hand, even managing to keep a smile on his face. It helped to know that what he'd started there would hopefully rip his organization apart bit by bit.

Landon's eyes were torn away as Bethany entered the ballroom with her family. That dress. Holy hell. Black, sparkly, accentuating her curves in every way that made him glad he was a man. And that he was going to be the one who got to enjoy those curves later tonight.

Yes, both Christiana and Angelique were thinner, more polished, but Landon couldn't tear his eyes away from Bethany to look at them for more than a few seconds in passing. Bethany had a fire, an authenticity, they didn't.

And that was without knowing how kind she was and her amazing work ethic.

Simon approached Christiana, so Landon quickly made his way to Bethany. Someone who looked as good as she did shouldn't be standing alone.

Or maybe he was worried that someone looking as good as she did *wouldn't* be standing alone for long.

She had a white mask attached to a thin stick and was looking over at the desserts to make sure everything was as it should be when he came up behind her and gently grasped her elbow. "May I have this dance, milady?"

Her eyes lit up from behind her mask. "Indeed, kind sir."

They flowed out onto the dance floor with the others. He knew enough about a waltz to keep them moving. Having her smile up at him while holding her in his arms was enough to make him feel like they were all alone in the room.

Boy, he had it bad. But he didn't even care.

After a few dances, her father called for everyone's attention from the microphone near the small orchestra. They stood still to listen.

"In less than forty-eight hours, my lovely Christiana will be married to the man who puts a constant smile on her face. I could not be more thrilled at her choice or the chance to celebrate the two of them all week with you. She is the apple of my eye."

"Hear, hear," someone called out, and everyone who had a drink raised their glass in toast.

Landon slid his hand around Bethany's. Her mask was figuratively and literally in place, but he knew the words had to hurt a little bit. These people didn't realize what a gem they had in her.

Or maybe they did. "I would also be remiss not to mention our other daughter, Bethany," Oliver continued. "If you've gained ten pounds this week, blame her and the delicious treats she's created. We're so glad to have her here with us where she belongs."

It wasn't as poetic as what he'd said about Christiana, but one look at Bethany's face told him it had been perfect for her. The key to Bethany's heart was respecting her hard work and talent, not complimenting her looks or status.

Oliver Thornton knew his daughters well.

Bethany was lit up. For the rest of the night, people were talking to her about her business. A few people had heard it was hers throughout the week, but now, everyone seemed to want to compliment her on her skills. He was happy to stand at her side and let her have the limelight. Would've stood behind her in support all evening.

Landon was prepared for it to be a long night. She deserved her chance to shine. No matter how much he was longing to get her out of that dress.

His time in the military had taught him discipline and patience, and he could admit it was taking all of that right now not to hoist her over his shoulder and make their way out.

They had a moment alone a couple hours later, and she lowered her mask, then peeked up at him before raising her mask again. She looked like she was going to say something but just blew out a little breath instead.

"You doing okay?"

Mask lowered again. "Would it make me a terrible person if I said I just want to get out of here?"

"What's wrong?"

She shrugged one soft shoulder. "What Dad said was perfect, and I think I'm going to end up with more business than I'd ever thought possible."

He trailed a finger down her cheek. "Well-deserved business. Is that okay?"

"Yeah. It's just…" She trailed off.

"A little overwhelming?" He finished for her. "A little

scary to know you'll have to take some big steps? A little hard to be the center of attention?"

She put a finger over his lips. "It's just that I'd like to get out of here and finish what we started this afternoon. I love that my business is growing in front of my eyes, but I can hardly concentrate on it because all I can think about is getting you naked."

Landon almost swallowed his tongue. "Then by all means, let's get out of here. Do you want to say goodbye to anyone?"

"No," she whispered.

Throwing her over his shoulder would be the most expedient way of getting them out. And he was tempted. Lord, was he tempted.

Especially when Mina stepped in front of them as Bethany and Landon were making their way, hand in hand, toward the door.

"Not now, Mina," Bethany said. "Whatever snarky thing you have to say can wait until tomorrow."

Mina's eyes narrowed. "Maybe I wasn't going to say anything snarky. Maybe I was going to say congratulations for getting the recognition you deserve."

"Oh." Bethany blinked at her, obviously caught by surprise. "Thank you."

Mina caught Bethany's other hand. "I'm happy for you. You've got a great business, and you two are so hot for each other that you're about to take off for a quickie."

There was going to be nothing quick about it, but the hot part was right.

"Who would've thought you'd be the one to have it all together," Mina continued. "How did you do it?"

Bethany grinned over at him. "Karma, I guess."

Landon leaned down and whispered in her ear, so softly Mina couldn't possibly hear. "I'm about to show you karma, Wildflower. All night."

God, if he didn't love the way her cheeks burned.

Mina cleared her throat. "I have to admit, you two do seem authentic."

He turned to Mina. "Not everything is for show. Bethany figured that out a long time ago."

"I guess she did." Mina pulled her mask back up to her face. "I'll let you guys get to wherever you're going."

They didn't say anything else, just held on to each other's hands as they darted for the door.

THEY DIDN'T TALK as they made it back to the suite. Landon didn't kiss her either. Because if he stopped to do that, he wasn't sure they were going to make it somewhere private before he had that dress off her and her naked body pressed up against a wall with him buried deep inside her.

Once they were in the room, with the door locked behind them, she took his hand and led them toward the bed, kicking off her shoes as she went. Only then did he pause, his conscience kicking in.

The mission was over, but that didn't mean he'd been honest with her. There was still so much between them that was built on half-truths.

This wasn't Landon's first rodeo. In their work at Zodiac Tactical, they always made sure they were the good guys. Which meant the ends generally justified the means.

Providing half-truths as to who he was and what he did to a few people was an acceptable trade-off for bringing down Frey and Martinez and their associates. In other missions, he'd told a lot more lies for a lot less gain.

But looking into Bethany's green eyes, he hated every

fucking lie that was between them right now. It was enough to have him pulling away.

Those eyes clouded over at his movement. "Change your mind?" she whispered.

"No. But…" Landon scrubbed his hand down his face. "There are things you don't know about me."

Things he had never planned on telling her because he'd never planned on letting things get this far. And even though the mission was over, he couldn't tell her right now. Maybe ever.

She narrowed her eyes. "Are you married?"

He shook his head rapidly. "No, never have been."

"Girlfriend?"

He continued shaking his head. "Not since before getting out of the Navy." He'd had a few flings along the way, but nothing remotely serious.

"Do you live in a bomb shelter and spend all your spare time prepping for the apocalypse?"

Landon had to laugh at that one. "No. But, I do actually know a couple of people who live that way."

She placed a hand on his chest. Right over that bullet wound. A constant reminder that none of us was guaranteed a tomorrow. "Do you have any plans to hurt me?"

His hand covered hers. "Never."

"Do you want me? Do you want this?"

"Almost more than my next breath."

"Then I think I know everything I need to know about you. The rest can wait for later."

Landon should've argued more, but she stepped closer, her softness pressing against him, her hand pulling his neck down so she could cover his lips with hers.

And then words didn't matter anymore. She was right; they knew enough. He knew that keeping his hands off her wasn't an option.

He turned her so he could slide the zipper down her dress, his fingers trailing the soft skin of her back as he went. It pooled on the floor at her feet, leaving her in her black bra and panties.

"You're so damned beautiful."

Landon thought she would get shy and make some sort of token protest, but she looked at him over her shoulder, her smile so full of confidence and heat he was afraid this might be over before they even got started.

He turned her and covered her mouth with his. He knew how to kiss a woman with finesse and skill, but not now, not with this woman. All he could do was devour her.

Fortunately, she didn't seem to mind. Her tongue matched his in the duel—her fingers coming up to wrap in his hair, keeping him pinned to her.

As if he was going anywhere.

Landon eased her back toward the bed, pulling his clothes off as he went. A low sound of need escaped him as she pressed closer. He trailed his lips down her jaw to her neck, sucking gently as she gasped.

He'd have to be careful not to mark her fair skin, surprised that he had to stop himself from doing so. He'd never had that urge before, but now, every part of him wanted to leave marks of his claim all over her body.

Most of those marks would be on places others couldn't see—her breasts, her thighs, her soft belly.

But also on her neck, where people would notice the little love bites and give them sly smiles, knowing what they'd been up to.

Knowing, without a shadow of a doubt, that he and Bethany were together.

Landon laid her down on the bed and kissed down to her full breasts before he could give in to those base urges to mark her neck. Not that her breasts were any less of a temptation. He teased one breast then the other with his lips and tongue and teeth.

"Mine."

He didn't even recognize his own voice and its Neanderthal traces as he pulled deeply on her nipple. Thank God she didn't seem to care. She moaned and pulled him closer.

He needed her. Needed to be inside her. Landon removed his lips from her skin, only to strip away the last of their clothes and pull on a condom—one he'd never thought he'd need on this trip.

"I want to be on top." She bit that full bottom lip, and it was all he could do not to reach over and do the same with his teeth.

This was going to be embarrassingly short if he didn't pull it together—especially once she was perched on top of him.

"Yes, ma'am," he managed to bite out. He lay down on the bed, swallowing his moan as she kissed down his chest, then straddled his hips.

"It's been a while," she whispered as she looked down at their bodies, so close to being joined.

"For me too." he ran his hand up her bent leg from her knee to her thigh. "We can go slow."

Landon watched, sweat breaking out on his forehead, as she lowered herself onto him one miraculously agonizing inch at a time. He closed his eyes at the feel of her soft heat engulfing him.

She worked herself all the way down, breath catching. "That feels so good."

He tried to reassure her that it was more than good, that it was bloody fantastic. But Landon, the guy with a charming quip always on the tip of his tongue, couldn't find his words.

All he could do was grip her hips as she began to ease her way back up then work her way back down on him, over and over.

"Yes," he finally muttered as she picked up speed. He opened his eyes to find her lush breasts swaying as she rode him, head thrown back, eyes closed.

It was so damned sexy.

"Fucking beautiful." He gripped her hips as she slid back up, holding her there, stopping her progress before he lost all control.

She let out a mewl, like a cranky little kitten, pressing downward, eager for him to impale her. Finally, he let her go, and as he slid into her, she crushed her mouth to his, pressing her tongue between his lips and swallowing his groan. Then she began to move, drawing herself up over him, then back down.

Slowly again. Excruciatingly slowly.

He fought the urge to grab her hips and drive her movements, wanting to let her have whatever control she wanted. But when she bit his lip as she ground against him, the act savage in its innocence, his good intentions disappeared. He growled before holding her against him and flipping them over, taking her completely.

Landon thrust into her again and again, relishing how tight her inner walls were as she clamped around him.

He couldn't hold on anymore. He was amazed he'd lasted this long.

"Come for me, Bethany." He was nearing the point of no return. "Come *with* me," he amended, his tone urgent as his breathing rate increased.

She tensed underneath him and pulsed around him, her orgasm taking her with no warning to him, and it was the last straw. He thrust harder until there were no thoughts in his head but her name and the pressure building through his system.

She cried out his name, her hands moving to his shoulders and clinging to him, riding out both of their orgasms. He inhaled sharply and held himself above her as he came with a force that shocked him.

Although, Landon didn't know why it should. Damned near everything about this woman shocked him.

She reached up and cupped his cheek, and he pressed a soft kiss to her lips as his hips slowed and their breathing crashed into each other.

"That was amazing," she whispered.

"Yes." Once again, he couldn't find any more words than that.

When they could finally both breathe again, he led her to the shower, washing them both off before taking her against the shower wall. They were both limp with exhaustion by the time they were done.

She smiled at him as he dried her off, and he had to close his eyes.

There were so many things Landon wanted to say to her, explain to her. Because all he knew was that there was no way this week was going to be enough for him.

Maybe when they got back to LA, he could tell her about the mission—but explain that it had been over by the time he'd slept with her. He never wanted her to think that he'd used her body for anything outside of pleasuring them both.

Landon wouldn't be able to give her specific details, but he could let her know about his true employment with Zodiac Tactical. Because he wanted her to meet everyone there. They were just as much his family as his mother was.

He had to believe that she would understand and forgive him. The alternative gutted him.

But right now, he wanted to hold her in his arms while she slept. That was all that mattered—the rest would wait. He might not sleep, but he didn't care.

She curled up into his arms, reminding him of an exhausted kitten this time, little claws pressing into his arm wrapped around her. He could feel her hair covering his chest, and he didn't ever want to move.

Soon, she was snoring in the most adorable way he'd ever heard.

The sun was coming up when his phone buzzed on the

nightstand. He wanted to ignore it but knew he couldn't. He hadn't slept much, but that didn't bother him at all. He reached over and grabbed the buzzing annoyance, careful not to disturb her.

Landon let out a curse when he saw the message from Tristan.

Computer transmitter you placed is a no-go. It's been wiped.

CHAPTER
TWENTY-TWO

BETHANY SLEPT MUCH LATER than she normally did. Her eyes blinked open, and the bedside clock told her it was already past breakfast hours and deep into brunch.

She stretched, laughing with a groan at the soreness in her body. The best sort of soreness. All over sort of soreness. An *I want it again!* sort of soreness.

She reached out to touch Landon, but the bed was empty. She sat up and looked around, but there was no sign of him. She remembered falling asleep in his arms last night.

She texted him.

Sleeping Beauty has finally awoken.

Bethany waited for a clever comeback, but nothing came. She didn't know why she was texting him looking the way she was anyway. If he burst in the door right then, she'd have to hide under the covers. Morning breath. Morning hair.

She dashed into the shower. He'd get her message and head back, probably with coffee and breakfast. Then she'd convince him to let breakfast get cold while she dragged him back to bed.

Because she wanted round two. Or round five, if you

counted how many times they'd made love last night. In the bed, in the shower, on the sink counter.

She truly expected him to be back by the time she got out of the shower. But he wasn't. And there was no response to her text either.

Okay.

She would try one more time.

Hey, you. I'm up and at 'em. Going to grab something to eat then get to work on tomorrow's cakes.

She cringed as she sent it. Was that the right mix of wanting to let him know she wanted to see him without seeming too clingy? She hoped so.

Still no response.

Where was he?

Bethany hung out in the room, taking time to get her hair fixed into a cute bun, putting on some makeup, hoping he'd show up. As noon came and went, she decided to go out to the pool area. Maybe he was working out or swimming—somewhere he didn't have his phone directly on him.

He'd aim those dimples at her when he saw her, and this ridiculous feeling in the pit of her stomach would melt away.

But he wasn't at the pool or the gym. And as time passed and she didn't hear anything more from him, the ugly feeling grew rather than melted until it was a huge ball of ice in her gut.

Landon was avoiding her.

Bethany hadn't seen that one coming. She forced herself to eat lunch—which did not do anything but make her stomach feel worse—then went back to the room. She looked at herself in the mirror, studying the care she'd taken with her hair and makeup. She wanted to scrub it all off and pull her hair down until it was a disaster.

But that was nothing but childish. She had work she needed to do. She had set aside today to finish the final wedding cake decorating. She'd already lost the morning, so there was no point in sitting around there feeling sorry for herself.

And there was definitely no point in sitting there wondering what had made Landon run for his life.

Part of her was still hoping it was all a big misunderstanding. That he'd come rushing in there at any moment with some crazy story about how a hut had collapsed on the beach and he'd had to single-handedly rebuild it using only duct tape and chewing gum. He'd been so busy saving some family's vacation that he'd lost track of time and forgotten to check his phone.

Until she glanced at her phone.

Read.

She had been left on *read*. He'd seen her message but hadn't responded. That told her everything she needed to know.

Bethany stuffed her phone into her pocket and headed toward the auxiliary kitchen. She was there to do a job, and that's what she was going to do. She wasn't going to let Landon derail her from her purpose there.

Even if it was a little bit difficult to breathe around the ball in her throat.

He and she had no promises. Hell, hadn't he tried to talk some sense into her before they'd had sex last night? Maybe he knew about his tendency to lose interest and become a complete jerk the morning after.

It came back to the fact that she really didn't know anything about her *fiancé*.

Bethany channeled her angst into working, blocking everything from her mind. Her hands weren't shaky today. Her heart might have taken a hit, but it wasn't going to show in her work.

It was almost dinner by the time she had the cakes exactly how she wanted them. They were ready. They were perfect.

They would sit in the cooler until tomorrow when they were moved for the reception.

Her job was finished. But as she came out from the cooler, all she could see were the cake stands in pieces over in the corner. Landon was supposed to have put them together that afternoon. Yet there they were, still in pieces.

That entire week, he hadn't given her any reason to believe he wouldn't have those stands set up in time. Until he went AWOL today.

Bethany rubbed at the tension that had settled in the center of her neck. She had worked hard all afternoon, and she was tired. Putting those stands together would take her hours—much longer than it would take Landon.

But she couldn't trust him to do it, and she wouldn't be able to do anything else or get to sleep tonight without knowing they were complete.

She grabbed her phone and pulled up the plans for building the elaborate stands. She'd built this business from the ground up by herself.

She was the only person she could count on. Something she wouldn't be forgetting again.

———

Landon

As soon as Landon had snuck out of their suite after getting the text from Tristan, he'd called him. He wasn't sure how bad the situation was, but he didn't want to lead Martinez to Bethany if he suspected he was undercover.

"What the hell happened? Am I compromised? Does Martinez know there was a transmitter placed on his computer?"

"Negative," Tristan responded. "It looks like this was more of a standard wipe. Something may have made him suspicious, but there was nothing to suggest the transmitter was found."

That at least meant his life wasn't in danger. "But we're back to square one when it comes to Martinez. And phone is my only option now."

"You can try again with the computer, but yeah, phone is best. At this point, we'll take whatever you can get." Tristan sounded as tired as he felt.

Landon rubbed his gritty eyes. "I thought this mission was over."

There was a long moment of silence. "Is your identity still secure?"

He knew what he was asking. Had Landon told anyone—particularly Bethany—what he was really doing there. "Yes. Mission isn't compromised. I just made some…decisions I wouldn't have if I'd known I was still in the middle of all this shit."

Visions of Bethany reaching for him, her soft smile lighting up her face, danced before his eyes. He never would've drawn her into the middle of an active mission, no matter how much he wanted her.

"Decisions based around a certain lovely baker? That's not your normal MO."

"I know." He rubbed the back of his neck. "I thought the mission was complete, or I never would've let anything happen."

"Does she suspect anything? Will it compromise your chance to get near Martinez?"

"No, she doesn't suspect anything." Because she trusted him. "But I'm down to the last transmitter, so I better make it count. I'm going to have to take some chances."

"Libra, I've got the full file on Joaquin Martinez sitting right here in front of me."

If Tristan was calling Landon by his Zodiac code name, he knew it was serious. "Not pretty?"

"Dude is the opposite of pretty. Frey may be dipping his toes into the human trafficking waters, but Martinez is up to his neck in it. As soon as Callum figures out the mole in his department, taking Martinez down is going to be his number one priority."

"Even more important for me to get this transmitter on him, then."

Tristan let out a sigh. "If he catches you, you won't make it off that island alive. He's ruthless."

"Then I'll have to make sure not to get caught."

"You don't have any backup. If I show up now to help cover you, it'll be suspicious. This was supposed to be an easy mission."

He rubbed his eyes. "I get it. You're like the rest of them, don't think I can handle it."

"Fuck off. That has nothing to do with it. I've argued to put you back on active missions since before you left the hospital. But that mind-set you've got—that you have something to prove more than anybody else?—that shit will get you killed if you're not careful."

He was right. It was his mind-set, and he hadn't even been aware of it. "I don't like you very much, Pisces."

He chuckled. "You don't have to like me. You do have to stay alive."

"I want to help take this bastard down. After what happened with Wavy and Bronwyn... I can't stomach a trafficker going free when I can do something about it. But getting near him is fucking tricky."

"How about I send a drone with a benzodiazepine strong enough to help with the job?"

"That's a good option. If I can't get near him today, I could roofie him at the wedding. Everybody's drinking at weddings, so hopefully he won't make too much out of a twelve-hour memory gap."

"It'll be at the drop point by this afternoon."

"Hopefully, I won't even need it." Getting something into Martinez's drink wasn't going to be much easier than getting to his phone.

"You have to be careful."

"What I have to do is get that transmitter on him."

"Listen to me, brother. I know you feel like you should've seen what was going on with Wavy, but it fooled us all. Planting the transmitter—which may or may not work in the long run—is not worth your life. I would be saying the same thing to any other Zodiac team member on this mission. Hell, I hope you'd be saying it to me if the roles were reversed."

"I would." And Landon would mean it too.

"Survival is always the most important thing. So, do what you can, but no matter what, you come home. We already came too close to losing you once."

Tristan was a good friend and a huge asset to Zodiac. Landon needed to make sure Ian was reminded of it. "Roger that."

After their call, he spent the entire fucking day trying to get close to Joaquin Martinez. He pushed every other thought —even the fact that he'd left Bethany alone in the bed with no idea where he was—to the back burner.

All that mattered was getting close to Martinez.

Getting back into his suite wasn't an option. He'd come down for breakfast like he had yesterday, but he had left one of his men guarding the room in the hallway. Using housekeeping to get in there twice wouldn't have worked anyway.

After breakfast, he'd gone back to his room. There was no following him from the inside, so Landon had rushed around to the outside of the building, climbing a damned tree so he could see into his balcony.

And he'd waited.

He'd gritted his teeth as he'd received the texts from Bethany wondering where he was. If he opened communication with her, he knew he'd lose any shot he had at getting close to Martinez.

Ended up it hadn't mattered anyway. He'd only left his suite twice throughout the day, and neither time had he been able to get close enough without making it obvious he was up to something. He would have to try tomorrow at the wedding with the roofie.

Shit.

The wedding.

The sun was already going down, and he hadn't put any of the stands together for tomorrow. And he'd been ignoring Bethany's messages all day.

There was only one way this could look to her—like he'd abandoned her completely after their night together in bed. Landon rushed to the auxiliary kitchen. Whether she was there or not, that was where he needed to be.

She was there.

And she'd put the cake stands together herself. She was putting the finishing touches on now.

Fuck.

She looked up when she saw him come in then concentrated her focus back down on the stands without a word.

"Bethany, I'm sorry." Landon had no fucking idea how he was going to explain this to her when the truth wasn't an option.

She didn't look at him. "None of your services—*any* of them—are needed any longer."

He scrubbed a hand down his face. "Bethany, I swear to you, I'm so sorry. I didn't mean for you to have to put this together yourself."

Now she looked at him. "But for clarification, you *did* mean to ghost me all day and not return my texts or talk to me at all?"

There was no good response for that either. "All I can do is offer my sincerest apologies."

She stood tapping the socket wrench in the palm of one hand. He was prepared in case that came flying at his head. "Are you some sort of commitment-phobe, Landon? Is that the big reveal from last night I wouldn't let you get to? You're a *hit and quit it* sort of guy?"

"No." Although he could totally see why she would think so.

She tapped the wrench harder. "Okay, then. Are you on drugs? Battling some sort of addiction?"

That was his easiest way out. She was tapping that wrench in a vaguely threatening manner, but her eyes were soft. She was too kind for her own good and willing to forgive someone who was suffering from some sort of addiction.

All Landon had to do was say yes. Hell, both his parents had been addicts—she already knew that. If he told her he had the same struggles, she would forgive him for today's silence.

But the line was right there. If he took that option and lied to her, it would mean the end of anything permanent between the two of them.

She might possibly forgive him working undercover and using her to get criminals, but lying to her to get out of personal trouble would be a trust broken that couldn't be rebuilt.

When Wavy had pointed that gun at him all those months ago, he'd been sure his life was over. There had been no way out and no options. All he could do was be a passive observer in his own demise as the bullet hit him in the chest.

Not this time. This time, he had choices. They weren't good ones, but they were choices.

Landon would not lie to her about this.

"No. I'm not on drugs."

She studied him silently for a long minute. "But you're not

going to tell me, are you? Whatever it is that's going on. And there is something going on."

"It's better if you don't know." He took a step closer. "I'll finish this if you want. I know you have to be tired. I can make sure it's ready for tomorrow."

"No. I'll do it. You go get your things out of the suite. Like I said, your services are no longer required. I'll finish everything here."

Everything in him wanted to stay and fight for her. To explain, with whatever lack of details he could, how much she meant to him. How much last night had meant to him.

But there was more at stake here than his feelings. If he wanted to help take down Martinez, he had to walk away from Bethany right now.

With a nod, and against every instinct Landon had, he turned and walked out the door.

CHAPTER
TWENTY-THREE

WATCHING Landon walk back out the door without a word, Bethany wanted to throw the wrench across the room. Or take it and slam it into the cake stands.

She had no idea how to make any sense out of him. She believed him when he said it wasn't drugs or having some sort of emotional withdrawal. There was something going on there, and she didn't know what it was.

And he wasn't telling.

She looked around her. Everything was finished and ready for tomorrow evening's wedding. The stands were stable and steady, the cakes were finished, decorated beautifully, and resting in the walk-in.

All she had to do was not have a breakdown before the wedding.

Whatever was going on with Landon wasn't her problem. He didn't have to explain himself to her, and obviously, what they'd shared last night wasn't a priority for him.

Bethany needed to let him go and separate herself, and her emotions, from him completely. Whatever secrets he had were none of her business.

But she found herself quickly locking up the kitchen and rushing back to the suite even though she knew Landon would be there.

Who was she kidding? *Because* Landon would be there.

She wanted answers.

The closer she got, the more she thought she had it figured out. The possibility had been running through her mind all day.

Dad had hired him as security for her.

Bethany's jaw clenched so tightly it was giving her a headache. She'd known for years that some of Dad's contacts were questionable, criminal even. He wasn't part of that life anymore, but that didn't mean they weren't still around.

She walked faster.

Dad had all but freaked out when he'd found out Joaquin Martinez was on the island. He'd told Mother, Christiana, and her to be sure to stay away from him. Maybe Dad had been afraid that warning her wasn't enough and that she needed someone nearby as a sort of bodyguard.

And who else better to protect her than a former Navy SEAL?

It made way too much sense. Made sense why Harley suddenly had a *family emergency* last week.

God, she was humiliated. Her parents had known from the beginning that Landon wasn't her boyfriend, fiancé, or anything. They'd humored her, barely short of patting her on the head.

And Landon had been in on it from the start. It was why he hadn't wanted to sleep with her.

Bethany stopped. Why had he slept with her if he was working for Dad? Because she'd asked him to? Had she been some sort of *pity fuck*?

She started moving again, now almost running. She wasn't sure she'd ever been this angry in her whole life. She burst into the suite, slamming the door behind her.

"Was I a pity fuck?" she yelled.

She screeched to a halt when she found Landon standing in the bedroom naked.

Their eyes met and held for a long moment until hers dropped to the evidence that he was growing, uh, very happy to see her.

He gestured to that mouthwatering hardness. "Considering this happens every time I'm within ten feet of you, or look at you, or think of you...I'm going to go with, no, not a pity fuck."

He stepped into the bathroom and came back out wrapped in a towel. "I didn't expect you here so soon. I wasn't sure where I was going to end up sleeping tonight, so thought I would grab a quick shower in case I didn't have one."

She couldn't stop staring at those abs, that chest. That bullet wound.

"Do you work for my father?"

His eyes narrowed. "Doing what?"

"Guarding me."

"*What*? No. Your father did not hire me for anything."

Bethany took a step closer. "Would you even be allowed to say if he did?"

He blew out a breath. "As a member of his security team? Maybe not, depending on what the contract paperwork stated. But as a member of his security, I would be the first to tell him that *secret guards* are a bad idea."

She crossed her arms over her chest, forcing her eyes to stay pinned to his. "You mean that me not knowing you were assigned to me as a bodyguard would be a bad idea."

"Yes. In order for someone to be truly protected, they need to be aware of what's going on around them."

"Sounds like you know what you're talking about."

He stilled then relaxed his shoulders in a deliberate move. "Residual knowledge from being a SEAL."

She called bullshit.

"You're not a carpenter by trade."

"I'm good at carpentry."

"This business your friend Ian started. Tell me more about it." Maybe he wouldn't tell her his whole truth, but with enough pieces of it, she could at least figure out the shape of the puzzle.

"Some things I can't discuss with you."

"Is your real name Landon Black?"

He nodded.

"And the other stuff? No wife? No girlfriend?"

"All true."

"Do you work for my father?" She asked again. She still couldn't let it go.

"No, I never met or spoke with Oliver Thornton before I arrived on this island."

"Did you sleep with me to get to something or someone?" She hated how her voice got weaker.

He took a step closer. "No. I promise you, last night was one hundred percent about me not being able to keep my hands off you and your sexy curves. Nothing more or less than that."

That at least made her feel a little bit better. She sat down on the edge of the bed. He was still standing in front of the bathroom door, towel low on his hips.

"I'm not sure what I'm supposed to think."

He scrubbed a hand down his face. "Let me shower, and we can talk some more. Although there's not a lot I can say. The most important thing is that I never meant to hurt you, and I'm sorry I did."

He disappeared into the bathroom.

Bethany lay back on the bed, bringing both arms up to cross over her face. She was tired. Not much sleep, then the worrying, and finally the work—hers plus his. She had reason to be exhausted.

And she was just as confused as she'd been when she got there. She had no idea what to believe about Landon.

Her phone buzzed with a text on the bed beside her, and she grabbed it. With her luck, Christiana had probably decided to call off the wedding.

Martinez is leaving tonight. You've got to make your move now.

What?

It took her a second to realize it was Landon's phone in her hand. Someone named Pisces had texted him.

About Joaquin Martinez.

Bethany dropped the phone like it was on fire and jumped off the bed. Landon needed to make a move with Joaquin Martinez?

Bile pooled in her gut. She'd been asking the wrong questions. She'd assumed that Landon was the hired muscle for Dad, but what if he wasn't on the right side of the law at all?

She stormed over to Landon's duffel. He'd already put his clothes in it, and it was sitting open on the luggage rack. She cringed but didn't stop herself from rooting through it.

She froze as her hand brushed something metal.

A gun.

Bethany jerked away like it burned her, then put her hand back in to grab it and pull it out to study. She didn't know much about weapons, so she held it by the butt so she didn't shoot herself.

This gun was small—her hand wrapped around it easily. She guess it made sense that Landon was going to have a small gun if he was going to try to wear it around there.

She dug back in his bag and found a holster. Not one that fit on a shoulder like on television shows. This one was small—it must go around his ankle. That was how he'd hidden it.

Bethany sat back on the bed with the gun in her lap, trying to figure out what to do.

She should leave. Go get security. And tell them what? It wasn't illegal for Landon to have a weapon.

Why did he need it?

He came out of the shower, that towel wrapped around his waist. He froze when he saw the gun in her lap.

"Wildflower? I need you to set that weapon on the bed next to you."

She kept her hand wrapped around it in her lap. "Why?"

"Because I don't want you to accidentally hurt me or you."

She stood, gun still in her hand. "I found it in your bag."

His eyes were glued to her hands as his weight shifted on the balls of his feet. "Yes, I had it in my bag. Can you please place it on the bed?"

"Why do you have a gun, Landon?"

She brought the weapon up to show him—as if he wasn't familiar with his own gun—and he moved faster than she'd ever seen him. Before she could even figure out what was going on, he had her wrist in his hand, ripping the weapon none too gently away from her. Her breath escaped in a little squeak.

"Sorry." He grimaced, stepping away, doing something to the gun so the magazine clip slid out of it. He set both on the dresser. "The last time someone as kind and gentle as you had a gun in her hand in front of me, I took a bullet to the chest."

Her eyes fell on that scar. She'd thought it was from something during his Navy SEAL years, but evidently not. She rubbed her wrist from where he'd twisted it to get the weapon from me.

"Are you okay?" he asked.

Was she okay? Her wrist was fine, but was she okay? No.

"Why do you have a gun?" she whispered. "If you don't work security for my dad, why do you have a gun?"

"I can't tell you."

"Because you're a criminal? Does my father know? Who do you work for?"

Bethany needed to get out of there. She started backing toward the door.

Landon was studying her with those intelligent hazel eyes. He should scare her much more than he did. Even right now, she wanted to understand what was going on more than she wanted to get away from him.

"I'm not any sort of criminal. I promise." He brought out his smile to attempt to put her at ease. "I have a legal permit for that gun. After my time in the SEALs, I feel naked without having a weapon."

That was probably true, but it wasn't the whole truth. Nothing with Landon this entire week had been the whole truth.

"I can't stay here with you. I have to report this to my father and the security team. I'd be a complete idiot if I didn't."

She turned for the door, tense for him to physically restrain her from doing so. That would tell her if he was a bad guy, wouldn't it?

It would also be too late for her to get away from him.

"Wildflower." The word came out as a sigh. "I'm here undercover for law enforcement."

Bethany froze three steps from the door.

"They sent me under to put a recording device on Vincent Frey's phone. He's a big-name criminal, and getting near him is almost impossible. When they found out he'd be here for the wedding, the Feds decided to make a move."

She turned to face him.

"This island has such strict security, it puts people—*criminals*—at ease. Cops can't just show up here. Invitations were closely guarded and monitored, so law enforcement had to find another way to send someone in."

"Me," she whispered.

"Your handyman Harley had a warrant out for his arrest."

"He did?" This kept getting worse.

Landon shrugged. "Nothing bad—a mistake, actually. A lucky break on our part. He helped me get in with you, and, in turn, we made that warrant go away."

She stood staring at him, trying to get her thoughts under control. "Is anything you told me the truth? Is your name even Landon?"

He took a step closer, and she wasn't sure if she should back away or not. "Yes. Anybody who searches my name will find some general info on me. Things that have been built to make me seem as boring as possible."

"So, you're a cop?"

"No, I work for a security company called Zodiac Tactical. That's the one my friend, and former SEAL teammate, Ian DeRose built. What I said about being a jack-of-all-trades is true. We do all sorts of work. A friend in law enforcement needed someone who could build for you and get the transmitter planted. I fit the bill."

"And I fit the bill as someone pathetic enough to believe everything a stranger would say."

Another step closer. "No. You had needs, and I could fulfill them. It got me on the island."

"And everything since then?" Bethany hated that her voice was weak. Why wasn't she screaming at him?

"Everything with you has been real, Wildflower. Not being able to stay away from you has been completely authentic. You blow my self-control straight to hell, woman."

"I don't know if I can believe you." But God, how she wanted to.

He crossed all the way over to her now, gently touching her arms. "I held out as long as I could. If—*when*—you found out about this, I wanted to be able to tell you that we didn't make love until after my mission was complete. I didn't want you to think I'd used you in that way."

Her brow furrowed. What about that text? "Your... mission is done?"

He let out a sigh. "I thought so last night when I made love to you. But there was an extra complication. That's where I've been all day."

"Was that complication Joaquin Martinez?"

His head snapped back. "Why do you say that?"

She shrugged one shoulder. "I didn't just randomly go digging through your duffel. You got a text about Martinez."

He dashed to the bed and lifted his phone. A vile curse fell from his mouth.

"I have to go." He forsook all sense of propriety, dropping the towel and pulling on his clothes. "Nobody knew Martinez was going to be here. He's an even bigger fish to law enforcement than Vincent Frey. I thought I'd gotten a transmitter on Martinez's computer yesterday, but it got wiped. I need to get a transmitter on his phone. I thought I had all day tomorrow."

"But he's leaving." That's what the text had said. "What are you going to do? Martinez isn't going to just hand over his phone."

He sat down to pull on his shoes. "I'll have to figure something out. It's critical. Martinez and Frey are neck-deep into human trafficking. If I don't get that transmitter on him, we'll lose the chance to gather critical intel."

"Martinez is dangerous. Dad didn't want me anywhere around him. He was very clear about that."

"Martinez is definitely fucking dangerous. But I've got to try. Lives are at stake." He grabbed something tiny out of his duffel. "I've got to get this transmitter on his phone." He slipped it into his pocket.

Bethany watched in silence as he grabbed his gun and put it back together, before slipping it into the ankle holster. She wanted to tell him not to go, but she already knew he wasn't going to listen to her.

He was completely focused—more of a Navy SEAL than she'd ever seen him. Ever seen *anyone*.

As he walked by her, he slipped an arm around her waist and placed his lips against hers. "Every kiss was real. Every single one. Don't ever doubt that."

He pulled away and walked out the door.

LANDON HAD MISSED eight texts from Tristan. He called him as he dashed out the door.

"Dude, I thought you were dead," he answered without any other greeting.

"What's going on with Martinez?"

"He called for a flight to leave tonight. Don't know why. No indication it has anything to do with you. He'll be wheels up in less than an hour."

Landon stepped out of the elevator and walked briskly through the hallway—just slow enough not to draw undue attention to himself. "Anything you can do to stall him?"

"I've already done everything I can on my end. We kept his jet on the ground in LA as long as possible. He was trying to leave a few hours ago."

"Let me know if anything changes. I'll keep you posted." He disconnected the call.

Instead of heading left, toward the interior of the hotel and the back patio, he went right, toward the front doors. He'd need one of the resort shuttles to take him to the island's tiny airfield. The shuttle stand was half a block from the lobby.

Landon would have no reason to be out at the airfield. Just showing up there was going to put Martinez and his men on high alert. Acting shit-faced drunk was probably his best bet. Hopefully, he could literally stumble into Martinez and get the transmitter on the phone. His security team would probably beat the hell out of him for getting too close, but he'd take it. And hope they didn't shoot him.

But he had to get to the airfield first.

As Landon exited the lobby doors, his luck turned. Martinez stood outside a limo at the shuttle station, his phone in his hand, waiting to get in. He stumbled in that direction, running his hand through his hair to muss it. It was still damp, but it would have to do.

A member of Martinez's security team walked around the limo and opened the trunk, placing luggage inside.

Landon half jogged, half stumbled forward. "Hey, you," he called, letting his voice slur. "I remember you. Go Dodgers!"

The security guy slammed the trunk and stepped between Martinez and Landon, but Martinez put a hand on the guy's back. "It's fine, Clark."

Clark stepped to the side, crossing his arms over his beefy chest, but he didn't move far.

"How's my cap? What's your name again?"

"Landon. I'm Landon. Your cap is fine." He looked around like he couldn't figure out what was going on. "Wait, are you leaving? You can't leave! What about the game tomorrow?"

He chuckled, shaking his head. "The wedding is tomorrow, so you won't be catching the game. And yes, I have to leave early."

"That sucks. I was looking forward to having someone who could help me sneak off and watch it."

"You're the bride's sister's fiancé. I think your absence would be noted."

He'd looked into him. Fuck. But evidently, his cover had held.

Landon made a face. "I'm still gonna sneak out. All I did was promise I wouldn't be watching the game during the ceremony. God, everybody is so uptight here."

"Oliver mentioned you and his daughter today at our poker game. He seems to like you."

He scrubbed a hand down his face in an exaggerated fashion, inching closer. "Look, I don't know how well you know Oliver, but I don't think this is gonna work out with me and his daughter. I mean, she's a good baker, but that's about it, you know? I never should've proposed. I got caught up in the moment. She's boring."

He stumbled just the slightest bit closer without touching him, hating what he was saying about Bethany.

He nodded. At least he seemed interested in the conversation. "You're young. You've got a lot to learn. You marry the good girls, Landon, keep that in mind. Marry the good girls and have your fun wherever you need to on the side. But the good girls raise good children for you and keep your home happy."

Landon's fingers itched to ball into a fist and clock him on the jaw right here. Bastard was going to stand there and talk about *good girls* when he was neck-deep in human trafficking?

Taking a chance at touching him with Clarky-boy nearby, he clapped Martinez on the shoulder with one hand and stuck the other in his pocket to work the transmitter off its backing so he'd have it ready to stick on his phone. "Wise words, my friend, but I'm going to have to find myself a different good girl. This one is too damn uptight."

Landon looked past him, hand still on his shoulder, at the limo. "Are you leaving?"

Bastard slid out from under his hand but at least didn't sic Clark on him. "I already said I was."

"Right. Right-Right-Right. I may have had a few too many.

Hey, listen, I know we don't know each other that well, but do you think you could give me a ride off this island? I'm done here. I need off."

He narrowed his eyes and shook his head. "I don't think that will work for me."

Shit, he was getting suspicious and starting to put more distance between them. He stumbled closer.

This wasn't working. Clark stepped forward, and Martinez was beginning to lose his amused demeanor. Landon's drunk act was wearing thin. He was about to stumble directly into Martinez and deal with the aftermath when Bethany's voice interrupted us.

"Mr. Martinez," she called.

What the hell was she doing here? Landon forced himself not to turn around and give himself away. Instead, he flinched and rolled his eyes.

"Damn it," he whispered to Martinez. "She found me. Help me, man. Get her out of here. Get *me* out of here."

Martinez chuckled.

Landon turned to see her hurrying toward them with a pastry box in her hands. "My father sent me with these." She beamed at them and held out a pink box in front of her. "He heard you were leaving and asked me to bring them out."

What the hell?

Martinez looked confused. Landon was sure he did too.

Bethany stepped directly in front of him, opened the cake box, and shoved it under his nose. "It's some of the desserts you'll be missing out on tomorrow. I'll admit, I insisted on bringing them to you. I think they're the best I've made this week. I'd hate for you not to get an opportunity to taste them. And tell all your friends if they need a baker for any events."

With her free hand, she reached back. It took him a second to realize she wanted him to give her the transmitter.

Oh shit.

Landon didn't want to do it. He didn't want her anywhere around this situation. If Martinez caught her…

She shook her hand in an obvious instruction that he was to give her the transmitter *now*.

Fuck.

Landon slipped the transmitter into her hand while Martinez and Clark were distracted by the treats in the box, praying he wasn't about to get both her and himself killed.

As soon as she had the tiny device, she stepped forward. "I'm sorry you couldn't stay." Lifting her chin, she held out her cheek, clearly indicating she wanted him to kiss her. "Please keep me in mind for any future baking needs you have. I put my card in the box."

He leaned in to press his jaw to hers in a polite, high-society kiss, but Bethany lurched forward, and the cake box flew into Martinez's chest. Clark moved with catlike reflexes to catch it, and he probably would have if Bethany hadn't been pushing it forward as she pretended to fall into Martinez.

Neither of them ended up falling, but they both ended up half bent over, near the ground. Clark yanked the bakery box away, and Bethany bent to pick up Martinez's fallen cell phone.

"I'm so sorry," she exclaimed.

"Jesus, Bethany, come on! What's wrong with you? You're so clumsy!" He stumbled over Bethany and hard into Clark, blocking his view of the cell phone. Bethany's body already kept Martinez from seeing it.

"Get it together, man," Clark whispered as Landon pushed his weight into him. "You're embarrassing yourself."

Martinez, with icing on his shirtfront, snatched the phone from Bethany. "I will keep your bakery in mind."

She nodded. "I'm so sorry! Can I pay to have your shirt laundered? I'm such a klutz."

"Yeah, she'll pay for it." He wavered on his feet to keep up his pretense as he made the obnoxious statement. Anything to keep him focused on Landon and not on his phone. The transmitter was tiny and wouldn't be noticed, but he only wanted Martinez remembering him.

He pulled a handkerchief out of his pocket and got up all the icing he could. "Don't worry about it. Laundering is not necessary. Let's go, Clark."

Clark jumped back and opened the limo door, the remains of the salvaged box in hand. Martinez slid into the limo, and Clark ignored them as he closed the door, then walked around them to get behind the wheel. They pulled away from the curb without a second's pause, moving quickly down the road toward the airfield.

Bethany and Landon stood there staring after them.

"I'm pretty sure I got it on the back of the phone. I didn't know if it had to go on a specific place or what." She bit her lip.

"Anywhere. As long as you got the transmitter on the phone, it can do its job from anywhere on it."

She glanced over at him. "Then I got it."

"You shouldn't have done that, you know." Landon crossed his arms over his chest. Now that Martinez was gone, all he could think about was how much danger Bethany had put herself in.

How much danger *he* had put her in. If Martinez had caught her…

The thought of it almost doubled him over.

"Why? I thought you just said I got the transmitter on the phone okay."

"Because it was dangerous, Bethany!" His voice got deeper with his emotion. "Because Martinez might have killed you if he'd caught you."

"I'm pretty sure he would've done the same to you if you'd been caught, and I had more excuse to be around him than you did."

She didn't get it.

For the first time, Landon had an inkling of how Ian and Sarge had felt when their women had been taken by criminals over the past year. The helplessness that had nearly drowned them. The bitter fury at the thought of Wavy and Bronwyn being hurt.

He was already feeling the same, and nothing had even happened to Bethany. Just the thought of it happening…

"But that's my job." He grabbed her hand and marched her a little farther into the privacy of the trees heading down toward the beach. "I have training and experience with this. You don't. You should not have put yourself in danger like that."

They went around a couple of trees and then ended up near the beach. No one was around. Good. He still had this yin and yang of icy fury and fear floating around in his veins.

Fuck being the one who always smiled. The one who was good with people. Right now, he could hardly get a handle on this storm blowing through him.

He wanted to throw Bethany over his shoulder and carry her somewhere safe and never let her out of his sight.

"Landon…"

He kept walking, her hand in his, as she rushed behind him to keep up. He didn't care that he was being unreasonable. He wanted her as far away from Martinez as possible in case he came back.

"You should've stayed in the suite," He bit out. "Do you know what Martinez would've done if he had even suspected you might be planting a transmission device on him?"

He couldn't even stomach it. The thought of it turned him into someone he didn't recognize.

"Landon, stop."

"Do you hear me? He's a human trafficker, and I'm not even sure that's the worst of his sins. Do you think that you being the sister of the bride would've stopped him from—"

She yanked on his hand and before he even knew what she was going to do had him pressed back against a tree and kissed him.

One of his hands immediately wound into her hair, the other wrapped around her hips and yanked her to him. Landon ravished those sweet lips like he'd been afraid he'd never have another taste of them again. Which wasn't far from the truth.

They were both breathing heavy as they broke apart.

"I think the words you're looking for are, 'Thank you, Bethany,'" she whispered with a smile.

He closed his eyes and pushed down the fear. She was right. He definitely owed her thanks.

"Thank you, Bethany," Landon repeated before kissing her again. "You saved lives today. My life definitely—because I was about to have to resort to desperate measures to get that tracker on Martinez's phone. But also the lives of the people who are going to be helped by law enforcement because of what you did."

He gripped her hips tighter. "But I still didn't like it."

She shrugged and gave him a gentle smile. "Placing the transmitter was worth the risk. It was more important than me or you."

He stared at her in the moonlight. *She got it.* Without any sort of training or military background, she understood the importance of what had needed to be done.

Even more importantly, she had done it.

He still didn't like it.

She put a finger over his lips. "Is your mission really and truly over now? No other bad guys going to burst through here at any moment, guns blazing?"

He kissed her finger. "Martinez was the last one."

He could see the gleam in her eye. "Good. Then I'd like for you to make love to me. *Here.* I need you inside me, right now."

CHAPTER
TWENTY-FIVE

BETHANY DIDN'T KNOW how to explain the adrenaline that was rushing through her blood, but she didn't have to. She could tell Landon already knew what it was all about.

He spun her so she was against the tree, and his lips began working their way down her neck, stealing her breath. One hand slid down her thigh and pulled it up over his hip so he could press against her right where she wanted him to.

Everything was so complicated. She was still confused and more than a little pissed that Landon had used her for this mission. But if he had to lie to her, at least it was for a good reason.

Stopping human traffickers was the best of reasons. It was why she had rushed over to the auxiliary kitchen and dumped some sweets in a box. Because if Landon needed help, she wanted to be able to give it to him.

And because she couldn't stand the thought of what someone like Martinez might do to him. Landon had been trying to get on Martinez's plane, for God's sake. There were so many things that could've gone wrong—all ending with Landon's body being tossed over the Pacific.

So yeah, Bethany wanted him to fuck her hard right up against this tree. For all the things that could've gone wrong but didn't. And most importantly because they'd just saved the day. She was giddy. And hot.

And already wet.

His lips moved against her throat as he lowered her leg and grabbed her panties under her skirt, sliding them down her legs. He unfastened his pants just enough for his hard length to spring free. She couldn't stop herself from wrapping her hand around him.

"Wildflower," he said through gritted teeth. "I don't have any protection with me."

"I'm on the pill," She responded without hesitation. "I'm okay if you are."

He leaned his forehead against hers, jerking as his fist closed harder around him. "Are you sure?"

"Very."

That SEAL speed again. Before she even guessed what he intended, he lifted Bethany off the ground and pressed her back into the tree, fitting himself against her. And then he was inside her, stealing her breath and trapping her between himself and the rough wood.

"Landon." His name came out as a half sob.

She was so full of him. Fuller than she'd felt last night. He was so deep he felt like he was a part of her, and he hadn't moved yet.

He gathered her wrists in one hand and pinned them above her head. Leaning forward, he kissed his way along her jaw to her ear. "You like living dangerously, don't you?"

She couldn't breathe, much less answer, as he moved his hips—a slow, rolling movement that was everything and still not enough.

"Please," she whispered.

"Mmm." He nuzzled his cheek against hers. "I like that. Please, what?"

"Please more."

He rolled his hips again with agonizing slowness. He still held her wrists in one hand, the other supporting her. She was trapped and helpless. Pinned to the tree. He knew she wanted more—rough, fast—and deliberately wasn't giving it to her.

Bethany squeezed down on him, and he groaned, thrusting in response. Two could play at this game.

She squeezed him again and moved her hips against his. But no matter what she did, he kept the smooth, steady pace. Every grinding movement brushed right against where she needed him, and pleasure rose like a tide that threatened to drown her.

Pulling against his hold, she wanted to move. She wanted to drag him against her and force him to move faster. "You're going to kill me," she breathed.

His low laugh sent goose bumps cascading down her whole body. Her nipples hardened against his chest. He kissed her, never stopping that infernal, torturous movement that was sending her higher and holding her back all at the same time.

Delicious friction consumed her. Lost in the sensation, Bethany couldn't keep her eyes open. She could barely keep herself from moaning loud enough to bring any passerby into their hidden area.

Out of nowhere, he let go of her hands and gripped her hips with a bruising force. He changed his motion, switching from a smooth roll to a deep stroke that hit her center so perfectly she saw white. He pulled back, almost all the way out, and slammed home.

Whereas the first rhythm wasn't enough, this was almost too much. She let out a sob that he caught with his mouth to keep her quiet.

Yes. This was what she'd wanted. He'd known it all along.

Pleasure splintered through her with each stroke—it felt as

if she were breaking, with glorious light shining through the cracks. She was shaking, clenching down on him inside her, trying to hold on through every stroke. Every driving movement of his hips was a new beam of light.

"Yes, yes, yes." The words were a soundless chant as he continued to give her what she wanted over and over, her body meeting his thrust for thrust.

It was a celebration of being alive, of surviving danger, of finally knowing each other on a true equal level.

Landon made no sound as he moved inside her, but Bethany could hear his breathing getting heavier, feel the tension racking his hard body as he got closer to release. He held her weight against the tree as if it was nothing, his hips picking up the pace and driving her over the edge.

Her nails scored into his neck as pleasure crashed over her, stealing her breath. He whispered her name like it was a sacred prayer as he found his own release.

Bethany's body went limp in the delicious aftermath as he buried his face in the side of her neck, breathing in her scent. He still pinned her to the tree. Her blouse was going to be ruined from scraping up against the wood, but she didn't care.

He finally moved back and lowered her to the ground. "That'll teach you not to put yourself in danger."

She laughed. "I don't know. I may not quite have learned my lesson."

He kissed her. "Then we'll have to get some more practice in. As long as it has nothing to do with Joaquin Martinez or Vincent Frey."

"Tomorrow is our last full day on the island. We better make the most of it."

He adjusted his pants then grabbed her underwear where they'd fallen to the ground and handed them to her. She used them to wipe herself off, then stuck them in her pocket.

He brushed her hair back from her face. She couldn't even

imagine what sort of mess it was. "Definitely want to make the most of tomorrow. But I'm also hoping you'll be willing to see me once we get back home."

"Really?"

"I've been racking my brain to figure out how I could talk you into seeing me once we got back to real life. I didn't want to lie to you, but I couldn't tell the truth either. Now, that doesn't matter."

"There's still a lot I don't know about you."

He leaned his forehead against hers. "And much I don't know about you either. Difference is, now we've got time to learn each other. And believe me, I want to learn all of you."

———

By the time they made it back to the suite, her legs were a little shaky. "Look what you've done to me, I can hardly walk."

He grinned over at her as he opened the door. "As much as I'd like to take all the credit, that's your body coming down from the adrenaline."

Bethany loved the feel of his hand at the small of her back as they entered the room. "I think I might have to try a little more monkey tree sex to see if that's actually the case."

He winked. "I offer myself as tribute. In the name of science, of course."

This man. She thought she'd liked him before. But now that she knew he worked to stop criminals, she could feel her heart doing backflips.

She needed to give her heart a stern talking-to about how it had been less than a week and it was way too soon to be feeling this way.

Somehow she had a feeling her heart would have no interest in listening to reason.

Bethany peeled off her clothes and got in the shower as

Landon checked in with…whoever he checked in with. She wanted to ask for more details, and she would. But right now, she just wanted to relax.

Having him join her and pull her close under the steamy spray and hold her—a gentleman who let her have the hot water hitting her in the back—did not make her heart do any fewer gymnastics.

He was staring at her as they dried off.

"What?" She asked him. If he wanted more sex, she was going to have to tell him…*yes, please*. No matter how tired she was.

"Once my team hears how you thought of bringing desserts to get close to Martinez, you're probably going to get hired by law enforcement. It was a great idea. I don't think he suspected a thing."

She gave him a goofy grin. "It was the first thing I thought of that would give me a reason for showing up. Actually, you're lucky…"

Wait. Bethany stopped drying.

"I'm damned well aware I was lucky you're so smart."

"No. I was going to say you're lucky because I ran over to the auxiliary kitchen, but I forgot my keys. The door happened to be unlocked."

He wrapped his towel around his waist. "Sounds like I was doubly lucky, then. If you'd had to come all the way back here then go to the kitchen again, you'd probably have been too late to help with Martinez."

She nodded vaguely, but that wasn't what was bothering her. "I know I locked the kitchen door when I left earlier. I was pissed at you because you hadn't set up the cake stands, and I decided I wanted to have it out with you. I am one hundred percent positive I locked the door."

His brows furrowed. "Okay, maybe the cleaning services came through? I'll still count myself lucky."

"I need to go lock the door. I won't sleep if I don't."

He nodded without argument. "I'll go with you."

She rushed to get dressed. All the good feelings that had been swimming around her belly had switched to dread.

Nobody should've been in that auxiliary kitchen except her. The resort staff had been very well aware of that fact—it was in her contract with them.

Landon was ready to go before her. He waited as she slipped on her shoes then grabbed her hand as they walked out the door.

They didn't talk on the way, but she knew he saw the open door to the kitchen at the same time as she did.

Bethany didn't leave that open. She knew no matter how much of a hurry she'd been in to get to Landon with the treats box, there was no way she'd left that door open.

"You didn't do that," he muttered.

She was thankful she didn't have to explain, but she knew this wasn't good.

The notion was confirmed as she made it to the doorway. She blinked as she took it all in. The cake stand she'd spent hours building was destroyed.

The door to the walk-in fridge was wide open.

And tomorrow's wedding cake was in pieces all over the floor.

CHAPTER
TWENTY-SIX

BETHANY STOOD THERE AND STARED. She couldn't believe it. The cakes she had carefully crafted back at her shop and then painstakingly decorated earlier were lying in multiple pieces on the floor.

This had been deliberate. An earthquake strong enough to topple the entire resort wouldn't have done as much damage.

"I think I'm going to throw up," she said to Landon.

He was standing next to her, muttering curses. "This was done on purpose. We need to call security."

Security wasn't going to help. They might be able to eventually pinpoint who the culprit was, but it wasn't going to make any difference in the fact that there was now no wedding cake for a wedding taking place in eighteen hours.

"It doesn't matter who did this." Her voice came out like a croak. "There's not going to be a wedding cake."

"Hey." He folded his hands around her arms. "It's going to be okay. We're going to figure this out."

She didn't know if he meant figure out who did it or figure out how to keep the wedding from being a disaster.

She gestured over at the cake stands that had been

destroyed too. She couldn't even wrap her head around it all. "I don't know what I'm going to—"

A screech cut her off.

"Oh my God, Bethany, what have you done?"

Landon and she both turned to see Mina standing in the doorway. Her eyes were huge.

"You sabotaged the wedding cake, didn't you? I *knew* it. I knew you would do something like this. I tried to tell everyone, but no one would listen to me. Wait until Aunt Patricia sees this. I tried to warn her."

Bethany swallowed a sob. That was what everyone in the family was going to think—that she had deliberately ruined the wedding cake. And she had no way of proving otherwise.

Landon crossed his arms over his chest. "What are you doing here, Mina? It's after midnight."

She didn't falter a bit. "I couldn't sleep. I had a bad feeling about tomorrow, and now I know why." She already had her phone out and was texting somebody. "I can't believe you would do this, Bethany. I just can't believe it."

She wanted to cover her ears so she didn't hear her accusation. She wanted to close her eyes and hide forever at the mess in front of her. She had ruined her sister's wedding even though she hadn't done anything.

"Step outside, Mina," Landon said.

"Why? I didn't do anything wrong. It's your *fiancée*." She spat the word. "Aunt Patricia is on her way. I can't wait to see her face."

"Out," Landon growled and pointed toward the door. Mina was actually laughing as she left.

"She did it," Landon said under his breath. "There's no way in hell she just happened to be walking by right when we discovered this. She's been waiting."

Bethany rubbed her hands up and down her arms to ward off a chill even though it wasn't cold. "Probably."

It didn't matter even if she had. It didn't change the fact that there was no cake for tomorrow.

Landon gently cupped her elbow. "Come outside. There's nothing you can do in here right at this second. We'll call somebody, get it cleaned up, and then we're going to come up with a game plan."

She blinked up at him. "There's no way I can recreate that cake in eighteen hours."

"But you can do something. It may not be the cake you've been envisioning, but I have no doubt you can make something beautiful for your sister."

Not that would feed hundreds of people and wouldn't look like it hadn't been bought at the local supermarket. She could only hope Mother hadn't actually canceled the reservation she had with the resort catering. They would have a team who could make it happen. She only had herself.

Bethany was still in a daze as Landon led her outside. A resort employee had come by to see what all Mina's screeching was about, and Landon requested that they send someone to clean up the mess and to help them figure out what was going on.

A few minutes later, Patricia arrived. Right behind her was Bethany's mother.

Mina shook her head slowly. "Aunt Patricia, Mrs. Thornton, look at what Bethany did. She sabotaged the wedding cakes just like I said she would."

Bethany looked at her mother. "I didn't do this."

"Where were you?" Landon asked Mina. "Where have you been for the past few hours?"

She crossed her arms over her chest, and her smile got smug. "I was with five of my friends and surrounded by multiple people on the dance floor at the oceanside gazebo. I'm pretty sure you can't blame this on me. Where was Bethany?"

"She was with me," Landon said.

"Ah." Mina nodded in a dramatic fashion. "She was with *you*, the surprise fiancé who happened to show up at the last minute, that none of us had ever heard of or seen. What a coincidence."

Bethany looked at her mother again. "I didn't do this, Mother. I promise."

She couldn't believe the words that came out of her mouth. "I believe you."

Neither could Mina.

"What?" she screeched. "I've been telling you this might happen all week, and now it has, and you're not even going to believe that she did it to herself?"

Mother turned to Mina. "My daughter has spent all week providing impeccable desserts for the guests and building up the name of her business. It would be counterproductive for her to destroy the wedding cake right as she is at the pinnacle of making such a name for herself. Bethany may be many things, but stupid is not one of them. She didn't do this."

She finally felt like some of the weight that had been on her chest was lifted. Mother believed her. She *believed* her.

"Thank you," Bethany whispered.

"No need to thank me." She raised an eyebrow. "There's still no wedding cake, but I know you didn't do this to yourself."

Faint praise, but she would take it. The important thing was she knew Bethany hadn't done this.

"Aunt Patricia." Mina turned to the other woman. "You can't be as blind as Mrs. Thornton, can you? Surely you can see what's happening here—"

Before Patricia could answer, a wild sound came out from the darkness. They all watched as Mina was tackled to the ground by some screaming banshee.

Christiana.

"You destroyed my wedding cake!" Christiana grabbed Mina by the collar and rolled her over.

"Christiana!" Mother, Patricia, and Bethany all yelled at the same time. She couldn't even believe her eyes.

"You destroyed my wedding cake!" Her tiny little sister was on top of Mina, pulling her hair. "I'm about to show you Bridezilla, bitch."

"Christiana, what are you doing?" If their mother had had her pearls on, she would've been clutching them. "Mina didn't destroy your cake. We don't know who did. She has an alibi. Stop this right now!"

Christiana was still straddling Mina. She grabbed her shirt by the collar and pulled Mina's face so that they were only inches apart.

"You shouldn't have sent that video, moron. Your little posse is not smart enough to keep things a secret."

Mina's face went pale.

"That's right," Christiana continued. "Whoever you paid to destroy the cake sent you proof, right? And then you couldn't keep it to yourself, so you sent it to your friends. And guess who got a hold of it?"

Christiana grabbed Mina's hair at the back of her head and slammed her head back. Mina was sputtering and trying to get a word in edgewise, but Christiana wasn't letting her.

Beside me, Landon chuckled. "And I thought the danger had left the island already."

"We should do something," Bethany whispered. "I don't want Christiana to go to jail for killing Mina."

Landon walked over much more slowly than she knew he was capable of, allowing Christiana to get a couple more hits in, before he picked her up by the waist and hauled her off Mina.

"That's enough, slugger. We don't want you to get arrested."

Simon came running in, along with both his dad and Bethany's. Then resort security showed up, resulting in mass chaos. Everyone was talking at once. Christiana was still screaming at Mina, and Simon was having to hold her back from doing further physical damage.

Bethany just stood there trying to figure out what she was going to do. Because no matter how much of a bitch Mina was, or how impressive her sister was when she really got angry, it didn't alter the fact that they still didn't have a wedding cake.

The cacophony got louder. Mina was protesting her innocence, now blaming Landon. Nobody cared. Security was trying to figure out what was going on, and both the bride's and groom's parents were looking about as dazed as Bethany felt.

This was going to take a while to sort out. And more importantly, it wasn't her problem.

Mina's plan had backfired. No one believed that Bethany had destroyed her own work. Their faith in her gave her the focus and adrenaline she needed.

She turned to Landon. "It's time for me to get to work."

She had a cake to make and a very limited number of hours to make it.

It took a couple of hours, but they finally got the kitchen cleaned up with the help of the resort staff. The manager had offered to wake some of the catering team members to help her make the cakes, but she declined.

They still weren't sure exactly who Mina had hired to do her dirty work. There could still be someone she was paying off. The last thing Bethany wanted was the entire guest list coming down with food poisoning from the cakes.

By the time the kitchen was cleaned up, she still didn't have much of a game plan. The multitiered fairy-tale castle design with geode towers was no longer an option. Neither were the six different flavors the cake was originally supposed to be.

So the guests would be getting her most unique flavor: vanilla chai cake. Even people not normally a fan of chai raved about it. And it was a tribute to Landon. His eyes had already lit up when he saw the cinnamon.

She needed to get the cakes made and in the oven as soon as possible. Cake for three hundred people was a huge undertaking.

Outside was still mayhem as she began to gather ingredients. Everyone was talking about whether to arrest Mina or just get her off the island, but Bethany didn't stick around to figure out what happened. Landon didn't either; he stayed by her side and helped her pull ingredients from the main kitchen.

Landon was going to be working all night too, trying to make a stand out of all the broken pieces currently lying outside. Even with both of them working at full speed, she wasn't holding out much hope.

Christiana came in and grabbed an apron.

"What are you doing?" Bethany asked her.

"I'm going to help. I don't want to be any part of that circus out there, and I think you could use all the help you can get."

Simon walked in behind her. "Me too."

She was going to argue, but the fact was, she did need all the help she could get.

Bethany turned to her sister and cupped her cheeks. "No way, hulk bride. You're getting married in just over sixteen hours. You don't need to stay here and help. You need to go back and rest."

Christiana didn't back down. "I'm not going to be able to

rest. Adrenaline. If you only knew what it was like to do something dangerous and crazy."

Yeah, if she only knew. She wondered what her sister would say if Bethany told her having fantastic sex against a tree might help her work that adrenaline out of her system.

"Okay. Just for a little while." She put them to work measuring ingredients for the cake batter, as she attempted to formulate a plan for decorating based on what they had available.

She wasn't surprised to find Christiana wavering on her feet after an hour. She caught Simon's eye and gestured toward her. He nodded. She needed to be in bed.

Bethany took the spatula out of her hand. "Time for bed. It's the night before your wedding, and I can't be responsible for you looking like a zombie tomorrow."

"But..."

She cupped her cheeks. "I promise I will handle this for you, my sister."

"I know you will." She kissed her softly on the lips. "You're the best sister ever."

Simon stepped closer and wrapped an arm around her shoulders. "Thank you, Bethany, for everything. For under-standing, and for going well above and beyond the call of duty. Whatever cake we have tomorrow, we'll be thankful for."

Christiana smiled up at him. "The important thing is that we'll be married."

"Out of here, you two." Bethany pointed at the door with her spatula. Simon led her out with a protective arm wrapped around her waist.

"Those two are going to make it," Landon said from behind her.

"I think so. The love is real. That's the most important thing."

"Yes, it is."

She turned to face him, running an exhausted hand down her face. Christiana wasn't the only one who was crashing. "Whether they have a cake for their wedding big enough for everyone remains to be seen."

Multiple layers were already in the oven, but there was still so much that needed to be done.

"We'll get it done." He kissed her softly.

Bethany didn't even have the energy to plaster a smile on her face and lie all chirpily to him. Sure, they would have something done. But she didn't want it to be too small or too plain.

She wanted the wedding cake to be reflective of what Christiana and Simon felt for each other.

And while she didn't regret sending them to get rest, the fact was, she couldn't get this done on her own. Even with Landon's help. And he'd already turned back to the stands he needed to piece together.

Bethany stared at the mess all around her. This wasn't how she normally worked. Her shop was neat and orderly.

She sucked in a deep breath. She wasn't going to fall apart now. There wasn't time.

She'd built Slice of Heaven by herself, and she'd do this by herself too. Even if the prognosis was grim.

The main set of cakes was out of the oven and in the chiller, and Bethany was in the process of making the frosting when she heard a timid knock on the kitchen door.

"Come in!" she yelled, not stopping her work. No more breaks.

"Is there some way that I could be of assistance?"

Bethany turned, eyes wide, to find Patricia standing in the kitchen doorway. She was wearing plain black trousers, a white sweater, and low heels. It was as informally dressed as she had ever seen her.

Patricia was wearing *work clothes.*

"I don't really have anything glamorous for you to do. At this point, it's tedious, messy, and hard work."

She walked farther into the room. "Believe it or not, I can do hard work and tedious. I would like to help if you'll allow me to, especially since it was my family member who got us into this predicament to begin with."

For the first time in hours, a little bit of hope trickled through her system. Patricia was nothing if not methodical. She could be trusted to make the frosting, which would allow her to start decorating.

"It's not your fault, but yes, I'll take the help if you can give it. Thank you."

She smiled, and it seemed quite genuine. "Thank *you*."

It was hard to believe how efficiently Patricia worked. She listened to Bethany's instructions and didn't complain at all, just went to it.

Landon had left to go find needed cake stand parts from the resort maintenance team. She worked side by side with Patricia for hours. They both worked hard.

The sun was starting to rise, and she could feel fatigue plaguing her entire body when more unexpected help arrived.

"I have double espresso for everyone, and we're here to work." Her mother and father walked in.

She blinked, then took the steaming cup with gratitude. "Thank you."

"Thank *you*." Mom echoed Patricia's earlier statement with the same emotion, then reached over and kissed her forehead. "I'm proud to be your mother."

Tears filled Bethany's eyes, and one leaked out. Her mother caught it with her finger. "Save those for the wedding. Right now, put us to work."

She did. And for the first time, Bethany had hope they were going to get it done to the level of beauty she'd envisioned. There were too many people in this tiny kitchen determined to make it so.

A few minutes later, she looked up to find Landon standing in the doorway with the tools he needed, smiling at the little workforce that had been created here in the auxiliary kitchen.

Her family had shown up when she needed them most.

CHAPTER
TWENTY-SEVEN

BETHANY'S SISTER might have made a pretty remarkable MMA fighter last night, but today, she made a truly breathtaking bride.

The wedding went off without a hitch. Landon and she finished the cakes and the stands and had them in place at the reception about an hour before she needed to go get ready. It wasn't as fancy—would never be the elaborate cake she'd originally had planned—but it still tasted great.

And even more, it was made with love. Not just love from her, but from the family members who'd come together to make it happen. Without them, there would've been no cake. Mother, Patricia, and Bethany had all shot smiles at one another as the cake had been served. Everyone loved it, including the bride and groom. What could have been a disaster ended up being a triumph.

Mina was gone. She'd been taken off the island, and Bethany already felt less stress knowing she was nowhere around. Nobody was going to press charges, but she had a feeling Patricia would go out of her way to make Mina's life miserable. Probably worse than being arrested, and Mina deserved every bit of it.

Exhaustion was catching up with her. What a crazy thirty-six-hour window it had been. First, making love with Landon, then thinking he wasn't interested in her, then dealing with the Martinez situation, and working all night on the cake. Bethany was ready to fall where she stood, but instead, she was in her gold dress and heels, watching her sister dance with her new husband.

Landon showed up at her elbow and extended the flute of champagne. She'd been enjoying his company all night—he'd been by her side almost every minute.

"Thank you." Bethany smiled up at him, trying not to be completely overcome by how he looked in his tuxedo. "I'll only have a couple of sips so you won't have to catch me as I fall on my face."

He trailed a finger down her cheek. "If you fell on your face right now, you'd still be the superhero who saved the day twice in the last twenty-four hours."

She shrugged. "I had help, especially with the cakes. Nobody wanted to see the wedding ruined but Mina."

"The help showed up because they believed in *you*. You'd already won your parents and the Carters over with your hard work and talent all week. Their helping was a response to that."

"I'm just glad everything went smoothly tonight. I'd half convinced myself there would be a problem. Don't they say bad things come in threes?"

He gave a wry smile. "With as many times as I've seen bad things come in way more than threes, let's just happily accept two this time."

She clinked her glass of champagne against his. "Deal. I'm too tired to borrow trouble."

"Are you too tired to dance with me?"

She cupped his granite jaw with her free hand. "Never."

He took their flutes and set them on a tray, and then he led her out onto the floor, pulling her close for a slow dance even though the music was more upbeat.

She looked up at him, her heart flipping over itself as he smiled at her—the most authentic one she'd seen from him since they'd met. Those dimples were out in full force, but this smile was different. Warm and tender.

"What?" he asked.

"I like this smile. Your megawatt grin is a sight to behold, but this one is…different."

He brought her fingers to his lips. "That's because this one is real. And just for you."

He danced with her every dance for the rest of the evening, keeping her in his arms like he couldn't stand for her not to be there.

In a lot of ways, this was their new start, a chance to get to know each other. The *real* each other, without any lies or secrets between them. Bethany hated that they had to leave the island tomorrow, but she believed him when he said that he wanted this to continue once they got home. She did too.

About an hour later, they sent Christiana and Simon off with a wave of sparklers. She knew her parents would leave the party open for as long as anybody wanted to stay, but she'd had enough.

"Do you want to walk with me on the beach since it's our last night?" Landon asked. "I know you're tired, so I understand if you just want to get to bed."

Bethany could sleep once she got home. There was nothing more she wanted than a stroll with him on their beach.

"That sounds great," she said, then spoiled it by letting out a huge yawn.

He laughed. "I don't think you're going to make it. How about if I go get us both a cup of coffee?"

"Perfect." Even coffee wouldn't keep her awake for long, but it would keep her awake long enough to steal some kisses

—maybe more—with him. "I'll meet you down on the beach."

She kicked off her heels as she walked from the outdoor reception venue into the sand with a sigh of relief. She walked until her feet touched the water, and she looked out at the moon, shining down on the Pacific.

In some ways, this week had been the hardest of her life. Bethany was looking forward to getting back to her bakery and normalcy. But no matter what, her *normal* had changed. She was leaving there with a lot more people in her life. Not just Landon, but her parents and sister.

Bethany saw the slight shadow move behind her. Landon had been quicker than she thought. She turned to smile, but a hand reached and covered her mouth and yanked her to the side.

Before she could figure out what was going on, she was being dragged down toward the isolated part of the beach, near the cliffs. It took a second for panic to set in, but once it did, she began to fight—clawing at the hand covering her face and jerking her weight from side to side.

The person had to be a man. He was much bigger and stronger than her. She tried to bite his hand. She needed to get a scream out, but he clocked her in the head with his fist, and everything started to spin.

"Shut the fuck up, or I'll kill you right here."

Through the haze, she recognized the voice. *Who was it?*

He continued dragging her down toward the empty part of the beach. She fought harder to get away. If he planned to kill her, she couldn't let him get her any more isolated.

Bethany kicked back as hard as she could, but her bare feet didn't do much damage. She tried to headbutt him, but that got her a fist in the gut. All the air flew out of her body, and pain took its place. Her weight sagged as she stopped trying to fight and started just trying to survive.

By the time she could get in enough oxygen to start

fighting again, he had her right where she hadn't wanted to let him get her—in the isolated, cliff section of the beach.

No one would come this way. Even Landon would assume if she'd started walking without him, she'd gone the other way.

The man punched Bethany in the gut again, right before throwing her to the ground. She was too busy trying to breathe to scramble away. He ripped her up by her hair, stuffed a gag in her mouth, and tied her hands behind her.

Through the pain, she blinked up at him and finally got a good look.

Fanshawe. That asshole from the bar.

He got right up in her face. "I bet you're wondering what I'm doing here, aren't you, bitch? Your *friend* got me back on the island and paid me to destroy your precious cakes. She said it would be the perfect way to get revenge on both you and your boyfriend, who got me fired."

Bethany tried to scramble away, but he yanked her back by her hair. "But it didn't work, did it? Everybody still loves you, and the wedding was a success. Mina will roll over on me the first chance she gets."

She looked around, but no one was nearby. It was just the rocky beach at their back and copses of trees all around them. No one would come here. Was Landon back from getting the coffee yet? Even if he was, he wouldn't know which direction she'd gone.

Fanshawe saw her looking around. "You like this place? Pretty secluded, isn't it? We're hidden from sight from everyone. The trees give us cover almost all the way to the water, but I can see if anybody's coming."

He bent close to her, and Bethany scooted back, making him laugh. "I'm sure your boyfriend's going to try to save you, but it's not going to work this time. As a matter of fact, I'm done playing by everyone else's rules. Time to do *me*. I'll prove to Mr. Frey that he should've kept me around."

She let out a sob behind her gag as Fanshawe pulled out a gun with a silencer on the end.

He was going to kill Landon.

Bethany had to warn him. She had to do *something* besides stay here trussed up like a fucking turkey.

She fell over to the side and Fanshawe laughed again, but she used the ground to get the gag out of her mouth far enough that she could scream.

And she did, as loud and as long as she could.

Fanshawe let out a curse, and the next thing Bethany knew, his fist crashed into her face. Agony exploded, and everything faded to black.

CHAPTER
TWENTY-EIGHT

LANDON GRINNED as he got the coffee from the elaborate machine in the resort lobby. Bethany was so exhausted she was about to fall down on her face, but she was willing to keep on trooping despite it.

The amount of grit he'd seen from her in the past twenty-four hours would put many of his Special Forces brothers to shame. She'd rolled up her sleeves—literally and figuratively —and worked the problem. Solved the problem.

Saved the day.

He'd only been half kidding when he'd told her law enforcement might try to recruit her. They'd probably try to get her to do double duty, baker and undercover operative.

He chuckled as he filled the second cup. Actually, that wasn't a terrible idea. She could probably get into places a normal agent couldn't, just by waving a box of her sweets under the bad guys' noses.

Not that Landon was letting her near any more bad guys.

As much as he enjoyed this tropical paradise, he was looking forward to getting back to the mainland and courting Bethany properly. Flowers and dates and long, long sessions in bed learning every inch of that beautiful body.

He got the coffees, adding sugar to his and cream to hers, and headed out to the beach, but he didn't see her. He turned back and looked around the patio. He wouldn't have been surprised if she'd curled up on one of the chaise loungers and fallen asleep.

Going all night without sleeping was par for the course for him, but not for her.

And if she was asleep, he'd be happy to dump the coffee and carry her back to their room for the remaining hours they had here. Even if it was just to hold her while she slept.

But she wasn't there or back at the wedding celebrations that were winding down. He looked at his phone in case he'd missed a message from her, but there was nothing.

Now he was getting a little worried.

Landon hurried to the other side of the patio to look in the gardens, in case in both of their exhaustion they'd misunderstood where they were meeting. None of the people strolling among the beautiful plants and flowers was Bethany.

He set down the coffee, his senses going on high alert. Something wasn't right. His gut had been nagging him about a problem through the whole wedding, but he'd ignored it, blaming the malevolent feeling on exhaustion and adrenaline from last night. There wasn't anyone left on the island who meant anyone harm.

He wasn't sure about that at all anymore. And every second he couldn't find Bethany had him more concerned.

Landon ran back to the beach, looking left and right. There were tracks going in both directions. He started off left, toward the main drag with soft sands and calmer waters, but that instinct in his gut had him turning back in the direction of the copse of trees.

That instinct had saved his life more than once when he was in the SEALs. He'd ignored it the day Wavy had shot him, arguing nothing bad could happen with her, and he'd ended up with a hole in his chest.

He wasn't ignoring that feeling anymore. Something wasn't right here.

A little farther ahead, Landon saw some sand that had been disturbed. His sense of unease intensified. Two dark spots on the beach made him rush forward to make sure he was seeing what he thought he was.

Bethany's heels. *Shit*. She wouldn't have left her shoes in the middle of the sand.

He peered toward the group of trees in the gathering darkness. He couldn't see that far ahead, but every instinct was pulling him that way. If he was taking someone from the beach, that's where he would head. The person in the trees had the tactical advantage—they could see someone approaching and pick them off. He was far enough away right now. But if he moved around the bend in the sand, he'd be in view.

A muffled scream from the direction of the trees proved his gut correct at the same time it drove a spike of terror straight through his heart.

That was Bethany.

Landon froze, taking in his options. He couldn't run toward her without getting himself, and maybe her, killed. The only options were to circle around from the trees, which would take time he didn't have or…

He looked out toward the rough waves of the Pacific in the dim light of the moon. His SEAL training had been in this very ocean. He knew how to swim these waters, had done it many times throughout his extensive training, even if that had been years ago.

Hell, even if he'd never dipped a toe in these waters, he'd still do it. Bethany needed him.

Within seconds, Landon had stripped out of his tuxedo. In his boxers, he ran for the water, pushing as far as he could on foot, then swimming even farther out, gritting his teeth against the icy bite. Once he was far enough that the waves hid him, he turned so he was parallel to the shore and swam with sure, even strokes, coming up for air every few moments to check how far he'd gone and to see if the trees had neared yet.

It wasn't long before Landon saw them. A man stood over a dark shape on the ground, presumably Bethany. He looked toward the sand—the direction he would've been coming from if he'd stayed on the beach. He kept swimming, going farther than he needed to, checking the man often. He didn't turn or even consider the fact that Landon could come up behind him in the water.

He pivoted toward the shore, easing back his strokes so he was more hidden in the ocean but still giving him as much speed as possible. He stayed low until the water was at knee-depth then slowly rose up out of it, his eyes on the man the entire time. Landon moved quickly to the tree line, ignoring the cold and lack of covering for his feet. The sound of the beach obscured any noise he made walking over the large leaves.

It didn't matter anyway; he obviously wasn't expecting Landon from this direction. When the man turned his head, he saw who it was. *Fanshawe.*

Landon had no idea how he'd gotten back on the island. He guessed Frey hadn't killed him as he'd half suspected.

As he got closer, Bethany wiggled on the ground. Relief spread through him to know she was alive. Until he saw she had blood all over her face.

Rage thrummed through Landon's whole body. He'd *hurt* Bethany. Sweet, kind, gentlehearted Bethany.

Now *he* wanted to kill the fucker. He sure as hell wasn't going to get the chance to hurt her again.

He strode out of the trees and up behind Fanshawe silently. Bethany's eyes widened slightly when she saw him, and unfortunately, he picked up on it. He whirled around, gun in hand.

For a second, Landon froze, hurled back into the past, as he stared at the barrel pointed right at his chest.

Fanshawe was completely different from Wavy. This beach was different from the penthouse apartment where she'd shot him. Everything about this situation was different.

But that bullet would feel the same as it ripped through his flesh and bone and organs. He didn't have to imagine the agony of the burn, the pain that swallowed you whole. Landon lived with the memory every day.

And right now, that memory threatened to drown everything else.

"I'm going to enjoy killing you and making her watch."

The rubber band of reality snapped back into place at his words. Instead of monologuing, Fanshawe should've killed him while he'd had the chance.

He wouldn't get another.

Taking advantage of the fact that he expected Landon to mutter some response to his asinine comment, he instead moved a step to the diagonal. Mostly to confuse him but also so that muzzle wasn't pointed right at him.

Fanshawe swung toward him, as he expected, but this time, Landon was ready. Using his momentum, Landon pulled him toward him, yanking the weapon from his grip. He unloaded it in a split second, dropping the cartridge case into the sand and tossing the unloaded gun several yards away.

He used the opportunity to swing at Landon's face and got in a hit hard enough to jerk his head around to the side, but he stayed on his feet. Fanshawe smirked at him as he spat out blood, obviously thinking he had the upper hand.

"You're not catching me off guard in a hotel hallway this time, motherfucker," he muttered. "You got me fired. Nobody believed you attacked me first. Now you'll really see what I'm capable of."

Landon shifted his stance so he was lighter on his feet.

There was no way in hell he was going down when Bethany was injured in the sand. He would not leave her unprotected against him.

Fanshawe was bigger than him, but that didn't stop him or worry him at all. He knew exactly how to handle him—he'd already shown him his weaknesses that week.

Landon let him get in another punch to his gut—doubling himself over at the blow. His response wasn't fake, but it wasn't the full truth either.

The bigger man grabbed Landon by the hair and ripped his head up so they were eye to eye. "Not so tough now, are you?"

"Tough enough to take an asshole who can't even keep a two-bit security job because he runs his mouth so much." Landon headbutted him.

He watched fury light Fanshawe's eyes, exactly what he wanted. Landon dodged his next set of blows easily. The angrier he got, the more he telegraphed what move he was about to make. Landon was easily able to avoid each hit.

"What's the matter, Fanshawe? Standing in the unemployment line zap all your energy?"

He dove for Landon, and all he had to do was step out of the way, let him get up, and do the exact same thing again. He was too angry to make any sort of smart blows at this point. Landon was careful to stay clear of his fists—his blows might be wild, but they would have the overwhelming power of his anger behind them.

He didn't have to beat Fanshawe. As he'd done all week, he was beating himself.

Bethany's whimper from over to the side jerked Landon back into the fight. He didn't know how injured she was.

It was time to stop playing. This time when he came at Landon, he attacked instead of defended. Three blows sent him to his knees, dazed.

He dropped beside Bethany and untied her hands and

removed the gag from her mouth. "Hey, Wildflower. You okay?"

"Yeah." She was coherent but had obviously taken a couple of hits to the face from Fanshawe. Behind them, he was staggering to his feet again, fists raised in the air.

Landon stroked a finger down her swollen cheek. "Stay right here."

The gun and bullets were within reach, and never had he been more tempted to use them on an unarmed man. But that wasn't who he was and, more importantly, wasn't who he wanted Bethany to see him as.

That didn't mean Landon wasn't going to beat the shit out of Fanshawe for daring to hurt her.

He didn't say another word to the man, didn't antagonize him, or wait for him to try to hit him.

And he didn't fight fair.

Landon got in two hits to his kidneys he knew would be particularly painful, followed by a jab that broke his nose. His head rocked back, and Landon spun, bringing his foot around in a quick roundhouse kick that had Fanshawe flying through the air and landing unconscious on the ground. He had to tamp down the need to continue pummeling the unconscious man.

Him, the person known for getting along with others so well.

Not someone who hurt Bethany.

Landon let out a breath and reeled in his anger—even though it took every bit of his training and focus. He took the rope Fanshawe had used on Bethany and tied his hands together, then tied his hands to his feet.

Gathering Bethany in his arms, Landon checked her over carefully. Her right eye was beginning to swell, and up close, he saw the blood had come from her nose.

"I'm so sorry," he whispered. "I should've been here for you."

She gave him a tremulous grin. "It's okay," she whispered. "You're here now, and that's all that matters."

She was right. Landon was here now, and he'd be damned if he was going anywhere any time soon.

They lay back, wrapped together. They'd have to get up in a minute, go find his clothes, call security, do all the stuff.

But for right now, Landon just wanted to hold her. The woman who would always be sweeter than anything she could ever bake.

"I think I might need a vacation from my vacation," she whispered.

"Wherever that ends up being, I hope I'm invited."

"As long as you don't bring any undercover work."

He kissed her forehead gently. "Deal."

CHAPTER
TWENTY-NINE

ONE YEAR *Later*

"Holy hell. You have got to marry Bethany." Tristan stuffed another of the individual cakes into his mouth. "Or, on second thought, don't. Then maybe I'll have a chance with her."

Landon looked over at Bethany, who was standing by Bronwyn Rourke, former Zodiac Tactical employee, both of them calmly supervising the distribution of the desserts throughout tonight's events.

"I wonder if Bethany will let us have a secret wedding like this one if I do." He said it as if he wasn't planning to marry Bethany no matter what type of wedding they had. He'd settle for anything from a Vegas quickie to a grandiose affair like Christiana's. As long as Bethany said yes.

Tristan grinned at him over yet another tiny cake, each of which had been painstakingly crafted with edible paint on the top to resemble one of Wavy Bollinger's colorful abstract paintings.

They'd all been brought there tonight in Denver to celebrate the anniversary of Wavy's first art show eighteen months ago. It had been in this very same building. Since then, she'd become famous, her art selling for more than he could comfortably afford.

She deserved it. She'd taken a tragedy that would've broken other people and turned it into compelling pieces of creative genius.

She now had shows all over the world, but she hadn't had one back here in Denver since the first. Hadn't been back in this building at all, as far as Landon knew. The building where she'd shot him.

So, he'd been thrilled she was having another art show here.

Except it had all been a ruse.

Landon should've known something was up with this *show* when every person who arrived were all friends and family. Zodiac teammates from all over the world, plus damn near the entire town of Oak Creek, Wyoming, where Wavy's two brothers—Finn and Baby—both had ties to Linear Tactical.

Tonight's show had contained no press, no strangers, no art critics. Just the people Ian and Wavy held most dear.

Ian had grabbed him the second he'd set foot inside the door. "I need you, Libra. Emergency."

If he'd had a weapon on him, he would've reached for it. But instead, his friend dragged him into a side room, set up with rows of chairs and an exquisite arch made of flowers at the front. The room was surrounded on all sides by pieces of Wavy's riveting art.

"Whoa, who's getting married?" Landon joked.

"Wavy and I are." Ian clapped him on the shoulder. "Need you to be the best man."

"What?" He knew his eyes were bugging out of his head, but he couldn't stop them. Landon pulled Ian in for a hard hug. "You son of a bitch. Good for you."

Ian was beaming. "I didn't want a big wedding. Neither did Wavy. And when she agreed to finally stop running and marry me a few months ago, we decided something like this would be perfect. We just had to get the details in place."

He couldn't even be mad at him. "Damn well is perfect. And I'm glad this building was where you chose to make it happen."

"We thought about Oak Creek, but this building was the start of everything—good and bad—for Wavy and me as a couple. We wanted to rewrite what happened here as something joyful and beautiful. That's if you're okay with it. If not, we'll shut this room off and just have a party."

Landon pulled him in for a second hug. "I couldn't be happier you're making your start as husband and wife here."

"I told Wavy you would feel that way."

He grinned at him. "You be sure to tell her that if it weren't for this building and getting shot, I wouldn't have been the one who got sent to that island a year ago. I would never have met Bethany. Damn well worth the bullet."

Thirty minutes later, to the surprise of all the guests, Landon stood beside Ian as he married the love of his life.

And then the party had really gotten started and was still going now.

He'd meant what he'd said to him about getting shot being worth it. It now seemed like a small price to pay for the privilege of being able to call Bethany his.

As soon as they'd gotten back from Santa Catalina, he'd started making up for the false start in their relationship. First thing he'd done was relocate himself permanently to Zodiac's LA office. Tristan had gotten to see more of him than he'd ever wanted to.

But living there had enabled Landon to court Bethany in the way he wanted to: slowly and with determination. Proving to her that she was worth it. Because she damned sure was.

In those early days, they'd gone on dates with lots of romance and no sex because he'd wanted to make sure she understood he was in this for much more than just her luscious body.

That had lasted for about two weeks.

By that point, Landon almost hadn't recognized himself. He was so desperate for her he'd dragged her out of a movie halfway through and taken her back to her house. He'd barely gotten her inside before taking her hard and fast on the kitchen table. Then another half dozen times the rest of the night. Neither of them could walk properly the next day.

He'd spent every night with her since.

He'd gotten worried about eight months ago when it became obvious he needed to return to Denver to run the Zodiac office there. Ian was spending more and more time in New York with Wavy, and Landon was needed. But he didn't want to be away from Bethany.

Her parents had stepped in and helped save the day. Oliver had invested in a second bakery for Bethany. So for the past six months, she'd alternated her time between two successful bakeries—the original Slice of Heaven in California, and the new Slice of Bliss there in Denver.

To Bethany's delight, Angelique had also gotten involved with the business and helped Bethany find the staff she needed to keep each bakery running smoothly. Michele managed the California shop, along with two full-time bakers Bethany had found and then Angelique had persuaded to join the team.

And there in Denver, another surprising professional ally had popped up: former Zodiac employee Bronwyn Rourke. Like Wavy, Bronwyn had had her life nearly destroyed by Mosaic, and she'd been slowly putting it back together. She was no longer capable of active duties for Zodiac and was taking literature classes at a local college.

Ended up, part-time work at Slice of Bliss was perfect for

her. And Landon hadn't been surprised for a second when Bethany's gentle presence and kind spirit meant the two women had become friends.

Sarge McEwan, as always, had quietly supported Bronwyn in what she wanted to do—encouraging her to branch out in her activities, but right there to sweep her up when she needed him. The love between the two of them was almost tangible.

He'd like to think the same was true for him and Bethany. She didn't need his overt protection like Bronwyn did from Sarge. But in all the other ways, they needed each other just as much. And more every day.

Landon caught her eye and smiled.

But she didn't smile back. In fact, she looked away, almost guilty.

What was that about? Everyone was enjoying her desserts —no surprise—and Bethany had rolled with the punches when the art show had turned into a wedding.

Or at least he thought she had. He'd been so busy with best man duties, he hadn't had a chance to talk to her since the nuptials had occurred.

She and Bronwyn had been working hard all week on those individualized cakes mimicking Wavy's paintings. Angelique had even come in to help, and Landon could've sworn he'd seen Sarge with a paintbrush in his hand when he'd stopped by the bakery a couple nights ago to drag Bethany home to bed.

The cakes worked perfectly, even if it was for a wedding rather than a show. But once again when he caught Bethany's eye, she looked away.

What the hell?

He ran through their recent conversations in his head. They hadn't had any fights or disagreements. But now that he thought about it, she had been a little distant all week.

Landon thought it had been the pressure for this event—Bethany was still building a name for herself.

But maybe it was something else entirely.

Tristan was still standing next to him making near-sex noises about the cakes as he studied Bethany. While Landon understood the sentiment, his mind was now focused on other things—like what the hell was going on with her.

He needed to find out what that was.

Landon glanced over at Tristan. "Don't gain thirty pounds tonight before you take over bodyguard duty of whatever movie star you're guarding next." He knew Zodiac had been contracted for bodyguard work of a well-known actress.

Tristan rolled his eyes. "Don't remind me. I've found that actresses are great with their public personas but tend to be much less likable when you get to know them in reality."

He chuckled. "Then hopefully you don't have to talk to her much and can just stop her stalker."

"That's the plan. Although I'd rather be undercover with Callum."

Callum had infiltrated Joaquin Martinez's organization in Vegas. They were both worried about him since the mole situation in his department had never been completely eradicated. He was having to do a lot of dangerous work without good backup.

"I wish someone had his back," Landon said. "Although you need to watch yours too with this stalker situation."

Tristan shot him a half grin. "Not my first day, boss."

"I know, asshole. Be careful all the same."

Tristan was shoving another mini-cake into his mouth as Landon headed off toward Bethany. She was now standing over to the side of the room by herself.

When she saw him, she rushed back into the catering setup room. She was actually avoiding him.

Oh, hell no.

He knew this building much better than she did and

ducked around the other side of the coat check room and headed her off at the pass. She was looking over her shoulder the other way and ran straight into his chest.

"Running away from me, Wildflower?"

"Landon!" Her laugh was anything but natural. "No, of course not. I just… I just needed to do some things for the bakery. For the art show." Her face blanched. "For the wedding."

He narrowed his eyes and ran a hand down her arm. At least she didn't pull away from his touch. That was a good sign, right?

"You want to tell me what's going on?"

"Nothing," she whispered, eyes dropping to the floor.

"Hey." Landon tried to pull her close to him, but she stiffened. "Bethany, what's wrong? Is it something with your desserts?"

"No." She shook her head. "Everyone is enjoying those."

"Of course they are." As expected.

"I didn't like it." Her voice was so low he could barely hear it.

"You didn't like what? The sweets you made?"

"No."

Landon's heart squeezed into a knot in his chest. She didn't like what? Them? Was that why she'd been distant the last few days? Had she changed her mind about them and didn't know how to tell him?

He tilted her chin up with his finger. The tears in her eyes had fear clutching his heart even more. "Talk to me, Wildflower."

"I can't do it anymore." She turned and ran into the coat check closet behind him.

Landon stared at the door. The tiny jewelry bag in his pocket—the one he'd been carrying around for days as he tried to decide the perfect way to ask Bethany to marry him—mocked him.

She couldn't do this anymore.

No. Landon wasn't going to accept that.

Eighteen months ago, doctors thought he wouldn't live after he was shot in the chest, and he'd fought his way back to life.

He'd fight for Bethany too, wear her down if he had to. Make sure she understood that whatever she needed, he would do his damnedest to make it happen.

She had given him another chance after how they'd started on the island. They'd come way too far to end it all now.

Not to mention, he couldn't live without her.

Landon followed her into the coat check room and closed the door behind them.

"I'm not letting you do this," he said to her back. "I love you, and whatever you need…whatever you think you can't do? We can work through this together."

She turned, face now pale. "Oh my God, Landon, no I—"

He couldn't stand the word *no* coming out of her mouth. He crossed over to her and pulled her against his chest. "Not no. *Yes.* We can figure it out. Don't do this to me, Wildflower. Don't do this to us. What we have is too good to give up on."

Landon was only a half-step up from begging, but he didn't care. He would beg.

"Landon." She pulled away from him. He closed his eyes and sucked in a breath. He had to focus. He had survived a bullet to the chest.

He wasn't sure he would survive this.

"I lied to you."

Landon's eyes popped open. "When?"

She shrugged one shoulder. "Well, I didn't really lie to you, I just didn't tell you the whole truth. I thought I would like it. Get back at you for what happened on the island."

For the life of him, he couldn't figure out what she was

talking about. "Just tell me how to fix this. Whatever you lied about, we'll work it out."

"I didn't like it," she whispered. "I don't want to do it again. I'm not you."

At first, he thought she meant she'd cheated on him. But that didn't make sense either.

Landon cupped her face. "I need you to tell me straight up what we're talking about. Because I don't understand. All I know is that I don't want to lose you."

"I knew this was going to be Ian and Wavy's wedding all week. They said I could tell you, but I didn't because I wanted to have the secret for once." Her big green eyes filled up with tears. "I'm sorry. I didn't like it. I should've told you."

This woman. Her big heart and her sweet spirit. She was feeling guilty because she hadn't told him this would be a wedding.

There was no way anyone could love another person more than he did her at this moment.

Landon brought his lips to hers gently. "I love you."

"You're not mad?"

"You're a naughty girl, and I might have to tie you to the bed later tonight to teach you not to keep secrets from me. But no, I'm not mad."

But he was relieved.

And determined.

And done waiting for the perfect time to tie her to him forever.

Landon stepped back from her. "If it helps, I've had a secret this week also. And I don't want to keep it to myself anymore."

She raised an eyebrow. "Looks like I'm not the only one who's going to get tied to the bed to be taught a lesson. What's your secret?"

He dropped to one knee in front of her and pulled the ring

out of the bag. It was an emerald. He'd gotten it because it reminded him of her eyes.

"Marry me, Wildflower. I'll do this again in a grand gesture befitting someone as beautiful as you. But right now, with just the two of us, promise me forever."

Her smile was breathtaking. "Yes. I love you, and I want forever with you."

He kissed her hand then slipped the ring on her finger. Hell, if his ring on her finger wasn't the rightest thing he'd ever seen.

Landon stood and pulled her in for a kiss. "You're mine officially now. No take-backs."

He felt her lips smile against his. "And no more secrets."

• • •

The Zodiac Tactical series continues with **CODE NAME: PISCES**.

ALSO BY JANIE CROUCH

All books: https://www.janiecrouch.com/books

LINEAR TACTICAL: OAK CREEK

Hero Unbound

Hero's Flight

Hero's Prize

ZODIAC TACTICAL

Code Name: ARIES

Code Name: VIRGO

Code Name: LIBRA

Code Name: PISCES

Code Name: OUTLAW

Code Name: GEMINI

GILDED EMPIRE (as MJ Crouch; series complete)

Broken Crown

Damaged Kingdom

Fierce Monarch

Vicious Throne

RESTING WARRIOR RANCH (with Josie Jade; series complete)

Montana Sanctuary

Montana Danger

Montana Desire

Montana Mystery

Montana Storm

Montana Freedom

Montana Silence

Montana Rain

LINEAR TACTICAL SERIES (series complete)

Cyclone

Eagle

Shamrock

Angel

Ghost

Shadow

Echo

Phoenix

Baby

Storm

Redwood

Scout

Blaze

Hero Forever

INSTINCT SERIES (series complete)

Primal Instinct

Critical Instinct

Survival Instinct

THE RISK SERIES (series complete)

Calculated Risk

Security Risk

Constant Risk

Risk Everything

OMEGA SECTOR SERIES (series complete)

Stealth

Covert

Conceal

Secret

OMEGA SECTOR: CRITICAL RESPONSE (series complete)

Special Forces Savior

Fully Committed

Armored Attraction

Man of Action

Overwhelming Force

Battle Tested

OMEGA SECTOR: UNDER SIEGE (series complete)

Daddy Defender

Protector's Instinct

Cease Fire

Major Crimes

Armed Response

In the Lawman's Protection

ABOUT THE AUTHOR

"Passion that leaps right off the page." - Romantic Times Book Reviews

USA Today and Publishers Weekly bestselling author Janie Crouch writes what she loves to read: passionate romantic suspense featuring protective heroes. Her books have won multiple awards, including the Romance Writers of America's coveted Vivian® Award, the National Readers Choice Award, and the Booksellers' Best.

After a lifetime on the East Coast, and a six-year stint in Germany due to her husband's job as support for the U.S. Military, Janie has settled into her dream home in Front Range of the Colorado Rockies.

When she's not listening to the voices in her head—and even when she is—she enjoys engaging in all sorts of crazy adventures (200-mile relay races; Ironman Triathlons, treks to Mt. Everest Base Camp...), traveling, and hanging out with her four kids.

Her favorite quote: "Life is a daring adventure or nothing." ~ Helen Keller.

facebook.com/janiecrouch

amazon.com/author/janiecrouch

instagram.com/janiecrouch

bookbub.com/authors/janie-crouch